PATRICIA WENTWORTH
FEAR BY NIGHT

PATRICIA WENTWORTH was born Dora Amy Elles in India in 1877 (not 1878 as has sometimes been stated). She was first educated privately in India, and later at Blackheath School for Girls. Her first husband was George Dillon, with whom she had her only child, a daughter. She also had two stepsons from her first marriage, one of whom died in the Somme during World War I.

Her first novel was published in 1910, but it wasn't until the 1920's that she embarked on her long career as a writer of mysteries. Her most famous creation was Miss Maud Silver, who appeared in 32 novels, though there were a further 33 full-length mysteries not featuring Miss Silver—the entire run of these is now reissued by Dean Street Press.

Patricia Wentworth died in 1961. She is recognized today as one of the pre-eminent exponents of the classic British golden age mystery novel.

GW00472342

By Patricia Wentworth

The Benbow Smith Mysteries
Fool Errant
Danger Calling
Walk with Care
Down Under

The Frank Garrett Mysteries
Dead or Alive
Rolling Stone

The Ernest Lamb Mysteries
The Blind Side
Who Pays the Piper?
Pursuit of a Parcel

Standalones
The Astonishing Adventure of Jane Smith
The Red Lacquer Case
The Annam Jewel
The Black Cabinet
The Dower House Mystery
The Amazing Chance
Hue and Cry
Anne Belinda
Will-o'-the-Wisp
Beggar's Choice
The Coldstone
Kingdom Lost
Nothing Venture
Red Shadow
Outrageous Fortune
Touch and Go
Fear by Night
Red Stefan
Blindfold
Hole and Corner
Mr. Zero
Run!
Weekend with Death
Silence in Court

PATRICIA WENTWORTH

FEAR BY NIGHT

With an introduction by
Curtis Evans

DEAN STREET PRESS

Introduction

BRITISH AUTHOR Patricia Wentworth published her first novel, a gripping tale of desperate love during the French Revolution entitled *A Marriage under the Terror*, a little over a century ago, in 1910. The book won first prize in the Melrose Novel Competition and was a popular success in both the United States and the United Kingdom. Over the next five years Wentworth published five additional novels, the majority of them historical fiction, the best-known of which today is *The Devil's Wind* (1912), another sweeping period romance, this one set during the Sepoy Mutiny (1857-58) in India, a region with which the author, as we shall see, had extensive familiarity. Like *A Marriage under the Terror*, *The Devil's Wind* received much praise from reviewers for its sheer storytelling élan. One notice, for example, pronounced the novel "an achievement of some magnitude" on account of "the extraordinary vividness...the reality of the atmosphere...the scenes that shift and move with the swiftness of a moving picture...." (*The Bookman*, August 1912) With her knack for spinning a yarn, it perhaps should come as no surprise that Patricia Wentworth during the early years of the Golden Age of mystery fiction (roughly from 1920 into the 1940s) launched upon her own mystery-writing career, a course charted most successfully for nearly four decades by the prolific author, right up to the year of her death in 1961.

Considering that Patricia Wentworth belongs to the select company of Golden Age mystery writers with books which have remained in print in every decade for nearly a century now (the centenary of Agatha Christie's first mystery, *The Mysterious Affair at Styles*, is in 2020; the centenary of Wentworth's first mystery, *The Astonishing Adventure of Jane Smith*, follows merely three years later, in 2023), relatively little is known about the author herself. It appears, for example, that even the widely given year of Wentworth's birth, 1878, is incorrect. Yet it is sufficiently clear that Wentworth lived a varied and intriguing life that provided her ample inspiration for a writing career devoted to imaginative fiction.

It is usually stated that Patricia Wentworth was born Dora Amy Elles on 10 November 1878 in Mussoorie, India, during the heyday of the British Raj; however, her Indian birth and baptismal record states that she in fact was born on 15 October 1877 and was baptized on 26 November of that same year in Gwalior. Whatever doubts surround her actual birth year, however, unquestionably the future author came from a prominent Anglo-Indian military family. Her father, Edmond Roche Elles, a son of Malcolm Jamieson Elles, a Porto, Portugal wine merchant originally from Ardrossan, Scotland, entered the British Royal Artillery in 1867, a decade before Wentworth's birth, and first saw service in India during the Lushai Expedition of 1871-72. The next year Elles in India wed Clara Gertrude Rothney, daughter of Brigadier-General Octavius Edward Rothney, commander of the Gwalior District, and Maria (Dempster) Rothney, daughter of a surgeon in the Bengal Medical Service. Four children were born of the union of Edmond and Clara Elles, Wentworth being the only daughter.

Before his retirement from the army in 1908, Edmond Elles rose to the rank of lieutenant-general and was awarded the KCB (Knight Commander of the Order of Bath), as was the case with his elder brother, Wentworth's uncle, Lieutenant-General Sir William Kidston Elles, of the Bengal Command. Edmond Elles also served as Military Member to the Council of the Governor-General of India from 1901 to 1905. Two of Wentworth's brothers, Malcolm Rothney Elles and Edmond Claude Elles, served in the Indian Army as well, though both of them died young (Malcolm in 1906 drowned in the Ganges Canal while attempting to rescue his orderly, who had fallen into the water), while her youngest brother, Hugh Jamieson Elles, achieved great distinction in the British Army. During the First World War he catapulted, at the relatively youthful age of 37, to the rank of brigadier-general and the command of the British Tank Corps, at the Battle of Cambrai personally leading the advance of more than 350 tanks against the German line. Years later Hugh Elles also played a major role in British civil defense during the Second World War. In the event of a German invasion of Great Britain, something which seemed all too possible in 1940, he was tasked with leading the defense of southwestern England. Like Sir Edmond and Sir William, Hugh Elles attained the rank of lieutenant-general and was awarded the KCB.

Although she was born in India, Patricia Wentworth spent much of her childhood in England. In 1881 she with her mother and two younger brothers was at Tunbridge Wells, Kent, on what appears to have been a rather extended visit in her ancestral country; while a decade later the same family group resided at Blackheath, London at Lennox House, domicile of Wentworth's widowed maternal grandmother, Maria Rothney. (Her eldest brother, Malcolm, was in Bristol attending Clifton College.) During her years at Lennox House, Wentworth attended Blackheath High School for Girls, then only recently founded as "one of the first schools in the country to give girls a proper education" (*The London Encyclopaedia*, 3rd ed., p. 74). Lennox House was an ample Victorian villa with a great glassed-in conservatory running all along the back and a substantial garden--most happily, one presumes, for Wentworth, who resided there not only with her grandmother, mother and two brothers, but also five aunts (Maria Rothney's unmarried daughters, aged 26 to 42), one adult first cousin once removed and nine first cousins, adolescents like Wentworth herself, from no less than three different families (one Barrow, three Masons and five Dempsters); their parents, like Wentworth's father, presumably were living many miles away in various far-flung British dominions. Three servants--a cook, parlourmaid and housemaid--were tasked with serving this full score of individuals.

Sometime after graduating from Blackheath High School in the mid-1890s, Wentworth returned to India, where in a local British newspaper she is said to have published her first fiction. In 1901 the 23-year-old Wentworth married widower George Fredrick Horace Dillon, a 41-year-old lieutenant-colonel in the Indian Army with three sons from his prior marriage. Two years later Wentworth gave birth to her only child, a daughter named Clare Roche Dillon. (In some sources it is erroneously stated that Clare was the offspring of Wentworth's second marriage.) However in 1906, after just five years of marriage, George Dillon died suddenly on a sea voyage, leaving Wentworth with sole responsibility for her three teenaged stepsons and baby daughter. A very short span of years, 1904 to 1907, saw the deaths of Wentworth's husband, mother, grandmother and brothers Malcolm and Edmond, removing much of her support network. In 1908, however, her father, who was now sixty years old, retired from the army and returned to England, settling at Guildford, Surrey with an older unmarried sister named Dora (for whom his daughter presumably had been named). Wentworth joined this household as well, along with her daughter and her youngest stepson. Here in Surrey Wentworth, presumably with the goal of making herself financially independent for the first time in her life (she was now in her early thirties), wrote the novel that changed the course of her life, *A Marriage under the Terror*, for the first time we know of utilizing her famous *nom de plume*.

The burst of creative energy that resulted in Wentworth's publication of six novels in six years suddenly halted after the appearance of *Queen Anne Is Dead* in 1915. It seems not unlikely that the Great War impinged in various ways on her writing. One tragic episode was the death on the western front of one of her stepsons, George Charles Tracey Dillon. Mining in Colorado when war was declared, young Dillon worked his passage from Galveston, Texas to Bristol, England as a shipboard muleteer (mule-tender) and joined the Gloucestershire Regiment. In 1916 he died at the Somme at the age of 29 (about the age of Wentworth's two brothers when they had passed away in India).

A couple of years after the conflict's cessation in 1918, a happy event occurred in Wentworth's life when at Frimley, Surrey she wed George Oliver Turnbull, up to this time a lifelong bachelor who like the author's first husband was a lieutenant-colonel in the Indian Army. Like his bride now forty-two years old, George Turnbull as a younger man had distinguished himself for his athletic prowess, playing forward for eight years for the Scottish rugby team and while a student at the Royal Military Academy winning the medal awarded the best athlete of his term. It seems not unlikely that Turnbull played a role in his wife's turn toward writing mystery fiction, for he is said to have strongly supported Wentworth's career, even assisting her in preparing manuscripts for publication. In 1936 the couple in Camberley, Surrey built Heatherglade House, a large two-story structure on substantial grounds, where they resided until Wentworth's death a quarter of a century later. (George Turnbull survived his wife by nearly a decade, passing away in 1970 at the age of 92.) This highly successful middle-aged companionate marriage contrasts sharply with the more youthful yet rocky union of Agatha and Archie Christie, which was three years away from sundering when Wentworth published *The Astonishing Adventure of Jane Smith* (1923), the first of her sixty-five mystery novels.

Although Patricia Wentworth became best-known for her cozy tales of the criminal investigations of consulting detective Miss Maud Silver, one of the mystery genre's most prominent spinster sleuths, in truth the Miss Silver tales account for just under half of Wentworth's 65 mystery novels. Miss Silver did not make her debut until 1928 and she did not come to predominate in Wentworth's fictional criminous output until the 1940s. Between 1923 and 1945 Wentworth published 33 mystery novels without Miss Silver, a handsome and substantial legacy in and of itself to vintage crime fiction fans. Many of these books are standalone tales of mystery, but nine of them have series characters. Debuting in the novel *Fool Errant* in 1929, a year after Miss Silver first appeared in print, was the enigmatic, nautically-named *eminence grise* Benbow Collingwood Horatio Smith, owner of a most expressively opinionated parrot named Ananias (and quite a colorful character in his own right). Benbow Smith went on to appear in three additional Wentworth mysteries: *Danger Calling* (1931), *Walk with Care* (1933) and *Down Under* (1937). Working in tandem with Smith in the investigation of sinister affairs threatening the security of Great Britain in *Danger Calling* and *Walk with Care* is Frank Garrett, Head of Intelligence for the Foreign Office, who also appears solo in *Dead or Alive* (1936) and *Rolling Stone* (1940) and collaborates with additional series characters, Scotland Yard's Inspector Ernest Lamb and Sergeant Frank Abbott, in *Pursuit of a Parcel* (1942). Inspector Lamb and Sergeant Abbott headlined a further pair of mysteries, *The Blind Side* (1939) and *Who Pays the Piper?* (1940), before they became absorbed, beginning with *Miss Silver Deals with Death* (1943), into the burgeoning Miss Silver canon. Lamb would make his farewell appearance in 1955 in *The Listening Eye*, while Abbott would take his final bow in mystery fiction with Wentworth's last published novel, *The Girl in the Cellar* (1961), which went into print the year of the author's death at the age of 83.

The remaining two dozen Wentworth mysteries, from the fantastical *The Astonishing Adventure of Jane Smith* in 1923 to the intense legal drama *Silence in Court* in 1945, are, like the author's series novels, highly imaginative and entertaining tales of mystery and adventure, told by a writer gifted with a consummate flair for storytelling. As one confirmed Patricia Wentworth mystery fiction addict, American Golden Age mystery writer Todd Downing, admiringly declared in the 1930s, "There's something about Miss Wentworth's yarns that is contagious." This attractive new series of Patricia Wentworth reissues by Dean Street Press provides modern fans of vintage mystery a splendid opportunity to catch the Wentworth fever.

Curtis Evans

Chapter One

ELIAS PAULETT sat in an upper room of his house in Glasgow and sipped from a tumbler of hot whisky and water. He was a very old man, and a very rich man, and a very successful man, but no one had ever loved him very much. It was now a great many years since anyone had loved him at all. It must be frankly confessed that he was not lovable. He had made his own way from poverty to riches, laying the foundation of his present very large fortune when, at the age of twenty-six, he married the daughter and heiress of Duncan Robertson, whose small proprietary line of steamers is now, like poor Jessie Robertson, quite forgotten. Elias Paulett used them, broke them, and went on.

He sat now, clasping his steaming tumbler and occasionally casting a glance of sardonic amusement at his great-niece, Hilda Paulett, who was reading aloud to him from *The Times*. She was a handsome girl in the late twenties. Her discontented dark eyes and the set of her full, sulky mouth proclaimed the fact that she was not interested in the City news.

Elias Paulett put out his hand and stopped her.

"That'll do. Anderson'll be back by now. I want to see him." He went on sipping and smiling to himself. It was not at all a pleasant smile.

Hilda Paulett went out of the room with an air of relief.

Presently the door opened again and Gale Anderson came in. He was a fair, good-looking young man of thirty-three or thirty-four. He had rather the look of having been a great deal indoors. His skin, and his eyes, and his hair were all a little paler than they ought to have been. He had the controlled manner which was natural in one who had been Elias Paulett's secretary for more than three years.

"Miss Paulett said you wanted me, sir."

Elias nodded. His thick, bushy white hair stood up in tufts, giving him something of the appearance of a cockatoo. His face was a mass of small puckered wrinkles out of which his deep-set grey eyes looked sharply.

"Yes, yes—Miss Paulett," he said—"my niece, Hilda Paulett. Do you call her Hilda?"

If Gale Anderson felt perturbed, he did not show it. He smiled very slightly.

"Well, sir, we've known each other for three years."

"You do, then?"

"Well, yes, sir."

"Ever kiss her?" said Elias Paulett.

Gale Anderson shrugged his shoulders.

"What do you expect me to say to that, sir?"

"Are you in love with her?"

"Or to that, sir?"

Elias Paulett looked at him with bright, wicked eyes.

"You might lie, or you might tell the truth. I'll save you the trouble, young man. You're putting your money on the wrong horse. I'd hate to see you fall down."

Gale Anderson's face showed nothing but perplexity.

"I'm afraid I don't know what you mean, sir."

"Oh yes, you do. You're not a fool, or I'd have fired you long ago. I'm telling you that you've put your money on the wrong horse."

"And I'm telling you, sir, that I don't know what you mean."

Elias Paulett set down the tumbler on the table at his elbow and pulled himself up a little in his chair. He wore a quilted dressing-gown of dark blue silk and had across his knees a plaid rug of Royal Stuart tartan.

"I wasn't asleep last night."

"I really do not know what you mean, sir," said Gale Anderson.

Elias Paulett laughed.

"You've a good poker face! I wasn't asleep last night when Hilda came up behind you and kissed you."

"I think you must have been dreaming, sir," said Gale Anderson.

"Dreaming, was I?" Elias swung round and pointed at the writing-table. "You were sitting there writing, and she came in and had a look at me. Then she said, 'He's asleep,' and she went across and leaned down over you with her arm round your neck and kissed you. And now perhaps you think I'm going to ask you your intentions. I'm not. I'm not going to ask you anything—not even how many times you've kissed her, or when you kissed her first, or whether it's stopped at kissing. I'm not going to ask you anything—I'm going to tell you something. You're putting your money on the wrong horse, and I'm going to tell you why. Someone's been making you believe I've left my money to Hilda. Well, I haven't. No—stand where I can see you and put that other light on! How's that poker face of yours? Let's have a look."

Gale Anderson was certainly very pale, but he had been so pale before that it was impossible to say whether he was paler now. There was a pendant light in the middle of the room. He touched the switch which lit a couple of brackets over the mantelpiece and turned to face his employer.

"It's very good of you to tell me all this, sir."

"Yes, isn't it?" said Elias with a grim twist of the mouth. "I've been good to myself all my life, and I'm keeping right on. I don't want you and Hilda to be thinking it's time I was out of the way, and maybe giving me a helping hand. I'll die when I'm due to die and not before." He took a bunch of keys out of his dressing-gown pocket and flung them on the floor. "If you'll open the third drawer on the left of the table you'll find the draft of my will. The original is in my lawyer's safe where no one can get at it. You can go through the draft at your leisure, unless you like to take my word for what's in it. I've got another great-niece besides Hilda—her name's Ann Vernon—and I've left my money to her. I've never seen her, because I quarrelled with her mother before she was born. If I saw her, I should probably dislike her as much as I dislike Hilda. At present I don't, so I've left her my money—provided she outlives me. If she doesn't, Hilda gets it. But I shouldn't waste my time making love to her on the off chance." He picked up his tumbler and drained it." Don't you want to read the draft?"

"I don't really feel it's my business, sir," said Gale Anderson.

"Willing to take my word for it, are you? All right—I don't want you any more. You'd better go and tell Hilda she's wasting her time too. You'll both need to marry money, so you'd best go courting where it's to be had. There's nothing coming to either of you from me, unless my niece Ann manages to smash herself up before I'm through."

Gale Anderson went out of the room without haste. He found Hilda Paulett in her own sitting-room on the ground floor. It was a dingy place and dingily furnished—old chairs that had been cast from the drawing-room; curtains of faded repp; a Brussels carpet whose pattern had almost disappeared; and an aged piano with flutings of discoloured green silk.

She looked up as he came in, and his face frightened her.

"Oh, Gale! What is it?" she said.

He shut the door and leaned against it. It was a minute before he spoke. When he did so, his voice was under control.

"Why did you lie to me about the will?"

The colour flew into her face.

"I didn't!"

"I think you did. You told me he'd left his money to you."

"Hasn't he?" The words came with a gasp.

Gale Anderson leaned against the door. He said coolly and quietly, "What made you think he had?"

She came a step or two towards him and then stopped, twisting her hands, her colour coming and going and her breath uneven.

"Gale—what's happened? You don't tell me. Has he altered his will? I saw the draft. I swear the money was left to me—I swear it!"

"You saw the draft?"

"I swear I did! It was the day he signed the will. When Mr. Everard had gone, Uncle Elias gave me his keys, and he said, 'This is the draft of my will. I'm keeping it for reference. Put it in the third drawer of the writing-table, and mind you lock the drawer.' So I went over to the table, and whilst I was putting it away he had a most frightful fit of coughing, and I thought I'd take a look and see if I could find out what he was doing with the money. His chair was turned round to the fire, so I was right behind him."

"Go on," said Gale Anderson.

"I got the paper open, and it was all that awful lawyer's language, but I made out that he was leaving everything to 'my great niece,' and then it got down to the bottom of the page and I didn't dare turn over, so I put it away quickly and locked it up and gave him back the key. That was good enough, wasn't it?"

Gale Anderson straightened himself up and came towards her. He took her by the shoulder, and she looked up at him in a puzzled, frightened way.

"Those words, 'my great-niece,' came at the bottom of the page?"

Hilda nodded.

"What's wrong—what's happened?"

With a turn of the wrist he pushed her away.

"You fool! Didn't you know he had another great-niece?"

She stumbled against the piano and caught at it to steady herself.

"Oh! You hurt me!"

"Do you expect me to say I'm sorry? You blazing fool! Did you hear what I said? There's another niece, and you don't get a penny."

She looked up wide-eyed, her full lips trembling.

"Gale—you didn't marry me for that? Gale, I didn't know—I swear I didn't! Oh, *Gale!*"

He said, "Be quiet!" and went to the fireplace and stood there looking down at the dusty paper between the bars.

She watched him, dabbing her eyes with her handkerchief and every now and then drawing a quick breath as if she wanted to speak but lacked the courage. When at last he turned round, the words broke out.

"Oh, Gale, are you sure? Don't I get anything?"

"Not unless something happens to Miss Ann Vernon," said Gale Anderson.

Chapter Two

ANN VERNON came up the steps of the Luxe with her chin in the air. If Charles Anstruther had been waiting for her, he would have reflected with a little stab of amused admiration that it was just like Ann to look as if she had bought the earth, in a dress which even to the male eye was tolerably out of date, and to cock her hat at an extravagant angle just because it had obviously borne the heat and burden of the summer.

Charles, however, was about a mile away. He was, for the moment, very much engaged with a pale, weedy young man whose uncertainty as to the respective functions of the brake and the accelerator of a very elderly car had caused him to shoot violently out of a side street. The consequences to Charles' car had been of such a nature as to stimulate his natural powers of invective to the uttermost. It was a hot day. A rich smell of petrol hung upon the air. There was the usual crowd. The pale young man dithered. Charles surpassed himself.

And in the lounge of the Luxe Ann Vernon began to feel justly annoyed. She was ten minutes late for lunch. Charles should have been at least ten minutes early. She had never kept him waiting less than quarter of an hour. On the face of it, it looked as if Charles was a bit out of hand.

Ann pressed her lips together firmly, took a slow look round, and then sat down with her back to the door in a recess behind a palm-tree and half a dozen hydrangeas. If Charles chose to be late, he could look for her. If he was more than five minutes late, he wouldn't find her at all. She toyed with the thought of sending him a telegram. Something on the lines of "Sorry forgot." Alternatively, she might ring him up—"It wasn't to-day I was lunching with you?"

"But I'm frightfully hungry," said the part of Ann that had no proper pride—"frightfully, frightfully, *frightfully*. I don't know who the idiot was who had the bright idea of calling bread the staff of life, but I bet he never tried leaning on it—not with all his weight, so to speak." Ann had. It was Wednesday. Since the previous Saturday she had breakfasted, lunched, and supped on dry bread, and she positively ached for the fleshpots of the Luxe. If Charles didn't come in five minutes, she would fade out of the side door, walk for about a quarter of an hour, and then come back again all late and haughty to find, she hoped, a champing Charles. Hang Charles! She didn't in the least want to get hot, and even hungrier than she was now. For one thing, it is terribly hard to be haughty when you are hot. Charles had to be frozen, and to freeze another you must be cool yourself.

The five minutes was nearly up. She was just going to lean sideways to look at the clock, when from the other side of the hydrangeas a voice said,

"A pity you can't marry her."

Ann stopped being interested in the clock. Theoretically, eavesdropping was a thing that you did not do. Actually, what a fascination there was in catching the little stray bits of other people's stories which came to you suddenly in trains, buses, restaurants, and crowded streets. You didn't know the people, so it didn't matter to them.

Ann felt a passionate interest in the voice from the other side of the hydrangeas. It was a man's voice, pitched very low.

"What a pity you can't marry her," it said. And then, "You're sure about the will?"

There was a little tinkling of glasses. There were two people there. Ann couldn't see a thing, but she heard another voice say,

"Of course I'm sure. Don't speak so loud."

This was too intriguing. Loud? The words had been barely audible, the voices so drained of tone as to convey no sense of individuality. Both voices might have been the same voice, only they weren't, One had answered the other with that fantastic "Don't speak so loud."

Ann was quite desperately interested. When you are alone in the world, you must be interested in other people or else you begin to die. Ann was very much alive. She leaned against a blue hydrangea and listened. The hydrangea tickled her ear. She heard the second voice say,

"She must be got away before she knows."

The first voice didn't say anything. The glasses chinked. The second voice went on.

"If he dies, the whole thing will be in the papers. She must be got away before she knows."

They were drinking something with ice in it. *Lovely!* Ann's tongue felt exactly like a dry biscuit. *Lovely clinking ice!* Hang Charles!

The first voice said,

"He's never seen her?"

The second voice said,

"And he's not going to. You must get her away at once."

"And then?" The words were hardly words at all. There was no sound behind them. Yet Ann had heard them.

All at once she wasn't hot any more; she was cold. A horrid little shiver ran over her. She didn't want to listen any more. She wanted Charles to come. *"And then?"* Those two words, which she couldn't really have heard, seemed to hang upon the silence. It was a horrid silence. The other voice did not break it. Only after an intolerable minute there was a scraping sound as if a chair had been pushed back.

Ann stood up, and as she did so the second voice spoke again, just a little louder: "Well, devil take the hindmost!" and she heard footsteps going away.

For a moment she stood where she was, because she was actually feeling as if she could not move. When she looked round the hydrangeas, there was nothing to be seen except two chairs and a table, and a couple of empty glasses.

Chapter Three

CHARLES ARRIVED full of apologies, but even more full of the damage to his paint and the enormities of a system which loosed half-witted invertebrate rabbits upon the highways in superannuated heaps of scrap iron.

"He calls the thing a car!" said Charles, still pale with fury. "Said he was learning to drive it! Will you have grape-fruit or *hors d'œuvres*? The thing would have dropped to pieces where it stood if it hadn't been for the rust! I can't think how it ever started, and I don't know now why it stopped short of smashing my petrol tank! Oughtn't to eat *hors d'œuvres*, you know—you'll spoil the rest of your lunch."

Ann took a delicious mouthful of sardine and egg. Lovely food! Lovely, *lovely* food—and lots of courses still to come! She smiled forgivingly at Charles and spoke the exact truth.

"I'm starving," she said.

"All right," said Charles, "put it away. I love to see you eating. You're about the only girl I know who does. I took a young thing out the other night, and she dined on four cocktails and two spoonfuls of grape-fruit. Most embarrassing for me, because I'd been playing golf and was all set for a good square meal."

Ann ate every scrap of her *hors d'œuvres*. There was Indian corn, and little button mushrooms, and Russian salad, and cucumber, and sardine, and anchovy, and egg, and a fat green olive. When she had finished the last grain of Indian corn she felt better. Charles' face came into focus again and stayed there. It was much more comfortable like that. She hoped he had not noticed anything, but for the first few minutes or so the room had been full of little dancing sparks, very horrid and dazzling, with Charles' face coming and going in the middle of them like a conjuring trick.

The waiter changed her plate and gave her a thick creamy soup with asparagus tips in it. After that there was going to be salmon, and cold pie, and *pêche Melba*. She smiled so sweetly at Charles that he very nearly lost his head, and only saved himself by immediately plunging into anecdote. He would certainly propose to Ann before lunch was over, but common decency forbids a host to offer marriage with the soup, because if the girl says no—and Ann was quite certain to say no—there is bound to be a blight over the rest of the meal. Besides, he had better tell her about Bewley first. He finished a story rather lamely, and said,

"I'm putting Bewley up for sale."

Ann laid her fish-knife and fork together upon an empty plate. *Hors d'œuvres*, soup, salmon—and she felt as if she had only just begun. She hoped there would be a very big helping of pie. Could you ask for a second helping at the Luxe? Charles had said something about Bewley. He was repeating it with that quick, dark frown of his.

"Bewley's got to go."

Why didn't she say something? Was it going to make a difference? Would she take him with Bewley, and say no if Bewley had to go? Did he want her if she was like that? He didn't know the answers to the first two questions, but he knew that one. Whatever she did and whatever she was, he wanted Ann. Lord—how he wanted Ann! He said sharply,

"Why don't you say something?"

Ann found something to say. She said,

"I'm sorry"; and then, "Is it because of money?"

Charles saw Bewley under the August sun—dark woods, moorland purple with heather, a blue edge of sea, security, five hundred years of possession, the oaks that were there when the Stuarts reigned and an Anstruther had ridden out to die at Marston Moor He said,

"I can't keep it up. The whole show's dropping to pieces—bottom falling out of everything. It'll have to go."

"You should look out for an heiress," said Ann lightly.

If she did not speak lightly and quickly, her voice might shake, and Charles might think—when really and truly it was only the dry bread, and walking the soles off her shoes looking for a job.

Charles smiled, and she would rather he had frowned.

"It's Bewley that's up for sale, not me."

"She might be an enchanting heiress," said Ann.

Charles agreed in the most reasonable way.

"She might."

Ann smiled. The pie had arrived. It was a lovely helping. Pastry was very, very filling. There was jelly. There were truffles. There were peas, and surprisingly young potatoes. She tried to keep her mind upon food, and how lovely it was not to be hungry any more. If Charles thought he could work on her feelings with something on the lines of "Bewley's mine to sell, but I'm yours," well, he'd better think again. A horrid dangerous little traitor thought kept bobbing up at the back of her mind. For twopence it would start signalling to Charles, the little beast. She boxed its ears, speared a truffle, gazed at it with dreamy affection, and said,

"You'd much better look for an heiress."

"Thanks," said Charles, still in that reasonable tone.

Ann found another truffle.

"Seriously," she said, "what's wrong with an heiress?"

"I don't want one, thank you."

"Bewley does if you don't. I suppose you'll fall in love with somebody some day. Why shouldn't you fall in love with a girl who's got some money? She might be a heart-smiter. There's nothing the least heart-smiting about being poor, you know. It's very deteriorating, because you have to keep on thinking about money all the time—horrid sordid things like, 'Will it run to a bus fare?' or 'Can I have butter to-day?' Everyone ought to have so much money that they never have to think about it at all. You've no idea how nice I should be if I had a thousand a year."

"It would take more than a thousand a year to save Bewley."

"Isn't there any way of making it pay?"

"Not without capital."

"Can't you let instead of selling?"

"What's the good if I can't ever go back? Besides, everything's going to rack and ruin—cottages, fences, everything. It's a hopeless show."

Ann said, "I'm sorry."

Charles went on talking about Bewley. Perhaps he found it a relief. Perhaps it was only because he had always found it astonishingly easy to talk to Ann.

Ann for her part found it quite easy to listen. She was feeling soothed and peaceful. She finished her pie and ate *pêche Melba* in a fond, lingering manner. Charles had a nice voice. Perhaps he wouldn't have to sell Bewley after all. If he married an heiress, she wouldn't be able to lunch with him any more. It had been a frightfully good lunch. She began to feel quite certain that she would get the Westley Gardens job. She needn't hurry, because her appointment wasn't until a quarter past three. It was going to be all right.

She smiled at Charles and said,

"You've got a positive network of aunts and cousins and people. Would you like to find me a job?"

Charles was slightly taken aback. He had been telling her about the death duties—three lots in ten years, enough to smash anyone. It took him a moment to switch over to the question of a job.

"Do you want one?"

"Darling Charles! Do I? As a matter of fa I hope I'm getting one this afternoon. Someone sent me a paper with a marked advertisement."

"Who did?"

"I don't know. Mary Duquesne, I expect. She's just gone off to India."

"What's the job?"

"Secretary to an old lady, I should think—Westley Gardens. I'm going to be interviewed this afternoon. But in case it falls through, if you *have* got an aunt up your sleeve—"

Charles frowned a little.

"Must it be an aunt?"

Ann put three lumps of sugar into her coffee.

"A cousin would do. I'm sure all your relations are fearfully respectable."

He frowned a little more. It is all right to have respectable relations, but they do not make a good starting-point for a proposal. Quite definitely a respectable cousin lacks romance. He stirred his coffee with ferocious energy. The idea of Ann as a companion or a secretary filled him with wrath. And then he looked up and met her smile. It began in her eyes with a half sleepy gleam of mischief and then just lifted the corners of a very attractive mouth. His anger vanished. He leaned his elbows on the table.

"If you really want a job—"

"And I really do," said Ann.

"I think I know of one—but I don't know if you'd like it or take it on."

Ann sighed.

"Oh well—one's got to live."

"You mightn't like it."

"I'd *like* to be an Idle Rich, but as I can't—what's your job?"

"Me," said Charles.

Ann felt as if someone had hit her. How *mean*! The traitor in her mind bobbed up and said "Hooray!"

"You!" said Ann.

"Won't you?" said Charles, and at the change in his voice something happened to Ann's heart. It was something very unexpected and disconcerting. There was a throbbing and a softness, and a feeling as if she might burst suddenly into tears. It was most frightfully disconcerting. Fortunately the feeling only lasted for a moment. She said,

"Charles darling, that doesn't sound at all respectable. I think it had much better be a cousin or an aunt."

Charles blazed into a dark fury.

"What do you suppose I'm asking you?"

Ann put her elbows on the table too. Her face, with its teasing eyes and the lips which were not quite as steady as they might have been, was only a few inches away.

"Is that a proposal?"

"Of course it is."

"Charles, how nice of you!"

"You will?"

"Oh no, darling. It's terribly nice of you all the same."

"Ann!"

Ann drew back.

"Oh no." She spoke a little too quickly, and Charles leaned nearer. "Why?"

"No experience," said Ann, and the mischief looked out of her eyes again. "It's the *very* first thing they always ask: 'What experience have you?' And if you haven't any, you either don't get the job, or else they take away the number they first thought of, and offer you about five shillings a week to do about twice as much as the last person did."

"It'll run to more than five shillings," said Charles. "If Bewley sells, we should be quite well off. There's a worthy and wealthy boot-manufacturer after it."

The "we" hit Ann hard. She turned rather pale and her mood changed. She said seriously,

"Charles, how long have you known me? Two months—three? And what do you know about me? You met me in June with the Duquesnes at Ciro's. Mary introduced us—you'd only met *her* twice before. Since then we've danced, gone on the river, bathed, and danced again. What do you know about me really?"

"What does one know about anyone?" said Charles. "I love you. I'm asking you to marry me, and we'll have the rest of our lives to get to know each other really well."

"Aren't you rather rash?"

Charles smiled.

"I know you rather well already, but I'm quite willing to know you better."

"What do you know, Charles?"

"You're proud, practical, generous, idealistic—a bit of a flirt, a bit of a tease, a bit of a mystery, and—" He hesitated.

"What?"

"I don't think I'll say."

"Yes, you must."

"You've been—disenchanted."

Ann nodded. She dropped one hand in her lap and leaned her chin in the other.

"That's clever of you! I suppose it's true. I'll tell you about it if you like. Then you'll be able to see why it wouldn't do for us to marry."

"I don't want to hear," said Charles quickly.

Ann laughed under her breath.

"Darling Charles—how chivalrous! But I haven't got a lurid past. I'm respectable through and through. I'd like you to listen if it won't bore you dreadfully."

"It won't bore me," said Charles.

"I'll make it nice and short," said Ann in her most reassuring voice. "Tabloid tales. Number one.... No, I can't joke about it, because it's not my tragedy—it's my father's and mother's. He was an American engineer, and he ran away with my mother. I don't think he had any near relations. She had an uncle who never forgave her. They took a cottage in the country, and he went up and down to his job. They were frightfully happy for a year, and then he was killed in a street accident. I was a month old. My mother wrote once to her uncle, but he never answered the letter, and she wouldn't write again. I believe he was rich. She never spoke about him. His name is Elias Paulett. I don't know if he's still alive."

"I know someone called Paulett," said Charles—"a girl, Hilda Paulett."

"Perhaps she's a relation. Do you know, I haven't got a single relation in the world that I know about except the wicked uncle, and he's probably dead. Is this Hilda person nice?"

Charles said, "So so. She stays near Bewley with people I bar."

"I don't really want to know any of my relations," said Ann. "If any of them had been human, they'd have helped my mother."

"What did she do?" said Charles

Ann's colour rose.

"She worked—" There was a pause, and then she added, "very hard—charing—anything she could get. When I was about five, she was doing regular daily work at the big house of the village. Mary Duquesne's people lived there. They let her bring me too. I played in the nursery with Mary. Sometimes my mother was there sewing—she sewed beautifully. Then Mary had a governess, and I shared her lessons. Mary was delicate. I was supposed to be good for her. I didn't know it at the time, but I was a prescription—like some thing in a bottle, to be taken daily, but take care it doesn't become a habit." She gave a little laugh. "Darling Charles, don't frown like that."

"It sounds damnable!" said Charles.

"Not a bit. Everyone was kind, and I was very happy. I loved Mary, and I didn't know that my mother was working herself to death. She died when I was fifteen, and Mary's mother took me up to live at the Hall. Mary had a finishing governess, so I had a really expensive education. Everything went on all right until Mary came out. Then there was a crash, because a man who had been asked down for her went off the deep end about me. I was such an ass that I thought he wanted to marry me. He didn't of course."

Charles said something under his breath.

"Thank you," said Ann. She was smiling. "That's when I learned what it meant not to have a background. You see, there wasn't really anything to choose between Mary and me. We'd done exactly the same things since we were five years old. A stranger wouldn't have known which of us was the daughter of the house and which—the prescription."

"Ann, do stop!" said Charles.

She nodded.

"I'm nearly done. Mary went to town for the season. Her mother got me the job of secretary to Mrs. Twisledon—Helena Forbes Twisledon. She was some sort of connection of theirs."

"Did you like it?"

Ann made a face.

"She was the most appallingly efficient person, not really human. You know, everything on a system. It was awfully good training, but a bit grim. I was with her four years. Then she died quite suddenly, and I had three rotten jobs one after another—a woman who drugged, an old horror who expected me to maid her, and a man who suggested week-ends at Brighton. I met Mary again in June. She'd just married Sir Henry Duquesne. They were quite nice to me. I was out of a job, and they took me about a bit. That's how I met you. Now we're up to date, and you know why I won't marry you."

"Do I?"

"You ought to." Ann took her elbow off the table and sat back. When Charles looked at her like that, it was very difficult to go on being cool and detached.

"If you wouldn't mind explaining—"

"I thought I had."

"Well, I've not got it."

Ann sighed.

"You're not trying," she said. Then, leaning forward again, "Charles, don't you *see*? I haven't got a single one of the things which your wife ought to have—background—standing—family—money. What's the first thing all your aunts and cousins will ask? *Who are her people?*"

"Ann!"

She gave a little angry laugh.

"It's true! And if I was fool enough to marry you, I should never be allowed to forget that I didn't belong. There's only one thing that would make them open their arms to me, and that's money. If I was a simply tremendous heiress, I don't suppose they'd bother about my father and mother, especially as they're dead." Her colour had risen and her eyes were a dark angry blue, but her voice was cool and sweet. She looked away from Charles to the clock on the other side of the room and pushed back her chair. "I must rush," she said.

Charles said nothing. He paid the bill and walked silently beside her to within a couple of yards of the swing-door which led into the street. Then he said,

"Just a moment if you don't mind. When am I going to see you again?"

"Next year—sometime—never—"

"Will you dine with me to-night?"

She shook her head.

"Why not?"

"I can't think why you want me to"

Charles looked at her.

"I haven't nearly finished proposing to you."

Ann felt happier. She loved the cut and thrust of a clash like this.

"Haven't you? But I've quite finished refusing you."

"I don't feel refused," said Charles.

"I'll put it in writing, if you like."

Charles shook his head.

"I might hold you to it, and then you'd be sorry. Eight o'clock here? Or would you like to do a show, in which case—"

Ann panicked. In half a minute she would say yes, and if she said yes, she was lost. She felt it in her bones. She said,

"I can't. Charles, I shall be late for my appointment."

"I'm driving you there—it's much too hot to walk. We can talk as we go along."

In the taxi he returned to the charge.

"Why can't you dine with me to-night? Is it because you're afraid?"

Ann flushed brightly. She opened her mouth to speak and then shut it again.

"Yes?" said Charles.

"No," said Ann.

Charles sighed heavily.

"I suppose you're trying to make me lose my temper. I'm not going to—it's too hot. Why won't you dine with me?"

"Do you really want to know?"

"Well, I rather hoped I'd made that clear."

Ann sat well back into the corner of the taxi.

"I haven't got an evening dress."

"Why haven't you?"

"Pawned," said Ann.

There was a short electric silence, and then Charles' hand came down hard on her wrist.

"Why?"

Ann tingled, but she kept her voice cool.

"Well, I'm out of a job—I've been out of one since June. Of course I ought to have saved whilst I was with Mrs. Twisledon, but I didn't. Charles, you're breaking my wrist!"

"No, I don't think so. Ann, call this damned appointment off and come somewhere where we can have the whole thing out."

"It's not a damned appointment. It's a lifebuoy in a howling storm. You've no idea how difficult it is to get a job."

His hand tightened on her wrist.

"Haven't I offered you one? Look here, Ann, there's only one good reason for refusing it, and that is that you hate the sight of me and never want to see me again."

"Perhaps I do."

"Oh no, you don't."

"You can't marry everyone you don't hate."

"You can marry me," said Charles.

Ann sat up, suddenly white and hard.

"Please let go," she said, and as Charles' grip relaxed, she took her hand away and laid it in her lap.

Charles said, "Ann—"

And Ann said, speaking low but very distinctly, "It's no, Charles, and it will always be no."

"Are you sure?"

The taxi stopped. Ann jerked at the handle and jumped out. She had run up three steps to a small pillared porch and was ringing the bell, when she heard the taxi start again and Charles come up behind her. She looked over her shoulder and smiled. She could afford to smile now that the door might open at any moment.

"Ann, will you ring me up? I suppose you won't let me wait for you?"

"No, you mustn't wait. I'll ring you. *Please* Charles."

"Ann, don't take this job. There's no need. Wait!"

A curious little jag of anger ripped through Ann's self-control. She said,

"*Wait?* I've been living on dry bread since Saturday."

And with that the door opened.

Chapter Four

A TALL YOUNG FOOTMAN preceded Ann up a thickly carpeted stair. He wore a chocolate-coloured livery with brass buttons. The carpet was of that bright shade of crimson preferred by hotels. The house was quite extraordinarily like an hotel—a sort of sublimated commercial hotel.

At the turn of the stair a mirror with a gilt border about half a yard wide reflected the footman's splendour and Ann's shabbiness. There was something about the chocolate and gold which made her look and feel most terribly shabby. There was a good deal of gold everywhere. The wall-paper had an immense gold pattern. It was improbable that the design was intended to represent golden cauliflowers trained up a crimson trellis, but it certainly conveyed this impression. On either side of the drawing-room door stood a shiny palm on a bright blue china pedestal.

The footman opened the door and announced, "Miss Vernon."

Ann came into the most dreadful room she had ever seen in her life. There was a great deal more crimson carpet, and a great deal more gilding. There were seven aspidistras, each in a brightly-coloured china pot. One of the pots was blue, and two were pink, and two were yellow, and two were green. There was a drawing-room suite very tightly upholstered in old-gold satin. There were at least five mirrors, and there were Nottingham lace curtains. The fireplace held a billowy mass of gilt shavings and a gilded firescreen.

From one of the old-gold chairs there arose a stoutish man of middle age with sandy hair that was beginning to turn grey. He advanced within a yard of Ann and made her a formal bow.

"Miss Vernon?"

"I came to see Mrs. Halliday," said Ann. "I wrote about this advertisement." She had the cutting in her hand and held it out.

The man nodded.

"Yes, yes—and you received an answer signed J. Halliday. I am James Halliday."

Ann felt the oddest sensation. Just for the fraction of a second it seemed to her that all this had happened before. There was a strange familiar unreality about the whole thing. It had happened before, or it had never really happened at all....

Then in a flash all that was gone, and she was saying,

"But I came to see Mrs. Halliday."

"Quite so," said the man. "Mrs. Halliday, as you say—my mother. Now won't you sit down, Miss Vernon?"

Ann sat down on one of the gilded chairs. It was even more unyielding than it looked.

Mr. Halliday resumed his own seat. He put a hand on either knee and bent a business-like gaze upon her.

"What Mrs. Halliday wants is a companion—and when I say a companion, that's just exactly what I mean. She's got her maid who looks after her—gets her up and puts her to bed and all that kind of thing—and if she should be ill, which I hope she won't, there'd be no expense spared. But what she wants is a companion, someone that will keep her bright, and make a bit of a fuss of her, and listen to her when she wants to talk, and let her be when she doesn't want to be bothered." He ran his hands suddenly through his hair and rumpled it. "I don't know if you take me?"

"Oh yes, I think so," said Ann.

Mr. James Halliday smoothed his ruffled hair.

"You wouldn't believe the trouble it is to get her suited. She likes them bright, but she don't like them uppish."

"I'd do my best to please her," said Ann.

"Well, there it is," said Mr. Halliday. "You see, it's this way—she's an old lady and she likes her own way. I suppose most of us do, but she's come to a time of life when she expects to get it, and if she doesn't get it there's trouble. I don't grudge a good salary to anyone who'll make her happy. There, you've got it in a nutshell, Miss Vernon. That's your job—to make Mrs. Halliday happy. When could you come?"

Ann was a little taken aback.

"I could come any time—I'm free now."

"Ah!" said Mr. Halliday. "That's right! Now, I've been on to that reference you gave—that Lady Gillingham who said you'd been brought up with her daughter—and I don't mind saying she spoke very highly of you. Let's get this clear. You say you're free. Does that mean you'd be free to come today?"

With the most extraordinary distinctness Ann heard Charles' voice saying to her in the taxi, "Don't take this job." She started a little, banged the door on Charles, and said,

"Oh yes, I could come to-day if Mrs. Halliday wants me to. May I see her now?"

Mr. Halliday rose with an air of relief and led the way back to the crimson-trellised cauliflowers. At a door on the right he knocked, and then preceded Ann into the room.

Mrs. Halliday was sitting bolt upright in a Victorian chair with a hard upholstered seat and back, and a frame of yellow walnut very uncomfortably carved. There was a crazy patchwork cushion on the floor as if it had just fallen. It was a relief to find that there was no gilding. The carpet was an old-fashioned one with a pattern of enormous pink and blue roses on a drab ground. There was a horsehair sofa, also with a walnut frame, and several odd little Victorian chairs covered in woolwork. The curtains were of crimson plush with an edging of ball fringe. There was a deep mantle-border of the same. A little round table with a maroon velvet top and a straight frill of hand-made crochet stood at Mrs. Halliday's elbow. Upon it reposed a large photograph album with gilt clasps and a massive workbox of Tonbridge ware.

Mrs. Halliday herself wore a little black silk apron over a full-skirted dress of black cashmere. She had a small black lace tippet about her shoulders, and an old-fashioned net cap upon her neatly brushed grey hair. The tippet was fastened by an enormous brooch which displayed a bunch of flowers worked in hair of different shades, the whole enclosed by a massive border of plaited gold. The cap was trimmed with bunches of narrow ribbon in two shades of magenta. Between the cap and the brooch there jutted out Mrs. Halliday's bristling eyebrows, her large bony nose, and her very determined chin. The eyebrows were grey and made a fierce slanting line above a pair of very shrewd grey eyes.

The face was long and thin. She put out a bony hand with a handsome diamond ring and said,

"Howdydo?"

"It's Miss Vernon, Mother," said Mr. Halliday. All at once he seemed nervous. He advanced a chair worked in pink and crimson cross-stitch, and was at once bidden to place it at a different angle.

"And then you can go, my lad. Her and me'll have our talk without you. Never knew two women yet as didn't get on better without a man between 'em." She spoke with a strong country accent, and ended with a chuckle. She had a row of large and even teeth which seemed, most surprisingly, to be all her own.

When the door had closed upon Mr. Halliday, she turned a sharp look on Ann.

"Vernon?" she said. "And what's your Christian name?"

"Ann."

"Just plain Ann?"

"Just plain Ann."

"And a good name too," said Mrs. Halliday heartily. "My grandmother called three of her fourteen Ann afore she could get one of 'em to live. She was a terrible persevering woman. That's a piece of her 'air in my brooch. The sprig of white heather, that's 'ers. Her 'air went a beautiful white afore she died. Seems like mine's going to 'ang on grey to the end."

Ann gazed enchanted at the brooch with its bunch of flowers.

"Are they all relations?" she asked. "I mean relations' hair. How thrilling!"

"Some of 'ems in-laws," said Mrs. Halliday. She unpinned the brooch and leaned forward with it. "That there buttercup, that was a bit of my mother's 'air when she was a young girl. So bright's a marigold— isn't it? Prettiest girl anywhere within fifty mile, so they did say. I don't remember 'er. And the little tiddy flower aside of 'er's, that's my sister Annie Jane what she died with. My father's sister, what had a turn for poetry, wrote an 'ymn about it:

'The lovely h'infant and the mother
Are gone,
And we 'ave left no other.'

Which it stands to reason we 'adn't, my father not being a bigamist. But that's the way with poetry. I can't say as it did my Aunt Maria any good. A kind of a mousey woman, she was. That's her 'air in the stalks—and about all it was fit for. A proper old maid, she was."

She replaced the brooch, fastened it with a snap, and said briskly, "Well, that's not business. 'Ow old are you?"

"Twenty-two," said Ann.

Mrs. Halliday nodded.

"Sixty years since I was twenty-two—sixty and a bit. Lemme see ..." The bushy grey eyebrows drew together. "I'd been ten years in the same service. Between-maid first—they don't send 'em out at twelve nowadays, but they did then, and we were a long family, five of me own mother's not a-counting Annie Jane, and four that my father's second wife brought with 'er from 'er first marriage, and another six that they went and 'ad to finish off with. Well, as I was telling you, when I was two-and-twenty, I was second 'ousemaid up at the 'All, and rare and pleased to be getting twenty-six pounds a year. As I says to the 'ussy as we've got now, 'You don't know when you're well off,' I says, 'And if I'd left dust in my corners same as what you leave in yours, I'd 'ave got a rare old telling-off.' There've been a lot of changes since I was twenty-two. Are you 'oping to be married?"

"Oh no," said Ann, and heard Charles' voice say *"Ann!"* in the back of her mind.

Mrs. Halliday nodded.

"Time enough," she said. "If girls knew what was in front of 'em, they wouldn't be in a nurry. When I was twenty-two I was walking out with the under groom, a very 'andsome young man and made the rottenest bad 'usband as you'd meet in a month of Sundays—but not to me, thank the Lord, though I cried me eyes out when he jilted me and took Dorcas Rudd for 'er pretty face, pore thing." She became brisk again. "What wages are you asking?"

"Mrs. Twisledon gave me a hundred," said Ann.

Mrs. Halliday clicked with her tongue.

"That's a terrible lot of money! But you'll 'ave to settle it with Jimmy." She chuckled. "Thinks 'e's made of money these days, Jimmy does! And I won't say 'e isn't a clever lad, and a good son too. 'E don't grudge me anything, I'll say that for 'im."

"Then you'd like me to come, Mrs. Halliday?" said Ann. "You think I'd suit you?"

Mrs. Halliday nodded with decision.

"I know a lady when I see one," she said.

Chapter Five

ANN RANG CHARLES ANSTRUTHER up from a telephone box in the nearest post office. The roar of traffic from the great thoroughfare outside was suddenly dead as she pulled the door to behind her. A light flashed on in the ceiling, and after that Charles was saying,

"Ann, is that you?"

Ann said, "Yes," a little faintly, because there had leapt into her mind the realization of what it might be to shut the door on the world and let it go by. The world shut out, and she and Charles shut in. An impossible dream, but unbearably sweet, as only a dream can be.

There was nothing dreamlike about Charles' voice as he said,

"What's the matter?"

"Nothing's the matter."

"Why did you speak like that?"

"I didn't speak like anything."

"Yes, you did. Ann, are you going to dine with me to-night?"

"No, I can't. Oh, Charles, I've got the job! Isn't it marvellous? What did you say?"

"I said damn," said Charles.

"Beast!" said Ann. "And when I told you I'd been living on dry bread!"

"Ann!"

"To-night," said Ann in a gloating voice, "I shall be dining with Mr. James Halliday. I should think we'd have hot-house peaches, and turtle soup, and asparagus, and strawberries."

"Out of season," said Charles morosely.

"Darling Charles, that's *why*. It's that sort of house—all plush, and gilding, and lincrustaed halls."

"Who is this man?" said Charles in a voice that jarred the telephone.

"Darling Charles, you'll bust the wire if you roar like that, and then I shan't be able to tell you about my nice job. But perhaps you don't want to hear."

"Who is this man?" said Charles, still with a good deal of vigour.

"It's all quite proper and respectable," said Ann. "He's old Mrs. Halliday's son, and I've been hired at the princely salary of a hundred and twenty pounds a year to listen whilst old Mrs. Halliday talks."

"Then why are you dining with Mr. Halliday?"

"Because Mrs. Halliday doesn't dine. She has what she calls 'a bite of supper and bed'."

Charles said, "Dine with me." Then after a pause he said her name—just "Ann"; but his voice made it sound like "Ann *darling.*"

Ann took a step back as if he were there and visibly trying to hold her.

"Charles, I can't."

"Where have you gone? I can't hear you."

Ann stopped forward again.

"I said, 'I can't.' I'm taking over the job at once—just going home to pack, and moving right in."

"When am I going to see you?" said Charles tempestuously.

"I don't know," said Ann. And then she said "Good-bye," and pushed the receiver back upon its hook. She couldn't hear Charles' voice any more.

It was perfectly idiotic for her heart to be beating so hard. She stood there until it quieted, and then she opened the heavy glass door and the roar of the traffic rushed in.

In the house in Westley Gardens Mr. James Halliday was also using the telephone. He said,

"That you, Gale?... It's all right—she's coming in to-night. How is he? About the same?"

Rather an abrupt voice answered.

"Of course he's about the same. He won't be any different till he's dead."

"Well, well, well," said Mr. Halliday, "there's no hurry about that, you know. If he can be kept going for a month, why, so much the better."

"A month? What's the good of saying a month? He might be gone to-morrow, or he might hang on for half a year. You've got to get her away. The minute the breath's out of his body there'll be a swarm of reporters nosing round, and it won't be twenty-four hours before someone gets hold of the terms of the will, and the next thing you'll know, she'll be seeing her name in the headlines with 'Rich Man's Heiress' underneath. You've got to get a move on or we're done."

"All right, all right!" said Mr. Halliday. "You know, Gale, you talk too much. I rang you up to tell you something, and you talk so much that you've pretty near put it out of my mind."

"Well, what is it?"

"And you're a lot too impatient too. It's a job that's got to be done carefully. I was going to tell you that the old lady asked her what we weren't sure about—whether she was thinking of getting married or anything of that sort—and she said no as cool as a cucumber."

A sound that was almost too angry for a laugh came to him along the wire.

"You make me tired! Do you suppose she'd give herself away at a first interview, and a business interview at that?"

Mr. Halliday assumed a tone of offence.

"Well, I'm sure Mrs. Halliday put it very nicely, and I don't see why the girl wouldn't have told her if she was engaged."

There was the angry sound again.

"Nice respectable middle-class mind you've got! Haven't you, Jimmy?"

The offence in Mr. Halliday's tone deepened.

"What's wrong with being respectable?" he said. "And what's wrong with a girl saying she's got a boy, even if she isn't right down engaged to him? The way I look at it is, she'd say so because she'd want time off to see him, and the old lady says she was very decided that there wasn't anyone." There was a pause. Mr. Halliday said, "You there, Gale?" and was barked at.

"Of course I'm there! When are you getting off?"

"Well—I thought about Monday," said Mr. Halliday rather dubiously.

"Five days? Much too dangerous."

Mr. Halliday coughed.

"The old lady don't fancy starting on a Friday—she's got an idea it's unlucky—nor she don't fancy a Saturday, nor a Sunday."

"What's this infernal nonsense?"

"I won't go against the old lady," said Mr. Halliday.

"What's wrong with Saturday?"

"She don't fancy it," said Mr. Halliday. "She isn't so downright set against it as she is against the Friday or the Sunday, but she don't fancy it much. I might try her again."

The man he called Gale fairly made the receiver crackle.

"She's got to fancy it! Do you hear?"

"Well, I'll try," said Mr. Halliday. "Good night to you, Gale." He hung up the receiver.

Gale was in a fume. Gale always did put himself in a fume. Elias Paulett wasn't going to die before Monday. He was just the sort to hang on, and on, and on. Still if there was any risk, they'd better shift on Saturday. That was the worst of dealing with anyone like Gale—you didn't know when to take them seriously. If Gale wanted you to do a thing, he'd pitch you a tale, and how were you to know whether it was a true one? He supposed they'd better shift on Saturday.

He set about making his arrangements.

Ann slept that night at Westley Gardens. Her room was over Mrs. Halliday's sitting-room. Mrs. Halliday had the bedroom over the drawing-room, and her maid, a stout elderly person of the name of Riddle, had a slip of a room between the two. It had been intended for a dressing-room, and it was a tight fit for Riddle.

Ann's room was a little smaller than the room below. It was furnished in bright yellow maple. The carpet, the curtains, the bed-spread, and the china were of a lively pink, but the bed was so comfortable that it almost made up for it.

Ann fell asleep and dreamed that she was running away from Charles down a primrose path. There was a bonfire at the bottom of the path, and someone whose face she couldn't see was feeding it with bright yellow furniture and bright pink china. The china crunched and smashed under her feet, but she couldn't stop. She ran right into the fire and heard the flames go roaring past, and old Mrs. Halliday said, "Girls wouldn't be in such a hurry if they knew what was in front of 'em." And then quite suddenly the fire was gone, and the light, and the noise. Everything seemed to have stopped, and she was in a dark place. Something moved, just out of reach. It moved again and came nearer, and in the last moment before she woke Ann knew what the something was.

But when she was awake she didn't know any more. She sat up in bed with her hand pressed tightly to her breast. There were beads of sweat on her forehead. Her hair clung to her temples. Something had made her afraid, and for a moment she had known what the something was. But now she didn't know.

It was a long time before she went to sleep again.

Chapter Six

THE NEXT DAY was Thursday, and in the course of it Mrs. Halliday imparted to Ann a great deal of family history. It made her head go round, because Mrs. Halliday ranged over some eighty years which she remembered herself, and another fifty or sixty which she had been told about by her uncles and aunts, and brought up, as from a crowded lucky bag, quarrels, courtships, births, marriages and deaths. You never quite knew to within fifty years what century you were in. At one moment Mrs. Halliday would be recounting the infant virtues of her son James—"'Is 'air curled lovely, and he weighed ten pound when he was born." And the next, with voice dropped to a whisper, she was imparting details of the scandal which had parted her great uncle Amos and his wife—"an 'ussy if ever I see one—not as I ever did see her, she being dead and buried afore I was born, and a good job too, coming mixing and meddling in a respectable family with 'er ringlets and 'er rooge."

By degrees, however, Ann gathered that Mrs. Halliday had married late—"I'd a brown cashmere dress wot my lady give me, and a black straw 'at with a nice bunch of cornflowers one side, and a pair of brown kid gloves with brass buttons."

Halliday, it appeared, had followed the sea—a north-countryman and close in his ways—not, Ann gathered, a good husband—"And few and far between they are Miss Vernon, my dear. A young man courting is one thing, and an 'usband is another—too loving to last is what I say, and it'll save you a lot of disappointment if you don't count on it. You take a good-living, respectable man with a bit in the bank—that's my advice."

"It sounds frightfully dull," said Ann.

"There's worse things than being dull," said Mrs. Halliday.

By way of an improving anecdote about a second cousin once removed who was so foolish as to marry a chance-come young man with a handsome face and a wheedling tongue, and who very properly ended in the workhouse, they returned to Mr. James Halliday. He was an only child and the best son that ever was. He too had followed the sea, and then he had a bit of luck and went into business—"'E's a great one for business is Jimmy, and set on my having the best of everything."

"Does this house belong to you?" said Ann.

"No, Miss Vernon my dear, it doesn't—not but what it mightn't come to that if 'e brings off something as 'e's got in 'and. 'E's got it furnished, and what they call a h'option, which is to say that 'e can buy it if 'e likes. But it belongs to Mr. 'Iggins—the Mr. 'Iggins as won the big prize in one of they Irish sweepstakes, pore feller."

"Why?" said Ann.

"'E got the money and 'e bought the 'ouse, and 'e done it up lovely from top to toe and furnished it fit for Buckingham Palace, and then if 'is wife didn't put 'er foot down and say she wouldn't live in it. Burst into tears right there in the 'all she did, and said as she wasn't brought up to it, and if she'd got to live in an 'ouse where 'er kitchen wasn't 'er own to sit in and she'd got to dress in velvet, she'd rather be dead and in her coffin right away and save a lot of trouble. Pore-spirited, I call it—put me in mind of my Aunt Maria when Mr. 'Iggins told me, and I said to 'im, 'Such being the case, better let 'er 'ave 'er kitchen, for you won't get any peace and quiet until you do.' Crying like a leaky tap all the time she was. So 'e let the 'ouse to James." She paused and added, "With a h'option."

On Friday morning there was a letter from Charles Anstruther. Ann opened it with a curious feeling of expectation. Which was absurd. The letter began with her name—just "Ann." This was, of course, highly compromising. It was more compromising than if he had said "Darling Ann," for nowadays everybody said darling and meant nothing by it. Just "Ann" meant, "I could call you such a lot of names if you would let me. Ann, don't you want to hear the names I've got for you?"

Ann bit her lip and read the letter:

Ann, do for any sake chuck this job. I don't like it for you. I'm sure I could find you something if you would wait. Ann, do wait, and let me lend you something to go on with. I promise I'll let you pay me back. If you won't take the job I want you to take, I'm sure I can find you something else. You don't know anything about these people, and I don't like what I hear. I've been nosing round, and no one seems to know quite where the money comes from. Some of it anyhow is from rum-running— some of it's possibly shadier than that. Quite definitely I don't like it for you. And I don't like your having had a paper sent to you with the advertisement marked. How do you know Mary Duquesne sent it? I don't believe she did."

Ann frowned and bit her lip again. Then she sat down and wrote to Charles:

Darling Charles,

What a fuss! You've been seeing films. The Hallidays are being frightfully nice to me. She's an old pet, and he's the best son in the world. She says so, and she ought to know. She's got a maid called Riddle who has probably been the most respectable person in England since Mrs. Grundy died. I suppose she is dead—or had you just been having a nice cosy heart-to-heart talk with her when you wrote to me?

She signed "Ann," and then wrote underneath:

Don't be a Maiden Aunt.

Boil the head till perfectly clear. One to two hours should suffice. (Mrs. Halliday has just been telling me how to make marrow jam. This ought to reassure you, because villains in films never make marrow jam.)

My Maiden Aunts told me never to allow young men to lend me money.

On Friday Ann began to settle down. It wasn't going to be too bad. Riddle looked after Mrs. Halliday till eleven o'clock, and then Ann took her over. After lunch she rested for two hours under Riddle's supervision, and at eight o'clock she went to bed. No, it wasn't going to be at all bad, and the pay was marvellous. If Charles thought she was going to throw up a job like this just because he chose to be a fuss, Charles had got to be taught to think again. Perhaps she would dine with him one day next week. She wondered whether she would have the nerve to ask for what Mrs. Halliday called her wages in advance. She couldn't dine with Charles unless she could get her dress out of pawn. Ouf! There was something horribly sordid about the idea of dining with Charles in a pawned dress—sordid, and salutary. If she was in any danger of weakening, the thought of the pawnbroker's shop would have a bracing effect. Yes, she would dine with Charles, just to show them both that she didn't care a damn.

And with that, Mr. James Halliday came into the room and inquired whether she had finished packing.

"Packing?" said Ann.

Mr. Halliday's sandy eyebrows rose.

"Well now! Hasn't Mrs. Halliday told you?"

"Nothing about packing," said Ann.

"No—no," said Mr. Halliday—"you've not seen her lunch, to be sure. Well, if you like to make a start, you could get in the best part of an hour before tea."

"But where are we going?"

Ann was in one of the old-gold chairs with a book on her lap. A hot, dusty ray of sunshine slanted between her and Mr. James, who stood a couple of yards away fingering the hard, shiny leaf of the aspidistra in the blue pot. He said,

"We're going on my boat. I hope you like sailing. It's too hot here for the old lady, and that's the truth. We wouldn't have been here now if it hadn't been for getting her fixed up."

"I *love* sailing," said Ann. "Where are we going?"

Mr. Halliday took out a bright magenta silk handkerchief and dusted the aspidistra. He had shrewd grey eyes and unusually thick sandy lashes. He did not look at Ann.

"Oh, up along the coast."

"And when do we start?"

"Nine o'clock to-morrow morning," said Mr. Halliday, and he put the magenta silk handkerchief back into his pocket and went out of the room.

It did not take Ann half an hour to pack. She looked at the clock, and wrote to Charles in pencil because there was no ink in her bedroom, and somehow—somehow she didn't want to write to Charles under the eyes of the mirrors and the aspidistras in the drawing-room. She said:

Darling Charles,

    Back to the films! Captions: "The Sinister House"—"The Lowly Companion"—"The Seven Aspidistras"—"Rum-runner's Gilded Hall of Vice"—"The Mysterious Yacht"—"An Unexpected Voyage." Take three long breaths and emerge into real life. We're off to-morrow on a cruise up along the coast. Isn't it simply too thrilling? I adore sailing. I'll send you an address when I've got one. If I don't, you'll know I've eloped with the run-runner to wherever he keeps his secret still—do you make rum in stills? I shall be able to tell you all about it if we ever meet again. Return to captions: "A Voice from the Ocean. Good-bye—good-bye—good-bye!" Slow fade out.

Ann.

    Isn't it too marvellous to be getting out of London?

Mrs. Halliday came down to tea in a very bad temper. Mr. Halliday did not come to tea at all.

"And I don't wonder neither!" said his mother, cutting a thick slice of bread viciously into squares. "It's right down put me out and 'e knows it, and if 'e's got any sense, 'e'll keep out of my road till I've slep' on it." She put butter on one of the squares, honey on another, marmalade on a third, and black currant jelly, strawberry jam, and apple cheese on the remaining pieces. "'E did ought to know better, and so I told him!"

"Don't you want to go away?" said Ann.

Mrs. Halliday took the square spread with honey in one hand and the square spread with marmalade in the other and took alternate bites from each.

"Acourse I want to go away!" she said angrily. "Monday we was going, and Monday was a good day to go—start of a week and start of a journey." She finished the honey and marmalade and went on to strawberry jam and apple cheese. "End of the week travelling's like end of the week washing—looks as if you'd been trying to get off since Monday and hadn't made it out. Wash on Saturday, wash for shame—that's what I was always told in my young days—I'd like some more milk in me tea. 'Ot and milky, and three lump o' sugar's the way I like it, Miss Vernon. So I says to James, 'Have it your own way, my lad, and don't blame me if things go wrong.' Another lump of sugar, my dear, and just a dab more honey. Him and me 'ad words, and if 'e goes without 'is tea it's no more than 'e deserves." Mrs. Halliday paused, licked a smear of honey from her forefinger, and went on to black currant jelly. "There won't be any good come of this, and so I told 'im. Dreamt I was packing last night and all, and woke up that put about because Riddle 'ad packed my best bonnet along of Jimmy's sea-boots. Another cup o' tea, my dear, and you needn't trouble to empty the dregs—I like to keep me sugar. I've had some terrible strange dreams in my time, and I don't hold with going against 'em. I dreamt one time that my laundry-line was blowing away, and I run out and tried to catch it, but I couldn't reach, so I got the kitchen table and climbed on it, and so soon as I got the line in my two 'ands it took me right off me feet and I couldn't let go, and I tore my best table-cloth clean in two and woke up crying my 'eart out, and that day three weeks I broke my leg through missing the top step of the stairs in the dark. So I don't 'old with flying in the face of dreams, and never shall."

When she had talked herself into a good humour, Ann said,

"Where are we going, Mrs. Halliday?"

Mrs. Halliday's long nose crinkled a little. Her head, with the grey hair banded on either side of a wide parting and surmounted by a white lace cap trimmed with yellow satin ribbon, nodded in time to her chuckling laugh.

"You wait and see, Miss Vernon my dear!"

Chapter Seven

CHARLES ANSTRUTHER got Ann's letter on Saturday morning. It disquieted him enough to send him straight off to Westley Gardens, where a young footman in undress informed him that the family had left, and that the house was being shut up. He didn't know anything about an address. Tipped by Charles, he believed that Mr. Halliday, and Mrs. Halliday, and Miss Vernon, and Mrs. Halliday's maid were going for a cruise on Mr. Halliday's motor yacht. He was very sorry, but he didn't know any more than that. He had only been engaged for the month, and it was the same with all the other servants. They were shutting up the house, and handing in the key to a firm of house-agents.

"I'm very sorry, sir, I'm sure, but I expect they'll have let the post office know about their letters, so if you was to write to this address, it would likely be forwarded."

Charles came away rather more disquieted than before.

He wrote to Ann, and presently got the letter back again. It was clear that, whatever Mr. and Mrs. Halliday had done, Ann had either not had an opportunity of arranging for her letters to be forwarded or had not availed herself of it. She had promised to send him an address, but none came. He began to rake London for people who might possibly know something about Mr. James Halliday. The man who had hinted at rum-running was a chance-met club acquaintance and had most inopportunely departed to Norway. Everybody Charles wanted appeared to be somewhere else.

He contrived in the end to meet unofficially one of the Assistant Commissioners of the Metropolitan Police, and of him made discreet inquiries. He did not find the interview a very reassuring one. On Charles' side Ann appeared as a cousin who had taken a job which worried her family. It is doubtful whether the Assistant Commissioner was deceived by this camouflage. On his part it appeared that, as far as the police were concerned, Mr. James Halliday had no history. He had never been in prison. He had never been in the hands of the police. Officially, there was nothing against him.

This should have been reassuring, but somehow it wasn't. As the Assistant Commissioner talked, Charles received a very definite impression that Jimmy Halliday—he spoke of him as Jimmy Halliday—owed this enviable state of affairs not so much to the innocence of his character as to the astuteness of his brain. "He looks like a mug and he talks like a mug, and if he'd been half such a mug as he looks, we'd have landed him long ago." Pressed by Charles, the Assistant Commissioner had almost as little to impart as the young footman at Westley Gardens.

"He's gone off on a cruise," said Charles.

"He started life as a sailor, I believe," said the Assistant Commissioner.

"Miss Vernon's on board as his mother's companion."

"Oh, then I should think she'd be all right," said the Assistant Commissioner cheerfully. "He's a very good son, I believe. Your—er—cousin will be all right if she's with the old lady. I can let you know where the yacht touches if you like."

It was ten days later that he got a line saying that the *Emma* had put in at Oban, and by the next post he got a picture postcard from Ann. It depicted the copy of the Acropolis which so incongruously crowns the hill above that West Highland port. Charles could have done without the picture and with more of the pencilled lines in which Ann addressed him as her darling Charles, announced that she was having the time of her life and was thinking of taking a permanent job as a cabin-boy, and concluded with the cryptic remark: "Films are off. This is the great out of doors." There was a little "Ann" in the corner just slipping off the card.

Charles called himself seven kinds of damn fool, had a couple of suit-cases packed, his car greased and filled up, and departed up the Great North Road, leaving the sale of Bewley hung up between the boot-manufacturer's latest advance and his, Charles', latest retreat.

The *Emma* stayed twenty-four hours at Oban, took Gale Anderson on board in an unobtrusive manner, and put to sea again in halcyon weather. Ann was enjoying herself so much that she was ready to be friends with all the world, but even on a day when the sea and the sky swam together in a blue and golden haze and only the faintest of clouds just touched the sparkling water with a passing shade of hyacinth or amethyst, she did not feel as if she could ever really be friends with Gale Anderson. It was a pity, because it would have been nice to have had someone young to play with.

Gale Anderson was young, in the early thirties. He was good-looking in a quiet, well-featured, fair-haired way—heaps better looking than Charles, who had a dark, ugly face which became ferocious when he frowned. On the other hand, when he smiled, you forgot all about his being ugly and you were put to it not to weaken.

Ann dragged herself away from remembering how Charles looked when he smiled. If it was undermining, the less she thought about it the better. Charles, refused, would probably marry the boot-manufacturer's daughter, which would be very nice, because then he wouldn't have to sell Bewley.

Gale Anderson neither smiled nor looked ferocious. He was pale, polite, and indifferent, and his cool blue eyes when they rested upon Ann appeared to find her of no more interest than if she had been a binnacle or a bulwark.

"Puts me in mind of a young gentleman that visited in my first place," said Mrs. Halliday. "Courting Miss Edith he was, and everyone said how lucky she was to get him, but it didn't turn out at all 'appy— not that there was anything against him, but he'd a sort of h'icy way with him that made me come up goose flesh all over, if you know what I mean."

Ann knew exactly what she meant, and said so.

"Then best keep mum about it," said Mrs. Halliday, "for him and Jimmy's as thick as thieves."

The words stayed in Ann's mind. They said themselves over once or twice when Jimmy Halliday and Gale Anderson walked up and down the deck talking in the low tones which never satisfied anyone else's curiosity. But of course there was nothing to be curious about.

They dawdled along among the islands and up the coast. It was all quite perfect. The weather went on being blue and gold for two days, and then broke in a thunderstorm. There was a flicker of lightning on the far edge of the horizon as the sun went down, and a lead-coloured bank of cloud crossed by puffs of white like the smoke from a heavy gun. The white clouds raced across the black one, and the black cloud itself came up and filled the sky. In a moment it seemed to be dark.

Ann was not at all pleased at being ordered off the deck. She wanted to watch. The wind came up in a squally gust and dropped again. For a moment everything held its breath, and then the lightning ran in a jagged scrawl across the zenith and a deafening clap of thunder followed. As James Halliday fairly pushed her inside the companion and slammed the door, a second squall struck the yacht and Ann was tipped down the companion with a noise in her ears that drowned the sound of the thunder. She got to her feet and slid across the saloon. As she caught at the handle of Mrs. Halliday's cabin, the door gave and she was flung inside. A brilliant flash lit the skylight overhead, but she could not hear the thunder for the noise of the wind. She would not have believed that wind could make so much noise. It was like thunder, and an express train, and a great whip cracking, and about half a million fiddles gone mad.

She steadied herself against the tilting of the cabin floor. Her blood was racing and she felt as if she had been running hard. It was all very exciting, but it was quite evident that neither Mrs. Halliday nor Riddle was enjoying it. Mrs. Halliday was in her berth with a frilled nightcap on her head and a fine knitted shawl about her shoulders. She looked white but determined, and at intervals of about half a minute she said, "Don't be a fool, Riddle!" You could see her saying it, but you could not hear the words because of the wind.

The impassive Riddle was completely dissolved in terrified tears. They rolled openly down her large pale face and fell unregarded upon her neat black lap. She sat sideways upon her bunk and clutched the edge. When the wind struck them with one of its heavier blows and the floor tilted, she screamed. Ann could see her mouth opening and the shriek coming out, and whenever it was possible to hear anything, Mrs. Halliday said, "Don't be a fool, Riddle!" And all the time the skylight brightened and darkened overhead as the lightning came and went. Then with a strange suddenness the fury of the squall was over.

Ann climbed uphill to the door, and then, as the boat went over, was shot right across the saloon. She wanted desperately to get out on deck again and see the lightning make its flashlight pictures of the black hurrying clouds and straining sea. She began to make her way towards the companion, but a sudden lurch flung her against the door of the cabin shared by Mr. Halliday and Gale Anderson. The door gave and she went slipping down against the bunks. In a moment there was water running down her neck, and her hands groped and slipped upon wet metal. The wind blew down upon her up-turned face. The skylight was an inch or two open, overlooked in the sudden flurry of the storm. It was raining now in torrents, and the water was coming in faster every moment.

She climbed on to the bunk to shut the skylight, and as she steadied herself, she heard Gale Anderson say, so close that it startled her,

"Damn fool to send her down! There'll never be a better opportunity."

The voice came through the open skylight. The rain splashed round the sound of it without confusing the words.

And then James Halliday said,

"The old lady sets a good deal of store by her. I won't have her put about."

Ann stood quite still.

There was no more to hear. The rain came down, and the boat rolled in the choppy sea.

She left the skylight open and the wet coming in, and made her way up the companion. She could not put any meaning to the words that she had heard. Mr. Halliday had made her go below. Why was he a damn fool to do it? Or weren't they talking about her at all? And what was the opportunity that had been missed?

She got the door open, and the wind met her. Not the raging fury of a little while ago, but a joyful, bounding wind that came hallooing across the open sea, flinging its showers at them and whooping off again. Ann held to the rail and looked out upon black tossing water. The lightning flickered away in the north, violet and green, and the clouds drove dark before the wind. On the western horizon was one pale streak of a light between green and grey.

Ann did not know quite when she began to have the feeling that someone was watching her. If she was visible at all, it must be only as a black blob. Why should anyone watch a black blob? Why for that matter should anyone watch Ann Vernon? She called herself an idiot and listened to James Halliday shouting out that there was another squall coming. She supposed she would have to go down again, but it would be much more interesting to stay there. She forgot the feeling of being watched as she looked out into the dark and heard the roar of the coming squall. Then, as she turned regretfully and groped for the companion door, something struck her on the head and she fell. There was a confusion of wind and water, an icy drenching, and a roaring noise. She was flung against something hard. Her hands clutched, and closed upon emptiness.

She had not time to be afraid before a grip that hurt was on her arm, her waist, and a moment later she was inside the companion, with Jimmy Halliday shouting at her. She could hear him above the wind, because it was he who was holding her. In a voice that sounded as if he was using a megaphone he was inquiring what the blank, blank, blankety something she meant by coming on deck when he had told her to stay below—"You blank, blank, blank little fool, you!"

Ann was so dazed that she just stared at him and went on staring. There was a little bright light just overhead. It showed Jimmy Halliday's face not six inches from her own, all puffed and scarlet under the wet sandy hair, whilst angry words and oaths came pattering out of his mouth like hailstones. She ought to have been angry, or frightened, or grateful, because she had very nearly been drowned, and he was swearing at her, and it began very dimly to occur to her that he had saved her life. But she wasn't angry or frightened or grateful, or anything at all except numb and dumb. Her head didn't feel as if it belonged to her, and when he gave her a push which sent her down the companion, she sat down in a huddle on the bottom step and shut her eyes. The wind drowned Jimmy Halliday's voice and the furious bang of the door above her.

She might have sat there for a long time if the boat had not been rolling so. She got up and made her way to her own cabin and lay down upon the berth. The squall lessened. The boat rolled. Once she heard Jimmy Halliday's voice pitched on a note of rage. He was swearing at somebody else now, which was a comfort. She rather gathered that he was swearing at Gale Anderson.

Then the voice was gone. She fell asleep.

Chapter Eight

THEY LANDED NEXT DAY in the very early morning. The wind had dropped and the rain was coming down, not heavily but in a fine weave of mist and water which blotted out both sea and hills. There remained a muddy foreshore sprinkled with boulders and coated with a yellowish rust, and above it a stretch of wet grey road, and a car.

The driver left his seat, exchanged a few inaudible words with James Halliday, and rowed off to the yacht. Gale Anderson took his place at the wheel. Mrs. Halliday and Riddle were helped in. Ann took a back seat and was barricaded with suit-cases. The rest of the luggage went on behind, and with Jimmy Halliday on the seat beside the driver they began to climb towards the unseen hills.

It wasn't a very cheerful journey. Ann's head ached. Riddle dwelt with mournful pride upon the certainty that she would presently be sick. And Mrs. Halliday, with her feet in cloth-topped button boots raised comfortably upon a couple of suit-cases, put her head back against a scarlet leather cushion and slept. She not only slept, but she snored in an awful rhythmic manner which reminded Ann of a cornet solo in an advanced modern symphony. The mist streamed by. Something rattled at the back of the car. It had the sound of metal upon metal, and it fretted Ann almost to screaming point. She put her hand to her head and felt the lump upon it. Something must have hit her very hard to make a lump like that. All through the business of getting up and getting Mrs. Halliday packed and landed Ann had been wondering just what it was that had raised that lump. She felt perfectly certain that she had not hit herself. She had been hit. Something had banged down upon her head and knocked her flying, and she had gone down clutching and slithering to the black drowning water that was waiting for her.

She looked round at Jimmy Halliday's bullet head with its short sandy hair and felt a belated gratitude. If he hadn't clutched her, she wouldn't be here now. She wondered where she would be. Her body would be swinging to and fro with the tide, and she would be somewhere else. The thought made her feel vaguely disembodied. She came back with difficulty to the question of what had hit her. There slid into her mind Gale Anderson's voice and Gale Anderson's words: "Damn fool to send her down! There'll never be a better opportunity."

They drove on into the mist and rain.

Presently Mrs. Halliday woke up and told a cheerful story about a young man that was hanged for sheep stealing.

"The last man in England to be hanged for it he was, and nothing but a lad of eighteen. He worked for his father, and there was a stray sheep come in along of theirs, so he asks his father what 'e shall do, and 'is father says, 'Some'un'll claim it,' but no one did. So it come to the sheep shearing, and the lad says to his father 'There's that sheep as come in along of ours—what's to do with it?' And his father says, 'Brand it and turn it in with the others,' and so 'e did. And it wasn't a week after someone come and claimed it. And they hanged the lad."

"Oh—they *didn't*!" said Ann.

Mrs. Halliday's bonnet hung at a jaunty angle over one large ear. She nodded her head against the scarlet cushion.

"Sure enough they hanged him. And my father climbed a tree to see it done, and fell down in a faint. Many's the time he's told me."

They drove all day in the mist. The hills were shapes, not so much seen as imagined. The sound of falling water came and went. Sometimes a great black shoulder loomed up, or the thick air parted to show a hill side hung with dripping pines, or a flat waste stretch of moorland dark with bog. Every now and then they passed another car or a group of stone cottages. Mrs. Halliday went to sleep. There were two picnic meals by the wet roadside.

Ann had plenty of time to think. She thought about the stormy night and being hit on the head. She thought about lunching with Charles at the Luxe. She thought a lot about Charles.

In the evening they stopped by the side of a loch. There was a boat by the shore. It was a relief to get out of the car and into the boat. James Halliday and Gale Anderson took a pair of oars apiece and rowed them out upon the loch. The shore faded.

Ann said, "Where are we going?" but no one answered her. They might have been going out of the world. She dipped a finger in the water, put it up to her lips, and found it salt. Was the yacht waiting for them out in the fog? She couldn't have got there. It came to Ann that she hadn't the faintest idea where they might be. They had driven all day, but they might have run in a circle for all she knew.

Out of the mist sprang a line of lapping ripples and a tiny white beach. The boat grounded, and the two men pulled her up.

A narrow path led up from the beach. It climbed by steps and steep slanting zigzags to come out upon a little lawn. And there, joyful to see, were the lighted windows of a house.

"And a nice cup of tea is what I want, if I never had bite nor sup again," said Mrs. Halliday.

Jimmy Halliday put his arm round her and lifted her over the threshold.

"You shall have as many cups of tea as you like, old lady," he said.

Chapter Nine

THE MIST WAS ALL GONE when Ann woke up. She ran to the window and looked out. Below her was the little green lawn, and beyond the lawn a straggle of bushes and trees, and beyond the trees the bright glancing of water blue in the sun, and the still clouded shapes of the hills. She washed and dressed quickly and ran down and out. It was all a wonder and an enchantment. The air was fresh and soft, and a thick dew drenched her feet.

She looked at the house from the lawn, and could have laughed, it was so out of keeping with its surroundings. A neat little villa with a bow window on either side of the front door and a cherub's head for a knocker. The room on the right was the dining-room. The room on the left was the parlour. Mrs. Halliday's room above it, the blinds all down. Her own room above the dining-room. All as tidy and small as if it had been picked up out of a row in Tooting—"It ought to be called *Mon Répos*, or *Sans Souci*, or *Il Nido*!" Her rather horrid forebodings of the day before were things to laugh about.

She ran round the house and stood still to stare. The villa front masked something very much older. The windows at the back were of the smallest, mere slits in thick old walls of weathered stone. There was a huddle of out-houses—a cow-shed, a pig-sty, a cobbled yard. She could smell the cows. There was more than one, by the fidgeting, breathing, munching sounds that came to her through the boarded doors. A cock flew up on to the yard gate and crowed. What an odd house to find in this wild place, so neat and smug in front, so old and ramshackle and untidy behind.

A path ran uphill between bushes. Ann climbed and went twisting and turning up a steep slope. The trees and a thick undergrowth hid everything except themselves. She came out at last on to a heathery knoll. The trees and bushes ceased, and the path came to an end. She went knee-deep amongst heather and tumbled rocks, and found herself at last at the top of the rise. She had made up her mind that she would not look until she had reached the top. Now, at the view-point, she saw water all round her, shining away in blue stretches to the precipitous shores of the loch. As she stood, the climbing sun was on her right. A very dark, frowning hill rose sheer from the water on that side. Immediately in front of her a black cliff streaked with red shadowed the loch. She turned about and saw, as it seemed a mere stone's throw away, the landing-stage from which they had come the night before and a bend of the road which had brought them.

She wondered what had happened to the car. It wasn't there any longer. Had it gone back and round the bend into the dark hollow between the pine-clad hill and the rough bare one which towered up into the clouds? She wondered who had made the road between the hills, and whether it had been a watercourse before it was a road. There was only that one break that she could see in the rugged wall of the loch. She could not even tell on which side lay the sea. If to the west, it was hidden by the sweep of the hills. She thought the light breeze came that way and that it tasted salt.

The island was quite small, perhaps four hundred yards across; she couldn't tell. She could only see its shore on one side, where it was very rocky. She thought the loch looked deep. There was no change in the colour of the water under the cliffs. She thought how sea-water changes to green and muddy yellow as it shallows along the coast. There was nothing like that here, and she pictured the loch as a deep chasm driven into the land, with the cliffs that edged it going down sheer under the water—down, and down, and down. She wondered what it was like down there in the depths. It ran through her mind that she had heard of a loch that was a mile deep. *A mile....* Ann shivered. It was a very long way down.

The thought stayed in her mind, and later on at breakfast she asked Jimmy Halliday whether the loch was deep. He raised his sandy eyebrows.

"Deep enough," he said.

"Yes—but how deep?" said Ann.

"Deep enough to drown you," said Jimmy Halliday.

Ann felt as if a very cold drop of water had run I down her neck. She gave a little shiver. And Mrs. Halliday nodded and said,

"That was a goose a-walking over your grave, Miss Vernon, my dear."

Ann laughed.

"I shall take care not to be drowned," she said.

Jimmy. Halliday didn't say anything for some time. Then quite suddenly he asked her if she could swim, and when she had said no, he relapsed into silence again.

Gale Anderson was not at breakfast. It presently appeared that he wasn't in the house at all, or on the island. Since he was gone, and the car was gone, it was to be inferred that they had gone together. Ann felt that she could very easily bear his absence.

After breakfast she explored the house. The two front rooms were exactly alike, and so were the two bedrooms over them, but the back of the house was all up and down, and in and out, with little rooms like cupboards, and at one corner a spiral staircase with steep worn steps in the thickness of the wall. It led from the kitchen to a tiny room which was scarcely more than a recess with a door to it. There was another stair in the front of the house, a proper villa stair with a painted banister and wooden treads carpeted in red. At the back of the house on the ground floor was a kitchen, and a very large wash-house. Both these had stone floors.

The work of the house was all done by a middle-aged woman with a vacant face. She was tall, and thin, and bent, and she wore a dark stuff petticoat and a little grey cross-over shawl. Her faded hair was screwed up into a knob at the back of her head, but stray wisps of it fell about her forehead and her large pale ears. She kept the house very clean and tidy and she was a good cook, but she never spoke. Only every now and then she would stop in whatever she was doing, straighten her back, and look at you through the falling wisps of hair. When she did this to Mrs. Halliday, the old lady would say sharply, "Get on with your work, Mary!" and then she would sigh and bend down again and go on working.

Now that they were actually here, Mrs. Halliday was quite willing to talk about the island. They came here every year, and she liked it well enough—though why she should like it, Ann couldn't imagine, since she hardly ever went out, and then never beyond the little green lawn.

Riddle hated it, as was to be expected. She became very low-spirited and gave in her notice regularly every morning after breakfast.

"What does Mr. Halliday do with himself?" said Ann.

It appeared that Mr. Halliday fished. In the boat-house beside the little landing-stage there was a motor-boat as well as the rowing boat which had brought them over. Sometimes Jimmy Halliday took one, and sometimes the other. He would be away for a few hours, or all day, or a day and a night. Sometimes he went out at night and came back with the dawn. Once Ann asked him to take her, and was astonished at the roughness of his refusal.

Mrs. Halliday nodded over a stocking she was knitting. She knitted all her own stockings in fine black wool with a broad rib.

"Sailors don't like drowned folk," she said—"and Jimmy's been a sailor same as his father. Thinks they follow them, sailors do—thinks they come up out of the sea and 'aunts them. I don't rightly know as I'd believe it myself, but my 'usband, Jimmy's father, he took it for gospel."

Ann went away and wrote a letter to Charles.

Darling Charles,

I love being here. I ought to be bored stiff, but I'm not. There's nothing here but rocks and heather, and water and hills and rocks, especially rocks....

It was quite a nice long conversational letter. When she had finished it, she went back to Mrs. Halliday.

"Please what's our address? I've just been writing a letter—"

Mrs. Halliday's needles clicked.

"'The House on the Island, Loch Dhu'," she said placidly. "Dhu—it's a silly-sounding name, isn't it and means black, so they tell me. Seems funny they should talk foreign, and all one country, and it'd be a lot handier if they called it The Black Lake and have done with it, though a lake it isn't, for it runs out into the sea over yonder."

Ann pricked up her ears.

"Isn't Loch Dhu near Arran?"

Mrs. Halliday shook her head.

"There's more than one, and this one's lonely enough. There's no one comes here now. There's been a cottage or two where the cliffs wasn't too steep, but they're all fallen in and the people gone—and there's nothing in all the world that I hate so hearty as a house without a roof."

"Why did the houses fall down?" said Ann.

"Because the folk went away and left them, Miss Vernon, my dear."

"But why did they go?"

"Some says one thing, and some says another," said Mrs. Halliday, and would say no more.

"And how shall I get my letters to the post?"

"Jimmy'll take them. There's a post-box over by the landing, and the postman comes that far and takes what's there and leaves what he's brought with 'im. He don't come every day."

Ann gave her letter to Jimmy Halliday, and began to wonder when she would get an answer. It would be nice to hear from Charles. It would be like hearing from someone in another world. She began to feel as if she had got over the edge of the world she knew and off the map. It would be very nice to hear from Charles.

She found she was counting the days. But of course if the postman didn't come every day, it was no good counting. Mrs. Halliday didn't seem to know how often he came, and when she asked Jimmy Halliday, he threw her one of those odd sideways looks and said.

"When he feels like it." And then he laughed, and Ann wasn't sure that she liked the sound of his laughter.

And then she found the piece of paper.

She was out at the back in the yard watching the hens feed. Mary had thrown them some house scraps, and now she came and went to the rubbish-heap beyond, bringing out her ash-bucket to empty. There was a high gusty wind overhead. A little piece of paper came blowing along the yard. The wind caught it, twirled it high, and dropped it at Ann's feet. She bent to pick it up, and it fluttered away from her as if it was alive. Laughing and breathless, she caught it at last where the path turned upwards amongst the trees. It lay in her hand like a little dead, captured thing. It had whirled away from her and danced on the wind, and now it was only a scrap of dirty paper. And then quite suddenly she stopped laughing and was hot through and through with anger. Under the smudges and stains she could see two words. They were words in her own writing. She had written them herself, and she had written them to Charles—"especially rocks." Part of "especially" was torn away, but she knew what she had written.

Someone had torn up her letter to Charles.

The heat of her anger burned her through and through. And then it was gone, and she was afraid. She really was over the rim of the world. Nobody knew where she was. Charles didn't know where she was. She wanted desperately for Charles to be able to find her.

Presently the fear died down, as the anger had died. She tore the scrap of paper in half and buried the pieces under a heather root.

She thought about writing another letter. She thought about complaining to Mrs. Halliday or to Jimmy. She stood there sheltered by the trees and argued with herself. The letter might have been destroyed by accident.... Oh no, she couldn't make herself believe in an accident. Then if it wasn't an accident, what was the use of complaining? A second letter would only share the fate of the first. She stood there for a long time, and then went soberly back to the house.

Chapter Ten

IN A FEW DAYS Ann had explored the island. It was a most irritating island, because there were only two places where you could get down to the water's edge.

There was the beach below the house, and away on the opposite side of the island another tiny strand not a dozen yards across. Everywhere else the sides of the island fell sheer or were banked with a huddle of great rocks and boulders. The beach below the house was a short semicircular stretch of white sand with the boat-house filling up a corner. On either side a tiny headland ran out into the water, and the water was deep.

Ann had a fright when she tried to paddle out to the headland. The beach shelved gently for a few yards, and then quite suddenly she was up to her neck. It was as if she had stepped down a yard. She stood there with the water moving her lightly to and fro. A ripple came up over her chin and touched her lips with salt. She had the feeling that before her was another deep step down, or perhaps the island fell sheer away to the bottom of the loch. She was afraid to move, but she had to move, and presently she turned round and found a foothold and climbed back into the shallow water. Her clothes hung about her heavy and cold, and she found that she was trembling a little. But all the same, now that she was wet, she meant to find out more about that sudden drop.

What she needed was a pole or a stick. She broke a long thin branch from one of the birches above the landing-place and measured it in yards, counting a yard from her outstretched finger-tips to her mouth, as all women do. It was not quite nine feet. She held it thin end up and went back into the water, feeling in front of her with the butt end of the branch. Everywhere at a distance of between three and four yards from the beach there was that sudden deep step down, and in some places the drop was more than three feet. Four feet—five—six—and once she could not touch bottom at all with her nine-foot bough. What would have happened to her if she had waded out in one of those deeper places? It was an easily answered question. Her own words came back and mocked her: *"I shall take care not to be drowned."*

When she had taken off her wet things she carried them down into the kitchen for Mary to dry. It was the middle of the afternoon and the house was dead quiet. Mrs. Halliday was having her nap, and Jimmy Halliday was out with the boat. When Mrs. Halliday slumbered, Riddle slumbered too. Ann thought it would be nice if no one but Mary knew that she had fallen into the loch. She came in with her dripping bundle, shut the door behind her, and put her finger to her lips.

Mary raised herself slowly in her chair. She had been sitting, as she always sat when she was alone, with her elbows on her knees, her chin in her cupped hands, and a drift of wispy hair across her eyes. Her blank look gave way to a startled one.

"I fell in and got soaked," said Ann. Her eyes laughed, and the air of an adventure hung about her. "Can you dry my clothes? I don't want everyone to know I was so stupid."

Mary put up a hand and brushed the wisps of hair aside. The hand shook. She got up out of her chair, came a step nearer, and said in a toneless, whispering voice,

"Did ye see it?"

They were the first words that Ann had heard her speak. She had thought her dumb, and now she wondered if the poor thing's wits were astray. She said very kindly,

"I just fell in. You will dry them—won't you?"

Mary came nearer and put out her hands until they rested on Ann's shoulders. They felt cold and heavy there. Mary didn't look at her. She stood with bent I head, looking down.

"Did ye see it?" she said again. The words were distinct, but separated from one another as if by the effort it cost her to speak them. It wasn't quite like a human person speaking. In the back of Ann's thought it reminded her of a gramophone record running down.

"I didn't see anything." She lifted the wet clothes between them. "Look—they're soaking. Will you help me wring them in the yard?"

There was just a moment's pause, and then the clothes were taken out of her hands.

Whilst they were wringing them out and hanging them before the fire, Mary was her vacant everyday self. Her strong hands moved efficiently and her blank gaze went past Ann as if she wasn't there. Only just at the end, when Ann put a hand on her arm and thanked her, she opened her lips as if she were going to speak.

"What is it?" said Ann.

The lips closed again. Ann had the feeling that they had spoken, and that what they had said was there between them in the room. It was rather a horrid feeling. She said with a quiver in her voice,

"What is it? Has something frightened you?"

The lips opened again, made an assenting sound, and shut in a grey, hopeless line.

"What is it, Mary? What's frightening you? Won't you tell me?" She put her arm about the thin shoulders and felt how tense they were. "Poor Mary! Do tell me."

The lips were very near to her ear. Again with a grinding difficulty words came from them.

"Keep frae the water or it'll get ye." And with that she twisted away and went out into the yard to the cow-shed.

It was next day that Charles Anstruther came to the shore of the loch and looked across at the island. There didn't seem to be any way of getting to it. He supposed that there must be some way, since the smoke of a chimney was rising from among the trees and he could see what was obviously a boat-house. He stood there and hallooed, but no one answered him and no one came. It began to look as if visitors were neither expected nor desired, and his suspicions of Mr. James Halliday took a new lease of life. It was a preposterous thing to immure Ann on an inaccessible island. The whole thing was preposterous. He felt a damned fool, standing here hallooing at a piece of perfectly unresponsive scenery. The place was as lonely as if it was back in the twelfth century. At the edge of the loch there was a stone cottage with its roof fallen in and foxgloves growing by the empty hearth, and that and the thread of smoke on the island were the only signs that any human being inhabited, or ever had inhabited, this loneliness.

He stood there wondering what he should do next. He certainly hadn't come here just to go away again. It was a long way from London to Loch Dhu. He had reached Oban to find the *Emma* moored there. It seemed quite easy and practicable to row out to her and ask for Miss Vernon's address.

There was a skipper and a boy on board. Not a sociable person the skipper. A few terse words of one syllable appeared to exhaust his conversation. All the same he managed to convey quite clearly that he hadn't got any address, and that he wouldn't give it if he had. It wasn't his business to give addresses; it was his business to wait for Mr. Halliday's orders and to stay where he was till he got them. At this point he walked away and leaned on the rail with his back to Charles.

Charles was aware of the grinning boy. He took out a cigarette and lit it, and at the same time allowed the crisp corner of a bank-note to appear. The boy's grin became fixed. His eyes goggled. Charles unfolded the note, refolded it, put it away, and caught the goggling eye. It seemed to him that it held a hopeful, lingering look. He addressed the skipper's back.

"If Mr. Halliday should send you an address, my name is Anstruther and I am at the Marine Hotel."

There was no response. Charles had not in fact expected one. He returned to the shore.

The question was, did the boy know the address, and would he be able to communicate with Charles if he did? His eye had certainly glistened at the sight of the fiver. Well, no address, no fiver.

Twenty-four hours passed, and it looked as if there was going to be no boy. The front at Oban affords a very beautiful prospect, but prospects were not being of any use to Charles. He walked up and down the long paved stretch and counted the hotels, and wondered why one of the houses had a roof like a bishop's mitre. These are occupations which pall. There were, besides, shop-windows full of strings of pink, and blue, and white, and purple stones. There was a beautiful Ionic cross of smoky cairngorm. Behind the surface attention that he gave to these things was a growing anxiety about Ann.

He was looking at the cross, when he was aware of a dark blue shoulder almost touching his own. He moved a little. The shoulder moved too. A quick glance of annoyance showed him the slightly ferrety features of the *Emma*'s boy. They wore a half embarrassed, half familiar grin. The pale blue eyes fixed themselves on Charles' face. Then, with an awkward thrust of the shoulder, he said in a hoarse whisper,

"Abaht that address—"

Charles' frown smoothed out. He looked encouragingly at the unpleasing youth and said,

"Can you let me have it?"

The grin widened. The embarrassment became more evident.

Charles took out his note-case and opened it.

"I'll give you a fiver—if you've got it."

"I got it all right," said the boy. "Skipper dropped a letter he was posting. I got it all right."

"Well?" said Charles. He unfolded the note and held it out.

"Skipper 'ud take the 'ide off me." His eyes sought Charles with a look of furtive intelligence.

Charles said briefly, "How much?"

The boy licked his lips. His heart beat with terror at his own audacity. The skipper would certainly have the hide off him if he knew. He said "A tenner," and had an awful spasm of fear lest he should get nothing at all.

He got the tenner, and Charles got the address.

In his relief the boy emptied out all the information that he had. It chiefly concerned the whereabouts of Loch Dhu. It was not to be confused with the better known loch of that name. The boy had been there once, and it gave him the pip—"fair made me 'air curl."

Charles got away with an impression in his mind about Loch Dhu. Now that he was standing upon its shores, the impression remained. The rugged and precipitous hills, the sheerness of their descent into the water, and that air of a place once inhabited and now deserted all went to deepen its influence upon his imagination.

He hallooed again, making a trumpet of his hands, and suddenly someone ran across the little white beach and stood at the water's edge. It was Ann. She stood there waving, in a blue cotton frock with the sun on her. It was late afternoon, and the shadow of the island was across the beach. Only Ann's head and shoulders emerged from it into the sunshine. He shouted, "Ann!" and across the water his own name came back to him with the echo of hers:

"Charles—Ann—"

He shouted, "Is there a boat?" dwelling on the o and prolonging it till the echo brought the sound again. In vivid pantomime Ann showed him a locked boat-house and a departed boat. Across some two hundred yards of water his name came to him again like a ghost that vanished before it could be grasped.

What a predicament! He had come to see Ann, and he saw her. And he might as well have stayed in town.

Ann, on her side, felt herself slipping from that high secure place to which the sight of Charles had lifted her. She had been on the heathery knoll when his first call came. It had been very pleasant there in the sun. The breeze came and went. It was very pleasant, but under the pleasantness there was something that she had to keep pushing out of sight. She wouldn't look at it long enough to be sure exactly what it was, but it rather spoiled the sunshine and the heather. And then Charles called, and Ann's heart came up into her throat and she started scrambling and running for the beach with an overwhelming joy and relief.

But now she saw him a long way off and with no means of coming nearer. It was the sharpest disappointment she had ever known, and beneath the disappointment the thing which she had pushed away out of sight began to stir.

Charles was shouting again.

"... back ..."

Did he mean that he would come back again? He was pointing at the sun, and the water, and himself. She couldn't make out what he meant. She shook her head, and Charles made strange signs with his arms. It would have been funny if it hadn't been heart-breaking. It was still more heart-breaking when, after a little more of this, he waved and turned from the shore.

Ann stood as near the water as she could and saw him go. She could only see a very little bit of the road, because it twisted away between the hills. At the turn Charles waved again, and then he was gone.

Ann went back into the house and listened to the life histories of the eighteen children of Mrs. Halliday's uncle, Ebenezer Todd—"Three pair of twins, and five of 'em foxy, and girls—and a red-'eaded girl is what I can't abide. Boys isn't so bad, but the boys was all dark except one, and he was so red you could ha' struck a match on his 'air." Mrs. Halliday turned her brooch to the light and displayed its bunch of flowers. "That's a bit of it down in the left-hand corner. Makes a nice rosebud, don't it, though there wasn't nothing of the rose about 'im— an impudent rapscallion if ever I see one, and the girls all after 'im like a lot of wasps after plum jam, and dear knows why, for he wasn't no beauty. Married a pork-butcher's widow in the end, and her in her fifties, and a very 'appy couple they made, only no children of course. And there was his sister Aggie, that was like a thread of cotton and no more colour than a bit of tallow, she married a widower with eight— more like a hank of tow her 'air was. There's some of it in that ivy-leaf. What I call a pore thing, my Cousin Aggie."

Ann's head was going round long before they had finished with the Todds. She hoped she wouldn't be expected to remember about them. She could really only think about Charles and the water that lay between them.

Chapter Eleven

JIMMY HALLIDAY HAD NOT returned when Ann went up to bed that night. They hung the key on a nail behind the big fuchsia at the front door. Ann always wondered why they locked the door at all, but neither Riddle nor Mrs. Halliday would have gone to sleep behind an unlocked door. It was a real villa door that shut with a spring lock, so they only had to hang up the key and give it a good bang—"And like as not Jimmy won't be back till breakfast time," said Mrs. Halliday. "Comes of a poaching stock on both sides of the family, and when it's that way, they'd sooner be out nights than in their beds."

Ann wondered when Charles would come back, or whether he would come back at all. The strange, floating sound of his voice rang in her head—sound without words, sound like water flowing, and in the middle of it one sharp island of a word—*"back."* She was sure that the word was "back." She went to her room, but she didn't undress. She knelt down by the open window and thought about what Charles would do. He would go away for the night and perhaps come back again in the morning, when he might hope that the boat would be in, and that there would be someone there to put him across. Very deep inside herself Ann had a feeling that Charles might come and Charles might call, but that no boat from the island would put out to bring him over.

She jerked away from this.

Perhaps Charles would hire a boat and come back by water. That would be much better. If she saw him coming, she could direct him to the one narrow place where a landing was possible on the other side of the island. She began to think that Charles would come in a boat, but she had no idea how far he would have to go to find one. She wished she knew more geography. She wished she knew where she was.

The day had been fine, but now the eastern sky had clouded over. Some light still lingered in the west. The high tops of the hills caught the last of it, but the loch, over which their shadows fell, was dark. The trees were dark beyond the lawn, and about the house it was dusk—a thin, clear dusk at first, but deepening every moment. Ann slipped down into a sitting position with her arms on the sill. Presently it would be cold, but just for a little the cooling air was pleasant. She did not feel at all inclined to go to bed. All sounds had ceased in the house. The trees were dead still—black painted trees on a background of grey. She could just hear the water moving and no more. Now it was so dark, she could not see where the lawn ended and the trees began. The clouds covered the sky. Somewhere behind them there should be a moon. She wished that they would break and let it through.

And then there was a sound. She could not tell what sort of a sound it was, but it startled her. She kneeled up and leaned over the sill, pushing back the hair from her ears and listening. She could hear something moving amongst the trees, and she wondered if Jimmy Halliday had come back. That only lasted for a moment. You didn't have to listen to hear Jimmy Halliday come home; he came clumping up from the beach after banging the boat-house door, and, day or night, there was no mistaking his tread. This was none of Jimmy Halliday. This was a cautious, hesitant step.

Ann jumped up with a beating heart. It couldn't be Jimmy Halliday. It might be Charles. She opened her bedroom door, took off her shoes, and, carrying them, went down in her stockinged feet. She had got the front door open and was out on the rough grass of the lawn, when something inside her said in a small, cold voice, "Suppose it isn't Charles." Ann rounded on the voice. "If it isn't Charles, who is it?" It might be—something else. She had a spurt of anger like a flaring match. "What?" she said. *"Something,"* said the voice, and died away.

Ann's spurt of anger carried her across the lawn and into the first shadow of the trees. They hung over her like a wave just waiting to break. She could see nothing, and she could hear nothing except her own pulses. And then out of the darkness Charles Anstruther said,

"Ann!"

"Oh!" said Ann with a sharp-caught breath, and in a moment Charles' hands touched her face, groping. His hands were wet. She stepped back and said his name.

"Charles!" And then, "You're wet!"

"Only my hands."

"How did you come?"

"I swam of course."

"Then you *must* be wet."

"I'm not. I rolled my clothes up in a mac and tied them on my head. It's what they always do in books, but I'd hate to do any distance with a wobbley bundle like that. If I'd had a bathing-suit, I'd have swum over this afternoon. But I told you I was coming back. You knew I'd come—didn't you?"

"I didn't think you'd come to-night. Charles, there'll be a most awful row—you'd better come farther away from the house." She touched him then for the first time, slipping her hand inside his arm and drawing him down the path.

Just above the beach a track went off to the left. Ann followed it for some twenty or thirty yards till it opened into a tiny clearing.

Above them, ringed by the trees, was a rift in the clouds and a patch of moonlit sky.

Charles put an arm about her.

"Ann—are you all right?"

Ann did not find the arm at all unpleasant, but she wasn't going to let it undermine her. Now that Charles had come, everything *was* all right. The things that she had had to push out of sight no longer needed pushing. They had gone back into the bottomless pit which produces nightmares, and a nightmare is a thing without existence. She said briskly,

"Of course I'm all right. Why shouldn't I be?"

"Why are you on this damned island?"

"It isn't—it's a very nice island."

"Friendly, hospitable place—isn't it? Do all your callers have to swim?"

"We don't have any. We lead the simple life. Presently I shall know all about *all* Mrs. Halliday's relations from their cradles to their having their pictures in the papers because they've been hanged or lived to be a hundred. She's got more relations than anyone I've ever heard of, and most of them had twenty children at least, so you see there isn't a dull moment."

"Do you think I've come here to talk about Mrs. Halliday's relations? I've come here to talk about you." His other arm came round her. "Ann, aren't you glad to see me?"

They were standing in deep shadow like deep; dark water.

"I *can't* see you," said Ann in rather a small voice.

"You can feel me. Can't you—*can't you?* Ann!"

Whether what she felt was the beating of her own heart or his, Ann could not have said. She was held so close that her breath was gone, and when Charles kissed her she kissed him back. But only for a moment. Then she pushed him away and stamped her foot.

"How dare you?"

"Ann—"

"I never said you could kiss me!"

"Ann—"

"I'm not the sort of girl who kisses people! I'm not! I think it's horrible, and vulgar, and cheap!"

"Ann!" Charles had her by the shoulders. He shook her a little. "I kissed you because I love you, and there's nothing vulgar and cheap about that! *Now* will you stop talking nonsense?"

"No," said Ann—"I won't! It's not nonsense—it's true! You're not to kiss me—you're not to touch me! I won't have it!"

Her thoughts hurried and were out of breath. If Charles kissed her again, she would let go. She was holding on desperately, but if he kissed her again, she wouldn't be able to hold on any longer. She would let go, and when it was too late she would be sorry ever after. Charles was in love, but that world well lost sort of business didn't last, and when he was sane again he would remember that he might have kept Bewley if he hadn't married Ann Vernon without a penny. And all his relations would remember it all the time. No—no—no—no—*no!*

"I won't!" said Ann, and did not know whether she said it aloud or not.

Charles' voice came from a yard away. The pale moony patch of sky overhead made the shadow between them seem darker. He wasn't Charles—he was danger. He was something she must hold her own against, even if it hurt—like this. He was saying, in a different voice,

"I won't touch you if you don't want me to—you needn't be afraid."

"I don't know why you came," said Ann, her voice stumbling on the words and a panic fear sweeping her when they were said, because now he would go and never come back any more. Relations looking down scornful noses didn't seem to matter when she thought about Charles going away for ever. But they ought to matter, they must matter, they *would* matter. She pinched her own arm very hard indeed and said, "It's no use your coming here. I didn't want you to come."

"I'm sorry," said Charles. He didn't sound sorry; he sounded angry. "I wouldn't have come if I'd known."

"You ought to have known!"

"I only wanted to make sure you were all right."

"Why shouldn't I be all right?"

"I don't know," said Charles. "But if you are, I'll be going."

It hurt more every minute. If it went on hurting like this, she couldn't bear it. She couldn't bear him to go like this. She couldn't bear him to stay. Waves of pain, and anger, and fear broke in her. She said in a polite, careful voice,

"It was good of you to come."

"Oh, damnably!" said Charles.

Why didn't he go? How could she bear it if he went? Oh, why didn't he go quickly?

And a yard away Charles, ragingly angry, was also wondering why he didn't go—and why he had come. And he would take his oath that she had kissed him. He broke into furious speech.

"I'm going! You needn't be afraid I'll bother you any more—unless you want me! I don't suppose you will, but you might! And if you do—is it any use asking you to write?"

"No," said Ann—"it isn't."

She didn't mean her voice to sound mournful, but it did. She saw in her mind the torn scrap of the letter which she had written to Charles, and which wasn't any use because it never reached him.

If her voice had sounded different, Charles would have turned on his heel and gone down to the water. As it was, he fired a "Why?" at her.

If she said that they had torn her letter up, he wouldn't go away at all. And he must go away—only not irretrievably.

"Letters don't always get posted here," she said.

"What do you mean?"

"They don't always get posted."

The anger that had swept between them like a sudden squall had died as suddenly.

"Ann, what do you mean? You must tell me what you mean. Do you mean you wrote to me?"

With a very little breath Ann said,

"Yes."

"I didn't get it."

"No."

"Why didn't I get it?"

"It didn't get posted," said Ann.

"Then how am I to know if you want me? Ann, you *might* want me."

Deep inside her Ann said, "Yes," and then, very urgently, "Yes, yes, *yes*." But she couldn't say it aloud. She could only say, "I don't know."

There was a silence between them. The clouds had moved overhead. The rift was out of sight. Everything was much darker. Then Charles said,

"Could you show a signal somewhere if you wanted me?"

"I don't know—I might."

"If you put a branch on the boat-house roof or anywhere on that beach, I should see it, and it's not a thing that anyone else would notice. It wouldn't be any use at night of course."

It came to Ann that if she were to need Charles suddenly, desperately in the night, she would be past helping. A kind of black gulf opened in her thoughts, and a shudder ran all over her. It was nothing. It was the dark. It was wanting Charles, and having to send him away. She said,

"Yes, I can do that. But I won't want anyone. Mrs. Halliday's very nice to me."

"And Halliday?" Charles' voice was rough.

"He's away fishing nearly all the time."

Suddenly it was quite easy to laugh—and oh, such a blessed relief! Charles—putting on a jealous voice for Jimmy Halliday!

"Darling Charles," she said, "you needn't worry about that. He'd take a lot more interest in me if I was a bit of bait or a dead fish."

It was nice to have got back to being friends again. She drew her breath more easily. The horrible tension was gone.

"Honest, Charles—you'd better go. Mrs. Halliday would have a fit if she found I wasn't in the house. It—it was nice of you to come—it was really. But there isn't anything you can do. It's a good job and good pay, and I can't afford to lose it. You will go—won't you?"

"I'll go—but I shall come back. You won't forget about the branch?"

"It's all nonsense, really," said Ann. She laughed again. "We're being romantic—knight-errant, distressed damsel, and all the rest of it! But there's nothing in it, and if you get me the sack, I shall sue you for damages. It would make a nice up-to-date ending—wouldn't it?"

"I prefer the old one," said Charles. "All right, I'm going. Good-bye."

Ann heard him going away along the path. She stood where she was for some minutes, and then she followed him. When she came to the turning which led to the beach she hesitated and then went down that way. Charles would be in the water by now. She thought she would wait until he was across. There would be plenty of warning if the boat came in.

It was very dark on the beach. The two headlands enclosed it and the island rose up behind. But out on the loch there was a little moonlight which came and went as the clouds moved overhead. In the last hour it had turned warmer. There must be a breeze high up, because the clouds flowed past without ceasing, but here, at sea-level, the air was perfectly still—still, warm air and warm, calm water. The clouds were not nearly so thick as they had been. They made an opal veil across the moon and parted to show deep stretches of blue-black sky. Ann could see a dark blur that was Charles' head with the bundle on it, and every now and then a little spray that caught the light as he swam, and then he was out of the water and shaking himself. And then he was gone. After a little while she thought she could hear the sound of his car going away behind the fold in the hills.

Ann went on looking at the water. She didn't want to go in. There were bright ripples in a wide path across the loch. The moon was not quite overhead. The clouds kept coming and going, and the ripples sparkled and dimmed and darkened. The stillness gave her a feeling of expectation. It was like the hush before something happens. Ann felt as if something was going to happen, but she did not know what.

Under the veiled half light she saw something that moved among the ripples—something without shape, a darkness in the water, a darkness that moved. The clouds above were denser, and the half light failed. She couldn't see. She couldn't see at all. She felt a cold and dreadful terror of the dark. And Mary had said, *"Keep away frae the water or it'll get ye."* She couldn't see, but she thought that she could hear the wash of that dark, moving thing. The cold fear broke into panic, and she ran, scrambling and slipping, up the steep path to the house. Half way up she looked back and saw that the clouds had shifted. The water lay bare and open to the moon. There was nothing there.

Chapter Twelve

GALE ANDERSON came back next day. Ann did not know when he came or how, but when she got down to breakfast he was there, and so was Jimmy Halliday.

She had heard Jimmy Halliday come back just as the light began to change towards the dawn. At first she had not slept, and then she had slept to dream that she was running across a desert of black sand with something coming after her like the wind. However fast she ran, she could never get away from it. The sand began to heave under her feet, and it wasn't sand at all, but water. And then, just as her heart stopped with terror, she heard footsteps come clumping over the lawn, and she was awake in bed, with her face half buried in the pillow and Jimmy Halliday swearing muffled oaths under the window because he couldn't find the key.

She wondered if he had brought Gale Anderson back with him. Perhaps he had. They certainly seemed to take each other very much for granted and made no attempt to talk.

No one talked except Mrs. Halliday, who was quite able to sustain the whole conversation. She went on pouring herself out cups of tea, each one weaker and more heavily sugared than the last. By the time she had reached six lumps in a pale straw-coloured fluid, she had told them all about Jimmy's great-grandfather Pointer, who was first mate on a sailing vessel, and who swore to seeing a ship with nothing but ghosts aboard her and all sail set in a gale that was fit to tear the solid land up by the roots and break it into islands—"And his mother says to him when he come home, 'If it's ghosts you want, you can see 'em as well at 'ome as abroad, any day. So you stay 'ome. And there's a haunted 'ouse right next the Jug and Bottle,' she says—'if you're set on such.' And Ned Pointer, he turned as red as a turkey-cock, and if she hadn't been his mother he'd have told her to shut her mouth, for he'd been sweet on Martha before she married Jem Ricketts that was landlord of the Jug and Bottle. And his mother ups and says, 'It's all right,' she says, 'Jem's been took, and if you're not afraid of his ghost, I dare say Martha'll take you into the business for the matter of a wedding-ring.'

And that's how you come by your great-great-grandmother—and a nice bit of money she had in her stocking foot."

The two men went off in the boat again after lunch. Ann watched them go from the high heathery knoll at the top of the island. There had been a mist all the morning, but the sun had drawn it up and the loch reflected the pale, cloudless blue of September. She saw the boat swing into the channel and pass out of sight under the lee of the island.

Could it have been a boat that she had seen last night?

No, it wasn't a boat.

Why wasn't it?

"I don't know—but it wasn't."

She put her head in her hands and tried to think why it couldn't have been a boat. Her closed eyes gave her the scene again—half light; and water; and something breaking the surface. That was it. A boat doesn't break the surface unless—A submarine would break the surface just like that. It would be very reassuring to think that what she had seen was only a submarine. Would it? *Would it?* She wasn't sure. The cold, black terror touched her again. She threw up her head and opened her eyes wide on the sunlight. She jumped up. She was a perfect fool to sit there frightening herself.

"I probably saw Jimmy's boat, and there's an end of it."

She looked out over the water and wondered where the boat was now. It ought to be coming into sight again if they were going out to sea.

When she had watched for ten minutes, she was puzzled. If they had gone up the loch, she would have seen them long ago. They must be close in under the island, or she would be seeing them now.

She went scrambling down towards the water until she came to the steep overhang, which stopped her. She worked along it in the direction of the house. Sometimes there was a slippery cliff, and sometimes a lot of great boulders piled cliff-high.

Quite suddenly she stopped. She thought that someone had spoken her name, and as she turned, bewildered, to see who it might be, it came again, and this time the direction was plain enough.

It came from under her feet.

She was in a cleft among the great huddled boulders, with the sea below her and out of sight. The rocks were over her head on either side, and behind her they ran away to a narrow rift down which a thread of water trickled. She had swung herself round one jutting point and was wondering whether she could manage the next. And then, there was her name echoing up from under her feet. It didn't come from the sea. After the first moment of astonishment she felt sure of that. It would have sounded clearer off the water—and different.

She turned her back on the loch and crept as far into the cleft as she could. When she couldn't get any farther, she bent down and listened again. A whispering of voices came indistinctly to her ear, mixed with the dropping of the tiny stream. The most devastating curiosity filled her to the brim. Whose were the voices, and where were they coming from?

As voices they had no more individuality than the rustling of dry leaves. They were just sound. And the sound came and went. Ann cupped her hands over her ears and leaned her forehead against the rock, and at once the sound changed tone and ran into a word—a strange and awful word which set her pulses thudding. One voice said, "Murder," and then another voice broke into laughter that crept and echoed in the unseen windings of the cleft. She felt her forehead wet, and did not know whether the moisture came from the clammy rock or whether it was the dew of sudden fear. The echo smothered whatever other words there were. She waited for it to die away, and all at once she heard Gale Anderson's voice: "You should encourage her to learn to swim. As it is, I suppose it'll have to be a boating accident." And then, whether because he turned his head or because he moved, the sound fell back into confusion. Once someone said, "I won't," and, "What's the hurry?" And then there was nothing but the whisper, whisper, whisper of two voices, and upon that there came to her, sharp and clear, the recollection of how she had sat in the lounge at the Luxe waiting for Charles and heard two voices whispering on the other side of a group of palms. What had they said?... *"You must get her away at once."—"And then?"* And after that a silence, and she had felt afraid without knowing why. And one of the voices had said, *"Well, devil take the hindmost."* And then they had gone away....

What nonsense to think of that now! All whispering voices sound the same. Those voices had said something about a will, and, *"He's never seen her,"* and *"He's not going to. You must get her away at once."* What had it got to do with her? It couldn't possibly have anything to do with her. One of those voices had said, *"It's a pity you can't marry her."*... One of those voices? Or—one of these voices echoing faintly in the cleft?... *"It's a pity you can't marry her."* ...

Ann turned giddy. She was too crouched together to fall, but for a moment she was not fully conscious. What had she heard? What had she *really* heard? Had she heard someone say, *"It's a pity you can't marry her,"* or had she only remembered hearing a whispering voice say it long ago at the Luxe?... It wasn't really long ago, but it seemed so. She felt immeasurably removed from the places she had known.

And what place was this, and what things were talked of here?... *Murder* ... The word had ceased to echo in the hidden places of the rock, but in the hidden places of her thought it echoed still.

The whispering fell to faint sound that just fretted the edge of her consciousness, and then the sounds of the air and of the water lapped over it and blotted it out.

Ann felt how stiff she was. She had only been crouching down in the cleft, but she seemed to have strained every muscle of her body. She crawled round the jutting corner, clung and scrambled a few more yards, and came out by the side of the house. She went up to her room, and was glad to get there unnoticed. She shut the door and sat down on the floor beside the window. She was shaking all over, and her thoughts shook too. She couldn't order them or get them to keep still.

The sun shone upon the lawn, and the sky was a clear, pure blue. The air came softly off the water. There were patches of green on the hills, and streaks of red, and black, and purple. Every now and then a scent of pines mixed with the faint salt smell of the sea.

Ann got up and looked at herself in the glass. There was a smudge of green slime across her forehead. Her eyes stared back at her.

"Oh, Ann! What a fool you are!" she said.

She poured cold water into the basin and washed her face and hands. Then she came back to the window again and leaned upon the sill. Her thoughts had stopped shaking and she began to sort them out.

She thought that the whispering voices she had heard in the cleft were the voices she had heard at the Luxe. She thought that the Luxe voice and the cleft voice had said the same thing—*"What a pity you can't marry her."* She thought those two things, but she wasn't sure.

It was maddening not to be sure. She tried to piece together what she had heard.

First of all, at the Luxe: *"What a pity you can't marry her."* And then, *"You're sure about the will?"* That was one man. And the other had said, *"I'm sure"*; and, *"Don't speak so loud"*; and, *"She must be got away before she knows."*

Ann thought about that. There was a girl who was coming in for money under a will, and she didn't know about it, because they had said, *"If he dies, the whole thing will be in the papers. She must be got away before she knows."*

There was a girl.... What girl?... How should Ann Vernon know?... Ann Vernon.... What girl?... Ann Vernon ...

"Nonsense!"

Ann said the word out loud in a clear angry voice. She went on saying it. "Nonsense—nonsense—*nonsense!*" If she said it often enough, perhaps that would make it nonsense. How could this girl, who was being left a lot of money, be Ann Vernon? Why, there wasn't a single solitary soul in the world who would leave her a penny.

Elias Paulett.

The name said itself with frightening distinctness.

Her mother's uncle, Elias Paulett.

"Nonsense!" said Ann again.

He was very rich. He had cut her mother off when she married. He must be an old man now....

"What nonsense! He doesn't know me—he's never see me!"

And at once the voices from the Luxe came tuning in: *"He's never seen her;"* and, *"He's not going to. You must get her away at once."* And—words with hardly any breath behind them; *"And then?"*

No one has answered that. Someone had said, *"Well, devil take the hindmost."* No one had answered that *"And then?"*—unless the whisper that had echoed in the cleft had answered it: *"Murder."*

Was it all nonsense?

The cleft voices repeated themselves—Gale Anderson's voice: *"I suppose it'll have to be a boating accident."* And it was Gale Anderson who had said, on the boat when the storm was driving them, *"Damn fool to send her down! There'll never be a better opportunity."*

Opportunity for what?"

The cleft voice whispered the answer:

"*Murder*."

Ann didn't say "Nonsense!" this time. She put her hands to her ears as if she could shut out the sound of that whisper, and she said, not loudly but in a hurried, stumbling undertone,

"Oh, no—no—no—no—*no!*"

A long time went by. She did not know how long. And then came the sounds of the two men returning—real sounds, loud and vigorous. Ann drew back from the window in a revulsion of feeling. The whispering voices fell away. She was piecing scraps together and making an ugly picture out of nothing.

She saw Gale Anderson come across the grass smiling, and behind him Jimmy Halliday, sunburnt and noisy, with a creel of fish on his arm. His voice came up to her like a blustering wind.

"Leaving me to do all the work, young fellow! What do you think these fish weigh? Give me a hand, can't you, and we'll show the old lady what we've brought her for her supper."

Gale Anderson turned just under Ann's window and looked back. He spoke with a laugh in his voice.

"Oh, devil take the hindmost!" he said.

Chapter Thirteen

MRS. HALLIDAY was very chatty at supper. She had two helpings of fish, and snapped Riddle's I nose off when, in handing her the second, she bent close to her ear and murmured what was apparently a protest.

"What's that? Speak up if you've got anything to say! And don't you go tickling me like that, Eliza Riddle, or I'll say something we'll both be sorry for—only you'll be sorrier than me! And if I want ten 'elpings I'll have ten 'elpings, so you keep your tongue where it was put and stop wagging it!"

Riddle sniffed silently. Her drooping, obstinate nose became slightly pink at the end. She continued to sniff whilst she cut and handed bread, and, still sniffing, left the room.

Mrs. Halliday chuckled.

"I'll get her notice when I go to my bed. She's been giving it me regular for five years, and she ain't gone yet and don't mean to. Makes her feel independent without having to act up to it. I've often thought it's a pity a wife can't give notice like that. I wouldn't wonder if there were a lot more 'appy marriages if the man didn't feel so almighty sure of himself. Why, the minute the ring's on 'er finger and the parson finished with his words, he thinks to himself, a man does, 'This here woman's my lawful wife, and what I do to her is nobody's business short of murder—she's got to cook for me, and wash for me, and scrub for me, and 'ave my children, and I don't 'ave to pay her a penny of wages.' If you ask me, there's ninety-nine men out of a hundred it'd do a heap of good to if the woman could up and give them notice. You just bear that in mind when your time comes, Miss Vernon, my dear."

Ann saw Charles' face sharp and clear, as she hadn't see it when she sent him away. It had been too dark to see it then, but she could see it now. Her colour rose, and Mrs. Halliday chuckled.

"It's no good my talking to Jimmy, nor yet to Mr. Anderson, because Jimmy's set on being an old bachelor, and Mr. Anderson's got a wife already."

"Pity you can't marry her" ... The voice at the Luxe—the voice in the cleft.... Gale Anderson couldn't marry her, because he'd got a wife already....

Ann's chin went up a little.

"Well, that's a comfort *anyhow*," she said to herself.

Gale Anderson was looking sulky. Mrs. Halliday chuckled again.

"Letting cats out of bags, am I? But if a nice-looking young man's married, it's better known from the outset, so as everybody can tell just where they are. It saves a lot of trouble in the long run. There was my cousin Jane Hollins' youngest, christened by the name of Gladys she was—Gladys Hollins—and she'd been going to the pictures regular for a year with a fellow before he 'appened to mention he'd a wife and three children in Leeds. Cried something cruel Gladys did, because she knew he was getting good money and she'd set her 'eart on a green plush drawing-room suite on the instalment system—got it all planned she had, and could see herself on the sofa beside of him holding his 'and. And *him* with a wife and three children all the time! I say a married man did ought to wear a ring same as a married woman and be took up by the police if he goes about without it."

Jimmy Halliday burst out laughing.

"I'd look nice in a ring—wouldn't I, old lady?" He put his hands on the table and grinned at them. "I've a nice hand for a ring—haven't I? I'll have diamonds and pearls, that's what I'll have—one on each hand. That'd be a bit of all right, wouldn't it, Miss Vernon?"

"Get along with you!" said Mrs. Halliday in high delight. "Who's going to marry an old bachelor like you? You've got to find a wife before you buy your ring."

Jimmy Halliday's grin took on a tinge of embarrassment.

"P'raps I've found one," he said.

Ann was thankful when the meal was over. She had never seen Jimmy Halliday in this mood. He had changed since they came to the island. The rather anxious politeness of his manner to her in London had vanished. He had been rough, surly, and uncommunicative. Now there was another change, and he was clumsily attentive. He pressed second helpings upon her, and attracted the ironic attention of Mrs. Halliday and the gloomy scowls of Mr. Gale Anderson, who was quite obviously in one of the worst tempers in the world. Ann felt sorry for his wife, whoever she might be.

As she wound wool for Mrs. Halliday, she was thinking hard. Where was Charles, and when would he come back to see if she had laid a green branch upon the strand? He wouldn't come every day—or would he? There were solid masses of comfort in the thought that he might.

If she only knew exactly where they were. She did know that supplies came once a week in a motor-van which dumped them on the shore for Jimmy Halliday to fetch. Tinned beef, tinned tongue, cheese, flour, butter, oil, candles, rice. Never any fresh meat. Did that mean that they were a very long way from a town? It was no use asking Mrs. Halliday; she only nodded and said, "I didn't have the education children have now-a-days. All that jography, and figuring things out on maps, that don't mean nothing to me, and so long as I get my food regular, I don't care a brass boddle where I am."

When she had finished winding the wool, Ann went down into the kitchen to Mary. Mrs. Halliday and Riddle were in the parlour, the two men in the dining-room. Ann went past the door without making a sound, and down two steps into the old part of the house.

The kitchen was warm and dark. There was a red glow from the fire, but no light. Ann shut the door and stood just inside it. She called, "Mary—" under her breath, and at once something dark crossed the glow and came towards her. She went back and struck the panelling as a hand brushed her shoulder and slid down her arm. Her wrist was clasped and held. The hand was very, very cold, and an involuntary shudder ran over her. Mary's voice said, "Whisht!" and she was drawn away from the door.

It was quite pleasant to get nearer the fire. The glow showed her no more than a shawled outline and a bent head with a ragged fringe of hair. She spoke at once to break the strangeness.

"It's lovely and warm down here. I've come for a talk. Let's sit down and be comfortable."

The hand relinquished its cold grip. The shawled figure retreated. Ann leaned to the fire, warming herself.

"What's the nearest town, Mary?" she said.

"I'm no frae hereaboots."

"Don't you know?"

There was a shake of the head. A straggling braid of hair showed against the glowing background. Ann thought that it trembled. She said, "Have you been here a long time? You don't stay here in the winter?"

"Ay."

"All alone?" said Ann in a tone of horror.

No wonder the poor thing was in such a state.

The head moved again, saying no.

Ann felt relief. Dreadful to think of someone in this lonely place through the winter dark and cold. She asked,

"Who stays here with you?"

"Ma man."

Mrs. Halliday's words came back—"I've often thought it a pity a wife can't give notice." She had wondered why Mary stayed in a place which obviously frightened her. Well, here was the answer to that. It was a pity she couldn't give notice.

"Where is he now?" she said.

"I dinna ken."

"Is he here in the winter?" said Ann.

"Ay."

"And you don't know where the nearest place is?"

Again that shake of the head.

"Don't you ever go away? Don't you ever go to your home?"

This time the answer was a most pitiful indrawing of the breath.

Ann caught one of the cold hands and held it.

"Oh, *poor* Mary!"

The hand was rigid in hers and even colder than she had thought to find it. It was drawn away to cover the hidden face.

"I couldna cross the water. I'll never cross it."

She thought she caught the words. And then, without any doubt, she heard Jimmy Halliday calling her name. In a flash Mary was across the floor and had the back door open.

"Rin aroond the hoose!"

Ann ran past her into the black yard.

She didn't know why she ran, or why she crept round the side of the house without making any sound. Why shouldn't she be in the kitchen with Mary? The answer to that was that it was Mary who had pushed her out and bidden her run. It was like a game of hide-and-seek.

She was laughing a little as she reached the far side of the lawn. And then suddenly the sharp beam of an electric torch struck her, and she stood still and put up a hand to shield her eyes. Jimmy Halliday's voice came from behind the beam, the rough voice which he had used since they had been on the island.

"What are you doing out here?"

Ann let herself say "Oh!" It wasn't at all difficult, for she had been really startled.

"'Oh!' isn't an answer," said Jimmy Halliday. He put a coarse mimicry into the word, and a hot rage whirled up in Ann.

She stepped out of the beam and said,

"I'm not doing anything."

"Aren't you? You're sure of that, are you? Sure you didn't slip out to meet that young man of yours?"

Ann began to walk towards the house. Jimmy Halliday walked beside her, swinging the torch so that it made a vivid emerald pattern on the dark grass. When they reached the front door, he stepped before her.

"You've not got an answer to that, have you?"

"No," said Ann. She was pleased, because her voice was quite steady and cool. Did he really know that Charles had been here, or was he guessing?

He made an explosive sound.

"Now look you here, my girl!" he said, and then caught himself up short. "Look you here, Miss Ann Vernon—there's something you've got to understand, and that's this. I don't come here to be pestered with visitors, and if that young man of yours comes here again, he'll come here once too often!"

"I don't know what you mean," said Ann.

The parlour window was only a yard away, and behind it Mrs. Halliday was knitting, and Riddle crocheting at a fine narrow strip which never seemed to grow any longer.

"Oh, you don't know what I mean, don't you? Well, I think you do, but if you don't, I don't mind helping you out." His hand went into his pocket and came out again palm upwards. He shone the torch upon it in a yellow ring. White and bright in the middle of it lay a silver match-box. It had Charles' name scrawled upon it, just like that—"*Charles.*" A flapper cousin had given it to him for his birthday. Charles had been at some pains to explain that she was a flapper—"Quite a nice infant."

Still in that cool voice, Ann said,

"What's that?"

Jimmy Halliday shoved it back in his pocket.

"Well, it isn't mine," he said, "nor it isn't the old lady's, nor yet Miss Riddle's, nor Mr. Anderson's. And since you're asking me about it, I reckon you're not going to say it's yours. Charles isn't any of our names that I know of, Miss Vernon, my dear." His voice took on a savage parody of his mother's, and again Ann was struck with anger.

"Please let me pass, Mr. Halliday."

"In a minute I will. But first you listen to me! I picked this up down on the beach, and I think you know who dropped it there. Now you listen carefully! This is a right down dangerous place for a stranger to go boating or swimming. Do you hear that? This loch's *dangerous.* Why aren't there any boats on it? The fishing's good enough. Why aren't there any houses? There are some, and they've been let go to ruin. No one lives here, and no one comes here. The people who live round about, they wouldn't come here if you paid them. And why wouldn't they? Because, I'm telling you, it's *dangerous*. It's dangerous and it's deep. Have you got that?"

"Oh, yes," said Ann. "But you and Mr. Anderson go out on the loch. It's very brave of you, isn't it?"

Jimmy Halliday made an angry sound and wrenched open the door. A very small oil lamp lit the narrow passage within. He plunged along it and into the dining-room.

Ann stood where she was for a moment. Then she went into the parlour and sat down by the window.

There was a rosewood table in the middle of the room. It supported a lamp with a green china shade. Mrs. Halliday sat on one side of the table and Riddle on the other. They were both dozing peacefully. Riddle's mouth was wide open, and the spectacles which she wore to do this fine crochet had slipped down to the end of her nose. Her right hand held a steel crochet-hook, and her left had fallen on to the arm of the chair, from which her strip of crochet hung down to the floor. Mrs. Halliday sat upright in a Victorian chair with her head supported by a little bolster cushion of black horse-hair. Her hands were folded in her lap and her deep rhythmic snores filled the room. It was a scene of the deepest and dullest domesticity. The lamplight and the walnut twirls which finished the arms of the chairs, the rosewood table with its polished surface and massive single leg, the faded green of the carpet, the faded crimson of the woolly mat upon which the lamp stood—how soothingly respectable an atmosphere did all these things disengage. Ann felt it seeping into her and lulling her anger and her fears to rest. How could you look at Mrs. Halliday's cap, with its crisp net ruching and its little bunches of black and violet baby ribbon, and believe that you were in danger? How reconcile Riddle—whose obstinate likeness to a sheep was even stronger in her sleeping than in her waking moments—how reconcile Riddle with murder? Ann became aware of a curious division in her mind. It was just as if there was a sheet of plate glass across it. On the one side there was the comfortable, safe dullness of this room and of its occupants. On the other there was a dark place full of shadows, with here and there a ghastly flash from some unseen fire. It was like the house, with its villa front and the old, dark rooms behind. She saw the kitchen, and Mary shuddering against the glow of the fire.

Quite suddenly she felt as if she couldn't bear it any longer. It wrenched you too badly to live on both sides of that division—to be dull, and safe, and Victorian, and respectable, and Mrs. Halliday's companion, and at the same time to be someone who was being plotted against—someone who had to be got out of the way lest she should find out about a will, someone who was to have a boating accident, someone who was to be *murdered*. You couldn't be both these people—you simply couldn't. And something kept forcing it upon you.

Charles must come and take her away. It didn't matter about his relations. From being the size of mountains, they had dwindled to indistinguishable specks of dust. As soon as everyone was asleep she would go down and lay a branch upon the strand—"And oh, Charles, please come quickly!"

Chapter Fourteen

WHEN JIMMY HALLIDAY plunged into the dining-room and banged the door behind him, Gale Anderson raised his eyebrows and, bending forward, knocked off the ash of his cigarette against the edge of the empty coal-scuttle, a smug wooden abomination with a design of three water-lilies in beaten copper. He was occupying one of the fumed oak armchairs which belonged to the dining-room suite. Jimmy Halliday flung himself into the other and swore.

Gale Anderson leaned back again.

"Well? What did she say? You needn't trouble to tell me what you said, because I could hear you."

"She didn't say anything."

The dining-room was lighted by a lamp which hung low down over the table. The draught of Jimmy's entry had set it swinging a little. It had an old-fashioned shade of pink fluted silk. As the lamp swung, the rosy shadow crossed the two men's faces and then again withdrew. Gale Anderson's handsome features were, as usual, rather pale. His light eyes wore an expression of cold resentment. He said, in his level voice,

"You don't mean that quite literally, I suppose?"

Jimmy Halliday was rather flushed. He reached over to the table for the bottle which stood there, poured himself out a good three fingers of whisky, and drank it neat. He set the glass down again with a thump.

"Now look here, Gale," he said—"you needn't trouble to use that fancy sort of talk with me—it gets my goat! If you want to know what the girl said, I'll tell you, and a lot of good it'll do you. She said she didn't know what I meant, and she said please to let her pass. And she said how brave you and me must be to go boating on the loch. That was after I'd finished telling her how dangerous it was."

Gale Anderson was sitting forward with his cigarette in his hand. A little thread of smoke went up from it.

"Yes—I heard you." He looked at the wavering thread of smoke. "I heard you—you said the loch was dangerous. What I want to know is just when she's going to find that out for herself. When is it going to be dangerous for her?"

"That's what I'm coming to." Jimmy Halliday's voice conveyed the impression that it would have been hearty if the private nature of the conversation had not called for something more confidential than heartiness.

"I hope you are. You've been taking your time."

"Dry up!" said Jimmy Halliday with a rasp. "I've got enough whisky inside me to make me feel I'd as soon have a row with you as not—so now you know! You listen to me, and when I've said my piece you can say yours, but you'd better be careful what you say. Rum's my drink, and when I've got whisky aboard I'd as soon quarrel as not. It's the way it takes me, so you'd better let me say what I want to." He got out a very foul old pipe and proceeded to stuff it with shag. When he had got it going he settled back in his chair and said, "I don't like this business—never did and never shall. It's too damned risky."

"If you hadn't interfered on the boat, there'd have been no risk at all. She was as good as overboard, and whose fault would it have been but her own? You sent her down, and she came up of her own accord."

"That's enough about that!" said Jimmy Halliday. "We had that out then, and I'm not going over it. And when you talk about no risk—anyone might have seen you give her that clip over the head."

"No one did."

"I'm not going over that. But I've told you all the time that the old lady comes first. You've got to get that in your head and keep it there. The old lady's back of everything—I wouldn't be touching this job if it wasn't for her. Things are getting a bit too hot in my trade, and I don't want to stay in it till I'm dropped on. If I was to get a stretch, it'd kill the old lady, so I want to clear out. When you came to me and put it to me that there's a share of a hundred thousand pounds to be had if a girl that don't know she's in the running for it can be kept out of the way, I told you straight I'd got to have half or I wouldn't lift a finger. Fifty thousand'll do me and the old lady very nicely. Well, that's what I said to you, and I said, 'Why don't you marry the girl and have done with it, a nice-looking young fellow like you?' And then of course you had to tell me you were married, and that it was your wife that would get the money if this girl was out of the way. And I reckon that was a bit of luck for your wife, because if it had been the other way round and it had been you that was in the running, I wonder how long it would have been before there was a funeral and you putting up a nice marble angel or something of that sort over her. You could afford to do it handsome if you married the other girl and had the spending of that hundred thousand."

Gale Anderson threw away the end of his cigarette and lighted another. He wore an air of bored tolerance.

Jimmy Halliday looked at him shrewdly from between his sandy lashes.

"Well now, all that sort of thing's a damned sight too risky. I don't take risks if I can help it—not that sort anyhow. You remember, I've said to you time and again, 'Pity you can't marry her,' which'd be a lawful legal way out, and no risk to anyone. And all the time it never struck me that if you couldn't marry her along of having a wife already, there was two of us in the business, and what was the matter with me?"

Gale Anderson withdrew his cigarette and emitted a cloud of smoke.

"And when did this brilliant idea strike you?"

"After we had that argument in the cave. Now you just listen to me! Putting on one side that I don't just naturally care about murder—"

Gale Anderson gave a short laugh, and Jimmy Halliday brought his fist down with a bang on the arm of his chair.

"I've got a right to my feelings, haven't I? You mayn't have any, but I have! But putting all such out of the way, there's two things against it. One's the risk—say what you like, it's risky."

"People are drowned in boating accidents every day, and you don't even have to have an inquest in Scotland."

The fist came down again.

"A risk there is! And I don't take risks when I needn't. Well, that's one reason against it. And the other's the old lady. She's got fond of the girl."

Gale Anderson's eyebrows lifted. His calm and prudent temperament enabled him to refrain from speech. Where his mother was concerned Jimmy Halliday was completely irrational. But he was wondering just what might be behind this concern for Mrs. Halliday. The result of the proposed marriage would be that the division of the spoil would lie with Jimmy and not with himself. He thought that he would prefer to take a risk and eliminate Ann.

Jimmy Halliday went on in a manner full of breezy good fellowship.

"Now, you just see how it works out. I put the old lady first, and it comes along like shelling peas. If anything had happened to that girl on the boat, the old lady'd have taken on a good bit. If anything was to happen to her now, she'd take on a good bit more—and taking on's not good for her. Keep her happy, and she'll live to be a hundred is what the doctors say. Now if I was to begin a bit of courting, there's two things that might happen, and maybe three. I figure it out this way. If the girl likes me and we fix it up, and the old lady's pleased, that's one way, and not a mite of risk to anyone. But suppose the girl isn't for it. Of course there's ways a girl can be brought to reason, and marrying's easy in these parts. I think she could be brought to reason. It's not her I'm troubling about—it's the old lady." He leaned forward and tapped with his pipe on his knee. "Do you know why I'm not married? Because every single blessed time I've thought serious about a girl, or a girl's shown any sign of thinking serious about me, the old lady's just about raised Cain. But look here—this time that's not going to matter. See what I mean? Either she'll be pleased and we'll get spliced, or she'll cut up rough, and then she won't mind what happens to the girl. Either way will be all right for her—and, as I told you to start with, I'm putting her first."

Gale Anderson got up and stood with his back to the mantelpiece. Between the smoke that filled the upper half of the room and the pink fluted silk which hid the lamp his features were hardly distinguishable. He said in a cool, cutting voice,

"You talk as if we had all the time in the world. Elias Paulett might die at any moment."

"Well?" said Jimmy Halliday, drawing at his pipe.

Gale Anderson's voice dropped smoothly.

"My wife comes in for the money if Ann Vernon doesn't—that is, she comes in for it if Elias lives longer than Ann. The minute the breath's out of his body Hilda's chance is gone, but if Ann dies first, Hilda gets the lot. We've got to get a move on."

"That's where my plan comes in," said Jimmy Halliday comfortably. "I marry the girl—she scoops the lot—no risk to anyone—and we divide."

Gale Anderson leaned back against the mantelpiece with folded arms.

"And if she won't marry you, neither of us gets a penny."

"She'll marry me if I want her to," said Jimmy Halliday. "I'll see to that. And once we're married she'll soon find out who holds the purse-strings. It's a good plan. You leave it to me and clear out. You oughtn't to have come within a hundred miles of this place. That boating accident you've kept talking about would be a lot more convincing if the man whose wife was going to get the money wasn't mixed up with it."

Gale Anderson's eyes narrowed for a moment.

"Is there going to be an accident?"

"There might be, if she didn't fancy me, or if the old lady cut up rough—there's always the chance of that."

Gale Anderson went back to his chair and lit another cigarette. He had made the most of Elias Paulett's condition because he wanted to force the pace. Delay was dangerous, but Elias wasn't dying—yet. Jimmy was an awkward customer to drive. He turned to what was an immediate emergency.

"What did she say about the match-box you picked."

"I told you she didn't say anything. She don't give much away. I like a girl with a bit of spirit."

"Do you think he's hanging around?"

Jimmy let out a puff of smoke.

"If he's been here, he must have swum. How did he know she was here anyhow? I tore up the letter she wrote him. He might have given her the matchbox—she might have dropped it herself—there's no telling. Or he might be hanging around. There'd be no harm putting up a bit of a show to scare him off in case he's anywhere about. There'll be a fine moon presently."

Gale Anderson frowned.

"That's a risky business if you like. You'll get a bullet in you some day, Jimmy."

Jimmy Halliday laughed.

"Not much I won't!" he said.

Chapter Fifteen

ANN WAS WAITING until she was sure that everyone was asleep. Mrs. Halliday and Riddle had been in bed for more than an hour, and Mary had come up the old winding stair and shut herself into the narrow, dark room which looked out on to the yard. But Gale Anderson and Jimmy Halliday had not come up.

Ann felt puzzled. She had been reading by candlelight, but now she put down the book and listened.

There was no sound at all. Her room was over the dining-room. At first the sound of the men's voices had come and gone as she read. She did not know when they had stopped, but it came to her that it was more than a little while ago. She leaned out of the window, and could hear nothing.

It was not so dark now as it had been an hour ago. Soon the moon would be over the hill. She went to the door, opened it, and listened again. She could hear Mrs. Halliday snoring in a droning, comfortable way, and when she went to the top of the stairs she could hear the ticking of the wall-clock which hung in the old part of the house where the passage went down to the kitchen. That meant that the door which shut off the back premises had been left open. Mary always kept it shut.

Ann came down the stairs till she could see the dining-room door. The hall lamp had been put out. The hall was dark, and the dining-room door was dark—no thread of light at the lintel. She wondered whether the two men had gone out by the back way. Why should they go out by the back way? She hadn't any answer to that at all. But she had to know whether they were in either of the front rooms. She couldn't go down to the beach and place the branch which was to be her signal to Charles unless she was sure that she would not be watched. On the other hand, if she didn't go soon, the moon would be up and the chances of being seen would be much greater.

She came down the rest of the way and opened the dining-room door. The heavy pungent smell of Jimmy Halliday's tobacco floated out of the dark room. It was quite dark. The windows were fastened and the curtains drawn. The drawing-room was the same, except that it smelt faintly of mould and of the peppermint and aniseed lozenges to which Mrs. Halliday was addicted. The front door was locked. The key was on the inside. There was no sound at all from the back part of the house. The kitchen was in darkness except for the very faintest glow from the sunk fire. The back door was locked.

She began to think that the two men had come upstairs without her hearing them. It had never happened before, but it might have happened. She had made herself read, and she had made herself think about what she was reading. She might have failed to hear what she had always heard before.

She opened the front door, closed it softly behind her, and ran across the lawn. It was getting lighter every minute. She must be quick if she didn't wish to be caught by the moon. She could have found her way in the dark; in this brightening dusk she could almost run. She broke a good-sized branch from a birch a little off the path, and, without going right down on to the beach, she managed to drop it so that it lay on the sloping roof of the boat-house. That was better than leaving it on the sand, where anyone might toss it aside. In this still weather there was no wind to move it.

She stood for a moment looking out over the loch. The great hill behind which the moon was coming up was as black as ink, and the water under it blacker still, but everywhere else there was a dusky softness which gave to sky and cliff and water the look of something not quite real. There was no edge, no outline, no definition, only that melting dusk. Ann wished that she could stay and see the moon come up. She mustn't stay. She must get back into the house before anyone knew that she had left it.

There was something queer about coming back into the house. She didn't know what it was, but it was queer. The queerness met her on the threshold, and she was glad to reach her room and shut her door upon it. She felt a very great sense of relief. Charles would come to-morrow, or the next day. He would take her away to a nice, safe, crowded place where cheerful, common, ordinary people were coming and going all the time, and there were policemen at the street corners. She thought with yearning of telephones, and buses, and theatre queues, and street musicians. Charles would take her back to the things. She needn't marry him if she didn't want to. She could get another job and pay him back.

She slipped out of her clothes and blew out the light. She said, "*Darling* Charles!" as she snuggled down in bed. "Angel darling Charles, do come quickly!" And almost at once she was asleep.

Dreams are such strange things. Ann slipped straight into the middle of one and found herself running hand in hand with Charles Anstruther down the long, steep slope of the Milky Way. The starlight swirled past them as they ran, like a mist which is driven by the wind. It didn't hide things as a mist does; it only made them look strange and far away. The Milky Way was very slippery. It shone under their feet as they ran. Charles held her hand in a very warm, strong clasp, and they went rushing down to the loch, which was as dark and as smooth as a piece of the midnight sky. The starlight didn't reach it at all. The water was cold to their feet, as cold as ice. They didn't sink down into it at all; they ran on the cold glassy surface. And then all at once there was a sound behind them. It wasn't a sound that Ann had ever heard before, but when she heard it in her dream her heart beat with one great hammer stroke and then stopped, because this was Terror itself coming up behind them, formless and dreadful. If the dream had gone on for another moment, the Terror would have had them both, but in that instant she woke and found herself sitting up in bed with her hands at her breast and her breath coming in gasps.

The room was not quite dark. The curtains were thin, and the moon made a pale square of the window. Against this square something moved. Ann's hands pressed down upon the leaping fear at her heart, and as she caught her breath in another gasp, Mary's voice said,

"Whisht!"

Ann was shaken by a shudder of relief. She didn't know what she had thought. She had not indeed had time for conscious thought at all, but the fear that had been in her dream had followed her. It fell back now into the darkness to which it belonged. She relaxed and said,

"What is it?"

The shadow that was Mary came a step nearer.

"Whisht!" she said again. And then she was on her knees by the bed and gripping the edge of it so hard that all the frame was shaken.

"What is it, Mary? Are you ill?"

She could see the shake of the head that meant no.

"What is it then?"

"I'm feared."

Was it Mary's fear that had been the Terror of her dream? She could feel it now, shuddering through the dark figure by the bed, shaking them both.

"What are you afraid of?"

"I'm feared for ye."

"For me?"

"Ay."

"But why?"

"Because of the water."

"What water?"

"I bade ye keep frae it, but ye'll no keep frae it—it'll draw ye."

"What do you mean?"

"There's a mune the nicht, and it's ay when there's a mune that it comes."

"What comes, Mary?"

"Souming in the water."

The broad accent puzzled Ann for a moment. She made a guess at the word.

"Swimming?"

Mary's voice dropped and flattened out. It was like hearing a ghost speak.

"Ay," she said, "souming in the water."

"What?"

"I dinna ken—I'm feared for ye."

Ann put out a hand and met a rigid shoulder. The shuddering had stopped. There was only a thin calico night-dress between her palm and Mary's cold flesh. It was very cold.

"Mary—what do you *mean*? You must tell me."

"Dinna go in a boat—dinna go near the water."

"Mary, is there really something in the water?"

"Ay."

"What is it?"

"It comes souming in the munelicht—I'm feared for ye. Keep frae the water."

"Ssh!" said Ann. "What's that?" She spoke with her lips so close to Mary's ear that the words could scarcely have travelled beyond it.

Out on the landing a board had creaked. There was a moment in which neither of them breathed. The board creaked again.

Ann slipped out of bed, went to the door, and opened it. If anyone was prying, she meant to know who it was. But the landing was dark and felt empty. Old boards creak sometimes of themselves, old stairs repeat the footfalls of the day. She struck a match and held it up. A momentary yellow flicker showed the landing bare of all but shadows. Like one of them, Mary slipped past her and was gone. The flame of the match dropped to a yellow point and went out.

Ann stepped back and shut her door. She felt a need for light. She went to the window and pulled the curtains back. The moon stood quite clear of the hills. It was very nearly full. It made strange shadows on the edge of the lawn. It showed the trees in a light that robbed them of life and colour, making them look like the forgotten trees of a dead world.

From her window Ann could see the water. Mary's words came back to her—"Keep frae the water." A light shudder went over her as she thought how near the water she had been that night—not quite down to the edge, but very near. What could there be in the water to hurt her, or to hurt anyone? She remembered something she had heard about another Highland loch—of how it was a thousand feet deep, deeper than anywhere in the North Sea, and that there were still people living who believed that it contained monsters, huge and shapeless, which rose up out of the deep waters for a warning of death. That was Loch Morar. Perhaps this loch had some story of the same kind, and Mary was superstitious. Perhaps ... But she *had* seen something move in the shadow after Charles had swum over the strait.

Ann began to feel cold and a little sick. If there was something in the loch, and if she had seen it moving there, then it had been horribly near Charles as he swam. Suppose the water had broken before him and given up some monster out of its depths....

"Keep frae the water or it'll get ye."

Ann put out a hand to steady herself against the wall. She had placed the signal that would call Charles back, and perhaps he would come as he had come before, swimming in the moonlight or in a moon-shot dusk—and then the waters breaking and something rising out of them.

A cold fear went over her from head to foot. Charles mustn't come—not yet. But if he mustn't come, then the green branch must be taken away from the boat-house roof, and it must be taken away at once. Charles would swim over in the dusk—early dusk or late. If *she* were coming secretly to the shore to look for a signal she would take care to come in the dusk before the day, at the loneliest hour in all the twenty-four. It was wearing towards midnight now. Suppose Charles was over there in the fold between the hills, waiting to come down to the shore as soon as there was light enough to tell green bough from shadow across the strait. She saw him, in a vivid picture, come down to the water's edge and strip and wade in. Everything was in shadow behind him, and the water like dark grey glass. She saw him swim. And then the waters broke and a blackness rose from them, and Charles was gone.

Almost as the picture was formed, her movement shattered it. She had slipped her night-gown off and was putting on her clothes. She was very quick and she made no sound. Instead of her cotton dress she put on a dark skirt and jumper. Then she took her shoes in her hand and went down in her stocking feet. The stairs had creaked all by themselves just now, but they did not creak as Ann went down. She turned the key, opened the front door, and when she had closed it sat down upon the step and put on her shoes.

Now she must cross the lawn, and if there were anyone to see her she would be seen. The grass was not green any more, but a blanched grey under the moon, with queer heavy shadows on the farther side. The dew wetted her feet as she ran. She had time to feel how damp they were when she stood listening under the trees.

The moon shone full on the face of the house. Ann's window was the only open one. The closed panes looked like blind eyes staring at her without sight. Her own open window showed the dark room behind it. Anything might be watching her from there.

"My own room—nobody's watching me." Nothing moved or stirred. One dark eye and three blank ones went on looking at Ann.

She gave herself a shake and turned down the path to the beach. She needn't go the whole way down. She could scramble along the steep bank to the place from which she had dropped the branch which was her signal to Charles. She broke another branch as she went. Now, if she caught this sapling in the crook of her arm, she could fish for the branch she had dropped. It was really quite easy to entangle the two boughs; birches had such a lot of small twigs.

With both branches in her hand she swung herself back to the track. You couldn't call it a path, for it was only a few inches wide, but such as it was, it seemed to run on to the headland on the right of the landing place. Ann pushed her branches away amongst the undergrowth and followed the track. She could not go back until she had looked out over the loch.

At first there was a tangle of trailing thorny growth—bramble or wild raspberry. Her skirts were caught and her stockings fretted. There were trees and bushes to hide her. Then the undergrowth ceased and the trees grew sparser. She was in full moonlight. The track ceased. The ground sloped down and then rose sharply to the piled boulders of the headland.

Ann climbed up to the highest point and stood there looking out over the water. She could see a long way. On the left the loch wound inland, and the last, least winding showed amongst the hills like melted silver. On the right it went away to the jutting cliff which hid the sea, long miles of it, shining under the moon. The island felt very small and dark on the bright mirror of the water. Right in front of her was the shore, and the ruined house, and the road which ran away to hide among the hills. The moon was almost overhead. Ann looked up and saw it very bright, and white, and clear, with a sharp cutting-edge that looked as if it would shear through any cloud. There were clouds about it now, light filmy vapours which shone with a reflected glow.

Ann looked at the sky, and the moon, and the water. The air was warm and very still. There was a sound somewhere, but she could not tell what it was, it was so faint. Then, as she turned her head to listen, it came again, a strange booming that put a tremor on the air and faded away into silence. Ann put her hand to her throat. What was it? It was so vague a sound, so hardly caught, and yet the air still shook with it. It would have been an eerie sound at noon under a high sun. At midnight in grey moonlight it set more than the air shaking.

She let herself down into a crouching position and held to a jutting point of rock. There was another sound now, a sound of water lapping. The first of the misty clouds just touched the moon and dimmed it as the polished surface of the water broke in foam. Ann saw the whitening ripples. The light dimmed, brightened, and failed. The surface of the water was an even grey patched with foam.

And then something broke the foam. The ripples fell away from it with a gurgling sound. Ann felt the terror of her dream. There was something moving in the water. The black line of it stretched to a monstrous length. It might be a shadow under the hidden moon—only no shadow moved like that and churned the water into foam. For a moment something reared up dark and formless. Then the strait foamed and the thing was gone. The wreath of cloud passed on, and the moon shone down. There was a line of white upon the water between the island and the shore. There was nothing else. The booming sound came again from very far away.

Ann put up her hand to her chin, because her teeth were chattering and she mustn't make any noise in this horrible shining silent place. There mustn't be any real sound. If you moved, something might hear you and come back, threshing the water into a white track of foam.

It was a quarter of an hour before she could force herself to move, and then only in the dark of a passing cloud.

The front door was as she had left it. She locked it and had lifted her foot to the first step of the stair, when she heard a sound in the house. There was no light. Her hand was on the baluster and her foot upon the stair. The sound came from the old part of the house. From the kitchen? She didn't know, and she didn't wait to know.

She ran up the stairs with her shoes in her hand, and was in her room with the door shut, whilst the blood still drummed in her ears.

She leaned against the panels, holding the handle in a hard terrified grip. There was no key that she could turn and no bolt that she could shoot. And there was someone coming up the stairs. Her terror took her past all reason. It might have been the formless shadow of the loch rising up into the house, by the fear she felt.

Then Jimmy Halliday spoke, and Gale Anderson answered him. She couldn't hear any words, only the two voices, and the sound of their feet. Both sounds died away. A door shut with a click, and another more softly.

Ann felt very cold. She took off her clothes with fumbling fingers and crept into bed. She did not think that she would sleep, but she slept at once, and only woke when the sun looked in through her uncurtained window.

Chapter Sixteen

WHEN CHARLES ANSTRUTHER got into his car and drove away he had every intention of returning to the island. He did not stay, because he could not continue to swim the strait every time he wanted to talk to Ann. He proposed, therefore, to find the nearest fishing village and there hire a boat. He supposed that this would be possible.

He came in the morning to Ardgair, which boasts a small square whitewashed inn and a cluster of little grey cottages down by the waterside. Having breakfasted, he inquired of the landlord as to whether a boat could be hired and of whom, and was presently in conversation with Mr. John McLean, a very polite old gentleman with a grey beard and frosty blue eyes. He had a boat to be hired—oh yes, by all means. And on this promising opening some pleasant digressions on the weather, the fishing season, and kindred topics—a conversation between gentlemen neither of whom would be so impolite as to hurry the other.

And where might Mr. Anstruther be wanting to fish?

Mr. Anstruther hesitated to confess that he didn't really want to fish at all, but this seemed to be the moment to mention Loch Dhu. And at once an unmistakeable blight fell upon the proceedings. There was some tacking backwards and forwards, and then a definite retreat.

When was it that Mr. Anstruther would be wanting the boat? To-day? Well then, he was afraid it couldn't be managed. To-morrow?—"Indeed, I am very sorry, Mr. Anstruther, but it just will not be possible." The day after?—"Perhaps there is someone else who could oblige you."

And so, with no reason given, the prospect of hiring Mr. McLean's boat receded and became one of the vast company of might-have-beens. Courtesies passed, and Charles went on his way. It took him, after recourse to the inn-keeper, to a black-haired and black-browed young man who was mending a net on the doorstep of one of the cottages. This, it appeared, was Donald McLean, part proprietor of a boat with his brother John.

Once again everything went smoothly until Loch Dhu came into the conversation, when the young man's black brows drew together and he said abruptly,

"We'll be overhauling the boat this week—we'll not be able to hire her."

Charles leaned against a low stone wall in front of the cottage.

"What's the matter with Loch Dhu?" he said.

The young man mended his net in silence.

Charles repeated his question.

He got a dark look and the rough side of Donald's tongue. The boat was his own and he was overhauling her, and that was the end of it.

Charles went back to the inn.

"What's all this about Loch Dhu?" he said. "Everyone's got a boat to hire until I say I want to fish Loch Dhu, and then they're off. What's the matter with it?"

The landlord was a little brisk man with a quick way of speech. He rubbed his chin and took up Charles' words as a man does when he wants to gain time.

"The matter with it? There's nothing the matter with it that I know about, but there'll be better fishing along the coast—oh, without doubt there'll be grand fishing if you go the other way. There's no fishing worth mentioning to be had on Loch Dhu. And that's not taking into consideration that there are very dangerous currents setting in that way, and the channel just crowded with rocks."

"Rocks?" said Charles with a sarcastic intonation.

The landlord nodded. He was another Donald McLean. His natural flow of speech returned. The blessed word rocks appeared to have restored it. Nowhere along the whole coast were there such rocks as beset the entrance to Loch Dhu. In fact, between the rocks and the currents, if you were to get a boat in without smashing her, you'd need to stay there, for you'd never get her out again.

"Then why don't those men say so?" said Charles.

Mr. McLean stole a sly look at his guest.

"They would not be wishing to give offence," he suggested.

"The last one didn't seem to be bothering himself about that."

The landlord rubbed his chin.

"Would that be Donald?"

"Yes."

"He is a rude fellow You will not be taking any notice of him. He is a good fisherman, but he has no manners."

Charles smiled.

"Yet he didn't tell me this story about rocks and currents. He said he wanted to overhaul his boat."

Mr. McLean shrugged his shoulders. Donald was a young man without any manners and quite unaccountable.

Charles continued to smile.

"Is there anyone in this place who will take me into Loch Dhu?"

In the end, and after a good deal of talk, he arrived at the conclusion that there was not. It was all very mysterious and very exasperating. Two undoubted facts emerged. Loch Dhu was considered dangerous. And no one would hire Charles a boat.

He sat down to lunch in a puzzled frame of mind. If Loch Dhu was dangerous on account of its rocky inlet and its currents, why didn't the men say so frankly? He had tried three or four of them, and they had all shut up like clams the moment he mentioned the loch. When questioned no one had anything to say. No one mentioned rocks or currents, no one mentioned anything. There was something odd about it.

He paid for his lunch and drove off. He certainly wasn't going to be put off, but it was no use going back without some means of reaching the island. He wanted,

1. A bathing suit, and

2. A collapsible boat.

Probably the nearest place which would produce both these things was Glasgow. His immediate objective, therefore, should be some place from which he could telephone to Glasgow. On the other hand, telephoning was a most devastating performance. He had a vivid recollection of a conversation with a motor-works in the Midlands from a Welsh village where he had broken a back axle shaft—and in that case he had at least known the name of the firm he wanted and every possible particular about the article he required. It had been a nightmare of voices off and sudden fadings out. A succession of people all most anxious to be helpful came and went upon the wire, whilst he automatically repeated the number of his car, the number of the chassis, the number of the engine, the year of manufacture, and a few more oddments of technical information. When some hours later he received a telegram inquiring the number of his car, words, perhaps fortunately, failed him. A further séance at the telephone resulted in the only possible train in the twenty-four hours being caught at the expense of a really prostrating effort on the part of everyone concerned.

Recalling this experience, Charles felt that he might be equal to telephoning for a bathing-suit, but not for a collapsible boat—definitely not. He could get to Glasgow by midday to-morrow if he hustled. A glorious afternoon's shopping, a night in bed, a start at cockcrow, and he could be back at Loch Dhu by nightfall. He thought he would add a tent to his equipment. He felt adventurous, and pleased with his dispositions. By taking a collapsible boat to the landward shore of the loch he would avoid the dangers of the inlet. If the weather held, camping out would be delightful. It was a good world, and with luck he would be seeing Ann the day after to-morrow.

He sang aloud as he drove. There were moments when, in addition to the bathing-suit, the tent, and the collapsible boat, he contemplated the expenditure of the rest of his bank balance upon an engagement ring. Ann having just refused him for the second time, the Highland air must be held accountable for this. It was indeed a most exquisite and intoxicating draught for a lover—cool under a cloudless sky, and full of the sunny fragrance of heather and pine.

Charles continued to sing.

Chapter Seventeen

Charles shopped with energy and enjoyment. He bought a bathing suit, and a collapsible boat, and a number of articles of camp equipment which he added to his bill under the persuasive eye of a salesman who would have inspired a maiden aunt with a desire to go camping. In retrospect, Charles thought himself fortunate to have escaped without buying a caravan or a tent. He managed to weigh one against the other and thus stave off a decision until he could nerve himself to say that he had an appointment and couldn't possibly wait any longer.

After this he thought he would have some tea.

He was threading his way amongst the small tables at Crawford's, when someone said his name—"Charles Anstruther!" and, turning, he saw Hilda Paulett smiling and beckoning. He had just time to think she was the last person on earth he expected to see, when he remembered that she lived in Glasgow—with an uncle. Yes, that was it—an impossible old beast of an uncle—horribly rich. The name escaped him.

He went over to Hilda, and found himself being invited to sit down at her table. She was alone, and she looked really pleased to see him.

Charles sat down, and was not quite sure whether he was pleased or not. On the one hand, he had never cared very much for Hilda Paulett. He didn't exactly dislike her, but he loathed her relations, the Craddocks with whom she stayed near Bewley. She had stayed with them every year for the last ten years, and he supposed he knew her pretty well, but as their acquaintance had never got beyond a little desultory conversation at a point-to-point, or an occasional dance at a hunt ball, it didn't amount to very much. On the other hand, it was pretty dull having tea by oneself, and he was bursting with conversation about camp equipment.

"What on earth are you doing in Glasgow?" she said.

"Shopping," said Charles, and ordered a comprehensive tea.

"Lucky you! I can't shop, because I haven't got any money, and if I were to run up bills, my uncle would hear of it and cut me out of his will."

Charles began to wish that he had not caught her eye. He loathed people who talked about other people's wills, and he remembered now that Hilda Paulett did it all the time. The uncle was rolling, and she would inherit, and she kept shoving it under your nose all the time. He said,

"I nearly bought a gadget that calls you in the morning, boils a kettle, measures out a spoonful of tea, puts in the milk and sugar, boils an egg, and fries a rasher of bacon. I didn't take it, because they wouldn't guarantee that it would cook sausages."

Hilda Paulett looked a little blank, and when she looked blank she looked sulky. She was dressed in the bright green which had been the fashion of a few months ago and was now dead. It could never have been becoming to her dark skin. Charles thought her gone off, and remembered with surprise that she was considered handsome. He answered a number of questions about the Craddocks—a revolting fellow Craddock—and was edging the conversation round to the point from which he might begin to talk about collapsible boats, when all of a sudden Hilda was saying earnestly,

"Charles, I want to tell you something—only you mustn't speak of it, please."

She had her elbows on the table and was gazing at him with an air of soulful secrecy which was very intimidating.

"Look here," said Charles, "here's a bit of advice—if you're going to confide in me, don't. You'll probably be sorry as soon as you've done it, and loathe me like poison for the rest of your life." He smiled at her pleasantly. "I'm assuming that you're going to confess to a murder or something like that."

Hilda Paulett had no sense of humour; he ought to have recollected that. He had meant to head her off any possible approach to a serious confidence, but to his discomfort she turned pale and said in a low, agitated voice,

"It isn't one yet."

"What isn't one yet?"

She looked over her shoulder nervously. It was rather late, and the two nearest tables were empty.

"Charles, I'm so awfully worried."

Charles groaned inwardly. Why had he not insisted upon conversing about his boat? Why had he flung himself to the wolves by asking her what she meant? He was for it now and had only himself to thank. An expression of pensive melancholy gave him a misleading air of sympathy, and would have encouraged Hilda if she had been in any need of encouragement. She had, however, reached the stage at which a confidant was a necessity, and it is to be doubted whether it would have been possible to head her off.

"I must tell someone," she said, and with a sharp sensation of surprise Charles registered the fact that she was frightened.

He said, "What's the matter?" and immediately there came tumbling out a lot of disconnected and agitated sentences. It was rather like having a jig-saw puzzle thrown at one.

"Of course he said no one must know." (Who on earth was he?) "And it was a legal marriage all right, because I went and asked a lawyer. And besides, he wouldn't be so angry if we weren't really married—would he?"

Charles threw a swift glance at her left hand and found it ringless. She must have seen the look, for she answered it.

"Of course no one knows—at least some of his friends do, but none of mine, and that doesn't seem fair—does it? But of course if Uncle Elias knew, I wouldn't have even an off chance of coming in for anything, so I do see Gale's point there."

Charles could see no point anywhere. But the girl undoubtedly had the wind up. He said,

"Do you mean you're married?"

And Hilda Paulett said, "Yes—*yes!*" and wrung her hands at him.

Charles felt extremely self-conscious.

"I say, don't do that," he said. "It looks as if we were having a row."

"I don't care! I've got to have someone to talk to! You don't know what it's like, thinking all sorts of things and then wondering whether you've imagined them!"

"Well, don't you think perhaps you have?"

"I don't know," said Hilda. She leaned towards him across the table. "There's such a lot of money, and she's got it all. Gale cares terribly about money. And you see, he thought I was going to get it, and so did I, so we got married—only of course we didn't tell Uncle Elias. And now I'm frightened."

"Why?" said Charles.

He leaned back in his chair. Even so she was very near him, and he could see that she was speaking the truth. She *was* frightened. Her nostrils quivered and her mouth twitched. She said,

"I don't know why. That's what frightened me. It's such a lot of money. Supposing anything happened to me, Gale would be free. He's awfully attractive—she might easily fall in love with him. But he couldn't be sure, and it would be an awful risk to take unless he was sure." She dropped her voice and said, "Supposing he is sure—suppose he makes her fond of him—then what happens to me? I wake up in the night and think about that. *What happens to me?*"

She was hysterical. Charles decided that with relief.

"Look here," he said—"do you want my advice? Go along home and sleep on all this. If you still feel worried in the morning, go and see your lawyer."

Hilda took out a handkerchief and dabbed her eyes. "I expect you think I'm silly, but it's dreadful to feel so frightened. Sometimes I'm frightened about myself, and sometimes I'm frightened about *her*—but I'm always frightened."

At the moment Charles thought she was making rather a luxury of being frightened. He felt like pushing her jig-saw puzzle back at her and saying, "Here, do the damned thing yourself!"

"You see," Hilda was saying in an earnest, shaken voice—"you see, if anything happened to her, I'd get it all. And once anyone begins thinking about that sort of thing it gets a sort of hold of them, so when he began to talk about a boating accident in his sleep it frightened me most dreadfully, and if he'd *asked* me to go out in a boat with him, nothing would have induced me to. But supposing it isn't me at all—supposing it's her and she doesn't know, and there's an accident—well, what would I feel like?"

Charles' head was going round. He said with conviction,

"I haven't the slightest idea," and glanced ostentatiously at his watch. The woman was balmy.

He pushed back his chair, and would have risen if she had not clutched him.

"Look here, Hilda—"

"I thought you'd help me. Aren't you going to help me?"

"I don't see what I can do. If your husband isn't treating you properly you'd better see a solicitor."

"A solicitor won't stop Ann Vernon having a boating accident," said Hilda Paulett.

Charles received the most frightful shock. All the pieces of the jig-saw puzzle rushed together and made the most terrifying picture. He remained where he was with one hand on the table and his muscles flexed. He had actually begun to rise, but the movement froze, uncompleted.

After about a minute he dropped back into his chair. He wondered if Hilda had noticed anything, and in the very act of wondering became aware that she was speaking—"If he had divided it, it would have been all right. There's enough for two. I can see Gale's point of view, you know, because it's a lot of money, and I don't suppose he'd have wanted to marry me if he hadn't thought I was bound to come in for it."

Charles spoke. His voice sounded harsh and abrupt in his own ears.

"We're not getting this straight. You thought your uncle had left his money to you, and he hasn't?"

"We both thought so. I saw it in the will—'every thing to my great-niece.' And the page ended there, but of course I thought it was me, because I didn't know Ann Vernon existed, and nor did Gale."

"You thought the money was left to you, and it wasn't?"

"That's what I've been trying to tell you, but you didn't seem interested."

A horrible griping laughter caught at Charles, but he choked it down.

"Oh, I'm interested," he said.

Hilda Paulett opened her bag and produced a mirror and a powder-puff.

"It's awfully sweet of you, and I feel ever so much better. You know, I think it does you a lot of good to get anything like that off your chest." She closed her eyes in order to powder the lids, after which she took out a lipstick and reinforced the discordant cerise of her lips. They were full, pouting lips and they took a good deal of colour. She managed to talk all the time.

"Gale's really very fond of me, and he's so good-looking. I'd love you to meet him. Of course we couldn't have got married without the money, and now it doesn't look as if we were going to get it. It was silly of me to say all that about Ann Vernon. She'll live to be a hundred—people always do if you want their money. I should get it if she died, you know. I shouldn't go into mourning if she had an accident, but of course I'd like to feel sure about it—about it's being an accident, I mean. But she won't have one."

Charles got to his feet. He was angrier than he had ever been in his life. For a violent minute he stood there and felt the room shake with his anger. Then he said, "No, she won't!" And what he would have said or done next he never knew, for at that moment a ginger-haired waitress arrived with the bill. By the time he had paid it he had himself sufficiently under control to bid Hilda Paulett a conventional farewell.

She did not appear to have noticed anything, since she repeated that he had done her a lot of good, and that she hoped that they would meet quite soon.

Charles evaded her hand, collected his hat and stick, and departed, hoping that he might never set eyes on her again.

Chapter Eighteen

CHARLES WAS ALREADY on the road when Ann woke next morning. The sun was shining in at the window, and as she sat up in bed, all the queer shadows of the night seemed to slip away from her. Whilst she dressed, she took herself to task. After all, what did it all amount to? Some broken scraps of conversation, and a shadow on the loch in the dusk whilst a cloud went over the moon. "But it wasn't a shadow," said something deep inside her. "It moved—and the water foamed."

She gave herself an impatient shake and stopped her ears. Those scraps of conversation—why need they have anything to do with her? This was a most reassuring thought. The two men were talking, and she had caught bits of what they said. They might have been talking about a book, or a play, or a case in the papers. Ann wished passionately that she could have found this a convincing line of argument, but she just couldn't get any mental grip on the idea of Jimmy Halliday and Gale Anderson discussing a play or a book. A case in the papers was a little more likely. But what case? Ann read the papers diligently, both to herself and to Mrs. Halliday. They arrived once a week with the groceries, and Mrs. Halliday took them in daily instalments—a morning paper in the morning, and an evening paper in the evening. Ann simply couldn't fit the scraps she had overheard to anything in the papers.

"Murder," and, "You should encourage her to learn to swim. Now, I suppose, it'll have to be a boating accident," and, "I won't."

There was more comfort in the last two words than in all her attempts to explain the rest away.

She went down, and found a very glum Gale Anderson and a spruce and sheepish Jimmy who sat between her and his mother and passed her everything three times until Mrs. Halliday, fixing him with a contemptuous eye, inquired what was the matter that he was behaving himself so silly, whereupon he blushed, chuckled, and upset his tea. Mrs. Halliday called him a great scummocking porpoise, and told Ann rather acidly to go and fetch something to mop up the mess. Jimmy did not offer to help her. He came of a class whose womenfolk wait upon them, and it was noticeable that since they had come to the island he no longer troubled to maintain the social veneer of Westley Gardens.

Ann mopped up the tea. There was a slight tension in the air when she returned after taking away the cloth she had used. Mrs. Halliday had pushed back her chair and risen.

"You come along with me, Miss Vernon," she said, and the customary "my dear" was lacking.

They went into the parlour and plunged into the day before yesterday's paper, but in the very middle of an exciting column headed *Film Star's Romance* Ann became aware that Mrs. Halliday's shrewd grey glance was fixed upon her. The shrewdness had a sparkle upon it, and the sparkle looked a good deal like anger. Mrs. Halliday's voice broke in, and the anger was unmistakable.

"Romance! I've no patience! Vanity and empty-headedness is what I call it! Anything to get themselves noticed, and not caring how it's done! You mark my words, Miss Vernon, it don't bring a girl to no good. A proper-minded young woman don't lay herself out to get taken notice of by a man that's old enough to be her father."

Ann had a lovely picture of herself setting her cap at Jimmy Halliday. She silently ejaculated, "Golly!" and said aloud, in a beautifully meek voice,

"Oh no—she wouldn't."

Mrs. Halliday gave a sort of snort. She was sitting up in a horse-hair armchair with a white antimacassar over the back of it and a lovely fat patchwork cushion made of hundreds of scraps of velvet and satin faggoted together with crimson silk behind her shoulders.

"*Wouldn't* she then? That's all you know about it! Though I don't suppose you're as innocent as you sound—girls never are. And I've had my experience of them. Jimmy wasn't only sixteen when they started after him, and that there Bessie Fox she'd have had 'im sure as nuts if it hadn't been for me. And where'd he have been now? Fox by name and Vixen by nature, that's what she was—a ginger-'eaded girl with a come-along-and-kiss-me look in her eye. But she didn't get Jimmy—no more did Mary Pott as set up to be a beauty and couldn't so much as darn 'er own stockings. Red staring cheeks like radishers and great gooseberry eyes, and didn't know how to cook a potato! A fine wife she'd have made!" She laughed a short angry laugh. "Well, she didn't get 'im—nor yet Susan Moggridge, nor May Fisher, nor Polly Pocklington, nor the widow that had the greengrocer's shop, and that was forty if she was a day, and talked a deal about what she'd got in the bank, and it come out afterwards that she hadn't nothing and was looking for a 'usband to pay 'er debts."

"How mean!" said Ann. She was glad to say something, because she wanted most dreadfully to laugh.

"Mean?" said Mrs. Halliday on a trumpet note of scorn. "The meanness of young women is past belief! Not as she was young—never see forty again she wouldn't—and artful. But she didn't get Jimmy. The nearest to it was Sarah Hollins, and if I ever 'ated a girl in my life, I 'ated 'er—with all 'atred," she added after a moment's brooding.

"Why?"

"Because she nearly 'ad my Jimmy—got as far as talking about putting up the banns they did."

"How did you stop them?"

"Told her he snored," said Mrs. Halliday—"something cruel, like a fog-horn. 'And no woman born as could stand it,' I says to 'er, and she ups and sauces me and says she can put cotton wool in her ears if such was the case."

"What did you do?"

Mrs. Halliday laughed grimly.

"I took and told 'im the same about 'er. 'And do she really?' says 'e. And I says, 'She do—and I give you joy of it, Jimmy my lad.'" She sniffed and looked pointedly at Ann. "The banns never went up after all. None of 'em didn't get Jimmy—*and none of 'em ain't going to.*"

The manner in which Mrs. Halliday delivered these last words was portentous in the extreme. She waited a moment for them to sink in and then took up the knitting which had been reposing in her lap.

"I don't want to hear no more of that there romance," she said. "You find me a nice murder, Miss Vernon my dear."

Ann felt that she had been warned.

After that it became imperative to discourage Jimmy Halliday— imperative, but very difficult. He waylaid her when she was going out after lunch and offered to take her up the loch. Twenty-four hours earlier she would have jumped at the offer. Now she wasn't going out in any boat with anyone. If you don't get into a boat, you can't very well have a boating accident. It might be boring to be confined to the island, but for the moment Ann was off boats. She said she was going to walk, and then thought how silly that sounded. You could climb, scramble, or slither, but you couldn't possibly walk on the island. However, one snub would do as well as another for Jimmy Halliday.

Jimmy wasn't snubbed. He looked at her sheepishly between his short, thick sandy lashes, fiddled with a handkerchief which had a lively pattern of scarlet anchors on a ground of Reckitt's blue, and once more invited her to come out with him on the loch.

An imp danced in Ann's eyes. She said in a meek, poor-companion voice,

"I'm afraid your mother wouldn't like it, Mr. Halliday."

Memories of Bessie Fox, Mary Pott, Susan Moggridge, Polly Pocklington, Sarah Hollins and the rest convinced Mr. Halliday of the truth of this statement. He blushed a vehement beetroot red and muttered something which Ann did not catch.

"What did you say?"

"I said she'd come off it."

"Do you think so?" said Ann. She shook her head mournfully. "I don't. You'd better take Mr. Anderson or Riddle—it will be safer. I hope you'll have a nice time."

She went back towards the house. Coming out of it she met Gale Anderson with a smile on his face. This was such an arresting phenomenon that she stopped to admire it. He really was good-looking when he smiled. Not that she herself had much use for pale regular features and blue eyes in a man, but the smile certainly did improve them. It also showed a row of teeth which were almost too good to be true. She wondered if they were true. And then she wondered what she had done to deserve this lovely smile.

Mr. Anderson addressed her with a good deal of charm of manner.

"Isn't it a beautiful afternoon?"

"Yes, isn't it?" said Ann.

After the weather gambit—what? The knights' move, with its stealthy sideways pounce? She wondered.

"It's far too good an afternoon to waste."

"Yes, isn't it?" said Ann; and forthwith she was being invited for the second time that afternoon to enjoy the loch from a boat.

"How kind of you!"

Gale Anderson told the truth.

"Oh, not at all," he said.

"What a pity I don't like boating," said Ann. Gazing with modest gratitude at the smile, she observed that it was no longer entirely effortless—a trifle fixed, a trifle strained—a hint of an approaching depression. "It is a pity—isn't it?" she said.

During the next five minutes Ann enjoyed herself a good deal. Gale Anderson, still smiling, expatiated upon the smoothness of the water, the steadiness of Jimmy's boat, and the ravishing beauty of the surroundings as seen from the loch. At every pause she looked a little more mournful and repeated a little more earnestly, "Yes, I know—but isn't it a pity that I don't like going in a boat?" In the end the smile came off with a jerk. Mr. Anderson went striding away across the lawn, and Miss Vernon entered the house humming to herself:

"Clouds were all around
Sunny days were few.
Then, just when I least expected it,
I met you."

She went into the parlour to look for a book. Mrs. Halliday and Riddle were napping, each in a horse-hair chair. Mrs. Halliday had her feet up on a large square foot-stool worked in cross-stitch with magenta roses on a crimson background. Each rose was the size of a well-grown cabbage, and the high lights on the petals were put in with shiny white beads. The rhythmic sound of two several snores rose and fell in the little room, Riddle's a faint alto to Mrs. Halliday's bass-baritone. The old lady had a white silk handkerchief over her face, and every time she snored it flapped against her chin.

"Golly!" said Ann to herself.

She picked her way to the book-case, avoiding Mrs. Halliday's knitting and the thread of Riddle's crochet, both of which had slipped to the ground. The book-case was in the corner between the window and the fireplace. It had scallops of green leather nailed along the edges of the shelves, and it held four rows of books. Ann knelt down in front of them with a sigh. Not a very promising lot, she was afraid.

She took out a book with no name on the back, discovered it to be the *Collected Sermons of the Reverend Henry Macdougal*, and put it back again on the bottom shelf. The remainder of the row appeared to be occupied by the works of Mrs. Henry Wood. Ann dipped into one of them, found herself in an intensive atmosphere of moral sentiment, said "Golly!" again, and abandoned this talented author without discovering her undoubted gift for telling a story. The title-page fell over as she was about to close the volume. In faint brown ink was the name, Jessie Paulett. Ann looked at it, frowning a little. Somewhere, if he was still alive, she had a great-uncle called Paulett. It wasn't a common name. And Charles had said he knew a girl called Hilda Paulett. Funny if she had some relations after all.... She wondered who Jessie Paulett was, and as she knelt there with the book in her hand, she had the strangest feeling of an unseen family circle closing in upon her. She didn't like it very much.

Jessie Paulett.... Like the faintest echo from that very far off time which was her childhood, she heard her mother saying in her pretty, tired voice, "I loved Aunt Jessie—but she died when I was fifteen." Aunt Jessie.... Was it possible?

She picked out a book at random and opened it. *Longfellow's Poems*, in brown cloth with a spray of gold lilies of the valley across the cover. Ann wasn't interested in the cover. She turned to the fly-leaf, and there, written right across the page, stood her mother's name in her mother's writing, a little firmer and more careless than Ann had known it, but quite recognizable—"Eleanor Paulett." Above, on the extreme upper edge of the leaf, very faint and spidery—"Dearest Nellie, from her loving Aunt Jessie."

Ann sat back on her heels and stared at the page. How did these Paulett books come to be here? This was her mother's book. Had her mother lived in this house?

She put Longfellow back and began to go through the shelves systematically, looking at the fly-leaf of every book. Most were blank, but there were two more "Dearest Nellies," one in a Burns and the other in a Tennyson. There were also some volumes of *The Canterbury Poets*, little square green books with gold tracery on the backs and "Eleanor Paulett" inside—*Keats, Shelley, Ballades and Rondeaus*, and the Border Ballads.

A very sharp stinging pain made Ann's eyes dazzle for a moment. Mummy—who had been Aunt Jessie's "Dearest Nellie," and had loved poetry, and had had such a hard, sad life of prose. It hurt frightfully for a moment. Why hadn't Elias Paulett helped her? She had written to him, and he hadn't even answered the letter—just because he was angry at her marrying an American.

Ann knelt there and wondered how you went on being angry with anyone for years and years and years. She could do a good hot boil up herself, but the idea of going on boiling for years or slowly freezing in a cold hell of resentment was absolutely staggering. She went on taking out books, and found two with Elias Paulett's name in a big square writing—one a thin paper pamphlet entitled *New Markets for Old Trades*, and the other a *Ready Reckoner*.

Ann put the books back carefully. She kept the *Border Ballads* with her mother's name in it, and was making her way towards the door, when Mrs. Halliday choked half way up a snore and sat up. The silk handkerchief fell off into her lap. She eyed Ann sternly and said,

"Who made that noise?"

Ann being at a loss for an answer, she transferred her stare to the unconscious Riddle.

"Snores something shocking—don't she? She did ought to have 'erself more under control. I've no patience with people making noises like that. Gave me a real start, she did."

"I'm so sorry," said Ann. And then, "Mrs. Halliday—who does this house belong to?"

"How do you mean, belong to?" Mrs. Halliday settled her cap, which was very crooked, and looked suspiciously at Ann.

"I mean the furniture, and the books, and everything. I've found some books with 'Paulett' in them. Used the Pauletts to live here?"

"What do you know about Pauletts?" said Mrs. Halliday sharply.

"I wondered whether they lived here."

"Why shouldn't they?"

Ann laughed.

"I don't know. Did they?"

"Seeing as how the place belonged to them, they did. And if the books have their name in them, it's no more than they've got a lawful right to."

"Does it belong to them still?"

Mrs. Halliday nodded.

"Belongs to Mr. Elias Paulett as lives in Glasgow—something in the shipping line, and a pile of money, so they say. My 'usband sailed in one of 'is ships, and my Jimmy done the same, and when he'd made his pile along of being clever and thrifty, he'd a fancy to take this place for his summer 'oliday. Take it he did, and we've come here every year. Pauletts haven't been near it, not in donkeys' years. And if you're going out, Miss Vernon, I'd be glad if you was to go and let me 'ave my nap—if so be that there Riddle don't wake me again, the snoring grampus!"

Chapter Nineteen

ANN TOOK HER BOOK and went round the house and up the winding path to the knoll at the top of the island. It was a very still, warm afternoon. The water of the loch lay like a sheet of blue looking-glass with the hills mirrored in it. So sharp, so clear, and so unblurred was the reflection that she could see every stone, every stain, every rift, and every cleft exactly repeated. There was not a cloud in the sky. There was a scent of heather and a scent of pine.

Ann sat down and began to read in the little green book with her mother's name on the fly-leaf. The ballads took her into another country—a country of hills, and haughs, and magical running streams—a kinder country than this. There were no lochs there with waters going down into terrible unknown depths. The nearest you got to it was in the company of Thomas the Rhymer.

> "O they rade on, and farther on,
> And they waded thro' rivers aboon the knee,
> And they saw neither sun nor moon,
> But they heard the roaring of the sea."

The sea didn't roar here. It lipped and lapped at the stones of the island, and sometimes when the tide was rising it came lifting in between the boulders with a strange sucking sound, and then it looked green with a foamy edge. Now it was all blue—smooth unbroken blue. The words went through her mind and broke suddenly, because for an instant the blue of the loch had been broken. Something dark showed and was gone again. Ann was left wondering whether she had really seen anything. She certainly couldn't have said what she had seen. The blue had been broken; that was all. She went on looking for a long time, but she saw nothing except the sun shining on the water, and the clear reflection of the hills. Perhaps what she had seen was the image of something moving upon the hillside ... No—because it was the blue that had been broken, and not the many-coloured reflection of the hills.

She went on looking for a little longer, and then went back to her book.

> "It was mirk mirk night, and there was nae stern light,
> And they waded thro' red blude to the knee."

Ann looked up with a shiver.

Someone was coming up the hill. She felt a certain degree of relief when she saw that it was Jimmy Halliday. She preferred him to Gale Anderson, and felt quite sure of being able to keep him in his place. He came up the slope, seated himself upon a large stone, and remarked upon the beauty of the day.

"It's a beautiful afternoon."

"Yes, isn't it?" said Ann.

Jimmy Halliday cleared his throat.

"It's a pity you didn't come out in the boat with me. It'd be grand on the water."

Ann shook her head.

"I don't like boating."

"I'd teach you to like it if you came out with me."

Ann shook her head again.

"It's too deep—you said it was yourself. I don't like lochs that go down for miles. Suppose I fell in and was drowned."

"I wouldn't let you."

"I don't think I like boating." She dropped her eyes to her book and read on.

Jimmy Halliday coughed.

"You and me's got to have a talk."

"Have we?"

Jimmy's voice became a good deal louder.

"I said we'd got to have a talk, and I meant what I said. If you'd known me a bit longer, you'd know that I always do."

"When you talk to girls?" said Ann brightly.

Her book slid off her lap. She had the pleasure of seeing Jimmy's colour rise.

"Look here, Miss Vernon—I want you to listen to me. A man's got a right to be listened to, hasn't he? You can say what you like afterwards, but you've got to listen to me first."

"Very well, Mr. Halliday, I'll listen."

Mr. Halliday ran a finger round inside his collar. The sun was hot. Mr. Halliday felt hot, and not unpleasantly embarrassed. There was a vein of sentiment in his nature which in time past had led him to succumb with fatal ease to the advances of Miss Bessie Fox and the other young women enumerated by his mother. From the moment that it had occurred to him how much pleasanter and more profitable it would be to marry Ann than to allow Gale Anderson to murder her this vein had fairly gushed. If Ann were murdered, Gale Anderson's wife came into Elias Paulett's money, and if Gale Anderson did the sharing out, Jimmy was under no illusion as to who would get the lion's share. If, on the other hand, he, Jimmy, married Ann, it would be he who would divide the spoil. And there would be no risk. Everything would be perfectly straight, legal, and above board. This was a great point. For some years now he had been living on the dangerous side of the law. He made large profits, but he ran great risks. The drug trade was no longer what it had been. The law was terribly active, and sentences ran high. Jimmy wanted to retire. A share of a hundred thousand pounds and a pretty young wife were gifts from the gods. Jimmy felt very warmly disposed towards Miss Ann Vernon, who was gazing at him with polite attention. He could have wished her plumper—he liked a good armful—but there it was, you couldn't have everything.

He cleared his throat and began.

"You're an unprotected young lady, and such being the case, it's natural you should look round for a chance to get settled in life."

That little warning sparkle came into Ann's eyes. It made them very bright. They were somewhere half way between grey and blue in colour, and they were shaded by very long fine lashes of a darker brown than her hair.

"Did you want to be settled in life when you were my age, Mr. Halliday?"

"Boys are different," said Jimmy in a moral tone of voice. "A young lady like you ought to think about getting settled."

Ann shook her head. The sparkle danced high.

"I don't want to be settled a bit—not for years and years and years. There are masses of things I want to do first. I want to go round the world, and fly to America, and shoot a rapid, and refuse a Prime Minister, and see Noel Coward's last revue. I'm not quite sure about the Prime Minister. Perhaps a Lord Chancellor would do, or I might have to put up with a plain Cabinet Minister. It's rather fun to think of all the things that might happen to one. For instance, I could vary the programme by flying with the Lord Chancellor, or shooting a Cabinet Minister."

Jimmy listened with disapproval tempered by the fact that Ann looked very pretty when she talked nonsense.

"A young lady like you doesn't want to get herself mixed up in any shooting affairs," he said.

"Oh, Mr. Halliday—just think of the headlines in the papers! I should just love to be in a headline, but I don't suppose I ever shall unless I go out with Mr. Anderson in his boat and he upsets her and drowns me. I might get a headline then, but it would only be a very little one."

Ann's innocent gaze remained fixed upon Mr. Halliday's face. The face remained a blank.

"If you take my advice, you won't go out in a boat with no one but me," he said without the slightest change of voice. "This loch"—he pronounced it lock—"is what I call tricky, and Gale isn't the hand with a boat that I am. You come out with me, and I'll see that there aren't any accidents."

Ann sighed.

"It's a pity I don't like boating. I did tell you that before, didn't I?" How many times was she going to have to say this, and when was it going to sink in?

As she spoke, she looked out over the loch and wondered just how deep it was, and how far down into those depths she would sink if she went out with Gale Anderson and his boat overturned. It would overturn; she felt quite sure about that. That is to say, it would overturn if Ann Vernon was ever fool enough to go out in it. Ann felt comfortably certain of never being just that particular kind of fool.

"Gale's my business partner," said Jimmie Halliday without taking any notice. "I've got nothing against him, but he's not quite the thing for a young lady like you. A married man didn't ought to get friendly with an unprotected young lady like you—it wouldn't look right, and it's not what Mrs. Halliday would care about neither."

"Mrs. Halliday didn't seem to care about my going out with *you*."

Jimmy was only too painfully aware of this. His spirits were a good deal dashed when he remembered the courtship of Bessie Fox, of the widow at The Stag, and his mother's reactions. The widow was an escape, and Bessie a brazen piece if ever there was one, but Sarah Hollins would have done him nicely. There was no doubt about it, the old lady was a fair terror when it came to him casting an eye on a girl, but so far it was all to the good, because here was the best part of a hundred thousand waiting to be picked up and no good thinking about it if he hadn't been a bachelor.

"She'd come round," he said.

"Does she as a rule?" said Ann.

Jimmy frowned and began to bluster a little.

"I'm my own master, aren't I? Nobody can't say that I haven't been a good son, but a man's got to settle some time, and it'd be best for her in the end. What the old lady wants at her time of life is a daughter. Maids and companions—what's the good of them? Here to-day and gone to-morrow. No—what she wants is a daughter. And who's going to give her one except me?" He took out a gaily coloured handkerchief and wiped a heated brow. "It may surprise you, Miss Vernon, and I don't want it to come too sudden, but the fact is I'm thinking of getting married."

"Oh—" said Ann. She wanted to laugh. She bit the corner of her lip very hard and gazed at Jimmy. "Does Mrs. Halliday know?"

"Not yet she doesn't."

Ann shook her head.

"She won't like it, Mr. Halliday. She's told me all about the girls who wanted to marry you when you were young—heaps of them. She said none of them had got you, and none of them were going to get you. I expect you'd better give it up. It would be horrid for the girl, you know, having Mrs. Halliday hate her—and I'm afraid she would."

Jimmy mopped his brow again.

"She'd come round," he said, but without conviction.

The laughter which she had been holding in threatened to be too much for Ann. She stooped, picked up a stone, and turning away from Jimmy, sent it skimming over the tree-tops. She looked down on them from where she sat—green tops of pines and delicate sprays of birch with the blue water beyond them. The stone went skimming over the green and dropped towards the blue. Ann watched it go, her lips parted in forbidden laughter. Then she lifted her dancing eyes and looked across the loch. As she did so, she saw something that stopped her laughter.

Just where the many-coloured reflection of the hills met the blue reflection of the sky, something moved. If she had looked just one split second sooner, Ann would have seen what it was that moved. By just that one flash of time she was too late. She was left with the knowledge that something had moved, and that she didn't want to laugh any more.

She put a hand down on either side of her, gripped the stone, and swung round on Jimmy Halliday.

"Is there anything in the loch?"

"In the lock?" His *lock* was quite uncompromising.

"Yes."

"There's a good bit of fish. The herring come in." His eyes shifted from hers.

"I don't mean herring—I mean something ... Mr. Halliday, what is it? I saw it one night in the moonlight. No, I didn't quite see it, because the moon went behind a cloud, but"—her voice fell—"I heard it, and I saw the wake it left behind. And just now—just now I thought I saw it out there." She lifted her left hand from the stone and pointed back towards the loch.

"It would have been just a shadow."

"It wasn't a shadow that I *heard* in the night—and when the moon came out again there was a track in the water, all foamy."

"What night was that?" said Jimmy in a quick undertone.

"Last night."

"What were you doing down by the water?"

Ann stared at him. He looked as if he was afraid.

"It was a lovely night. I couldn't sleep."

"You're to keep away from the water!"

He spoke roughly, and she was reminded of Mary's words: "Keep frae the water." Mary had said that, and Mary had said, *"Or it'll get ye."*

"What is it, Mr. Halliday?"

Jimmy gave her a queer look.

"I've told you the loch's dangerous. You keep away from the water and you'll be all right. Don't go out at night or it'll be the worse for you—let alone that it isn't at all the thing for a young lady like you. I'm not saying what you saw or what you didn't see—there's things I wouldn't like to talk about—but as for your seeing anything out there just now, that's all my eye and Betty Martin."

Ann gave her head a small obstinate shake. She hadn't seen anything, but there had been something to see—if she had looked a moment sooner.

"There was something," she said under her breath.

"And I say there wasn't," said Jimmy Halliday. Then all of a sudden he laughed. "Have it your own way! But remember the loch's dangerous. And if that young man that came along in his car a couple of days ago comes back, he'll be likely to find it out for himself."

"Will you tell me what you mean, Mr. Halliday?" said Ann.

Jimmy Halliday got up and stood over her, his hands in his pockets and his sandy brows frowning.

"There used to be bits of houses up and down the loch—fisher folks' cottages. There's one of them over there in ruins now—you've seen it for yourself. Why did the people go away? I'll tell you why. They were scared. If you ask me what scared them, maybe it was the same thing that scared you—maybe they thought it was risky living down so close to the water—maybe they were afraid of getting their feet wet. Anyway they quit." He turned away and began to go down over the slope of the knoll. From below her he looked back and spoke again. "What did you think you saw just now?" There was an anxious ring in his voice.

Ann hesitated.

"I just missed it. When I looked, it was gone."

He moved his shoulders like a man easing them of a weight.

"You didn't see anything," he said, and walked down the hill.

Chapter Twenty

ANN SAT STILL and thought about her talk with Jimmy Halliday. One thing emerged. She had begun by being amused, and had ended by being rather frightened. She wasn't afraid of Jimmy Halliday. She felt quite sure of being able to keep him in order, and if she couldn't, Mrs. Halliday could and most certainly would. No, she wasn't afraid of Jimmy. He had undoubtedly signified his intention of making her the offer of his hand in marriage. Why? Propinquity, sentiment, a desire to settle down, a filial ambition to provide Mrs. Halliday with a daughter—*or* some reason connected with those odd bits of conversation about a will? Whose will?

She could very easily believe that Jimmy Halliday would like to provide for his old age by marrying an heiress, but it was very difficult to imagine that that heiress was herself. Who was there to leave her money? Elias Paulett? Why, he had never seen her or taken the slightest interest in her. As far as he was concerned, she might have starved or gone to the workhouse.

Well, she would just have to stave Jimmy off. He did not appear to be an ardent wooer. According to Mrs. Halliday it had usually been the girls who had done the wooing, so it ought not to be too difficult to keep him at a good safe distance.

She dismissed Jimmy's courtship and turned to the other part of their conversation. There was something here that puzzled her a good deal. After insisting that the loch was dangerous, and appearing to lend quite a ready ear to her account of having seen something swimming in the strait at night, Jimmy Halliday had gone off the deep end at the idea of her having seen the same something by daylight. Her thought became momentarily more impressed by this discrepancy. He didn't mind her believing that she had seen something by moonlight, but he had been disturbed—was that the word, or was it alarmed?—at her insisting that she had seen, what she had just missed seeing, under the eye of the sun. She thought there was something odd about this—odd, and a little frightening.

She stood up and looked out over the water for a long time, but there was no more to be seen than hill and sky above, and below, again hill and sky, like a clear transparent picture upon the surface of the loch. The sunlight made all the colours quiver as if they were alive.

Ann went back to the house with regret.

The rest of the day wasn't at all comfortable. Mrs. Halliday was cross because her nap had been interrupted, and both Jimmy Halliday and Gale Anderson gave her plenty to be cross about. Ann was responsible for bringing down a storm upon Mr. Anderson's devoted head. He had spoken to her in a low voice, and she at once repeated his remark for Mrs. Halliday's benefit.

"Mr. Anderson is shocked to think that I can't swim."

They were all out on the lawn, Mrs. Halliday in a black silk mantle, a black feather boa, and a bonnet with three purple ostrich feathers placed at a rakish angle over one ear. One of the horsehair chairs had been carried out for her, and her feet, in elastic-sided boots, were raised from the grass on a little round walnut footstool with a beadwork top. At the word swim her head went up like a war-horse. She repeated sharply,

"Swim? What does a young lady like you want to swim for?"

"I don't," said Ann, sitting down on the grass.

"And what's it got to do with Mr. Anderson?" said Mrs. Halliday, using very much the voice with which it may be supposed that Job's war-horse said "Ha!" among the captains.

"He thinks I ought to learn."

Gale Anderson stood a yard or two away and gazed past the ostrich feathers. Jimmy Halliday had gone down to the boat-house.

"And him teach you?" said Mrs. Halliday very sharply indeed.

"That was the idea, wasn't it, Mr. Anderson?"

Up to this moment Gale Anderson had regarded the removal of Ann as a matter of business, but under the faint mockery of her voice he felt that for once business and pleasure might be combined. She'd laugh at him, would she, and let him in for a tongue-lashing from the old harridan? Well, they laugh best who laugh last.

Mrs. Halliday snorted.

"Not in my *h*ouse!" she said, using an aspirate of alarming intensity. "Not in my *h*ouse he don't! Nor you neither, Miss Vernon!"

Ann had a lovely picture of trying to swim on the parlour floor, but it was swept away by the spate of Mrs. Halliday's virtuous wrath.

"There won't be none of this there mixed bathing in my house, Mr. Anderson—not while I'm above ground there won't! And Jimmy did ought to know better than to allow you to speak of such a thing—never brought up to suchlike he wasn't!"

"I told you Mrs. Halliday wouldn't like it," said Ann in a virtuous voice. She gazed sweetly at Mr. Anderson from her seat on the grass, and was repaid by seeing him struggle with a scowl. It defeated him, and he turned and went away round the house.

Ann was watching his retreat with satisfaction, when the storm broke over her.

"And let me tell you, Miss Vernon, a young lady with proper feelings don't get asked to go bathing with married men, nor with single ones neither! Hussies, I call those that do, and *worse*! And I tell you straight I'm surprised at you, Miss Vernon! When I was in service, the young ladies did use to bathe, and maybe their brothers and a gentleman friend would join them in the water. But how was they dressed? Many's the time I had Miss Sophy's and Miss Gwendoline's bathing-dresses to dry—and what was they like? 'Igh up to the neck and a decent sleeve—blue serge piped with white, and a proper full skirt that came down below the knee and covered the pants. That's what Miss Sophy and Miss Gwendoline wore in the water. And what did I see the last time I was at the seaside? 'Ussies, and worse! Next door to naked, with their backs showing down below their waists and about as much stuff on the rest of them as 'ud make a pair of silk stockings, and clinging so tight it didn't hide nothing and wasn't meant to!" Mrs. Halliday gave a snort at which the ostrich feathers quivered. "And that's what *your* bathing-dress is like, I'll be bound!"

Ann was sitting up clasping her knees.

"I haven't got one. And, dear Mrs. Halliday, I don't want to bathe the least bit in the world—and certainly not with Mr. Anderson—not even if I'd got a bathing-dress exactly like Gwendoline's and Sophy's with yards of blue serge and little white squiggly edges, and Riddle to chaperone us all the time he was teaching me to swim."

"Let him teach 'is own wife!" said Mrs. Halliday severely.

"Perhaps she doesn't want to learn," said Ann. "I'm sure I don't—I keep telling you so. I should hate him to teach me anything. I should think he's got a perfectly horrid temper. I don't like him a bit. Do you?"

Mrs. Halliday drew herself up with an air of offence.

"And it's not for you to say who you like and who you don't, Miss Vernon—not in my house nor yet in Jimmy's, seeing as Mr. Anderson is his friend."

Ann bit her lip. She would have liked to shake Mrs. Halliday. She would have liked to trample on the ostrich feathers. She would have liked to give notice. When you have no home and no money, you can't afford the luxury of losing your temper. She had not lived all her life in other people's houses for nothing. She bit her lip very hard, and the colour ran brightly up to the edge of her hair.

Mrs. Halliday gave a rather lesser snort like an engine letting off steam and cooling down.

"You mind your manners, and I'll mind mine," she said. "A good talking to don't do a girl any harm—and I'll say this much for you, you don't answer back. Jimmy ain't asked you to go swimming with him, has he?"

"Oh no, Mrs. Halliday."

"And better not," said Mrs. Halliday darkly. "I'll take a couple of turns round the lawn if you'll give me your arm, Miss Vernon, my dear."

Chapter Twenty-One

CHARLES DROVE ON through the lovely weather. The clear arch of the sky was of a tender and melting blue. The hills that rose against it showed every gradation of colour from dark pine-green to the heather tints and the bright light leafy mist of the birch. There was black rock and grey rock, hillsides scarred with the red of rusty iron or dropping in ledges of purple shale. Here and there great streaks of yellow ochre dazzling to gold in the sun, and here and there a sudden gleam of white marble looking like frozen snow. The road climbed and fell across wild high moorland where the bog-cotton blew and dark water stood among tussocks of coarse faded grass.

All the time he was getting nearer to Ann.

The sun went down before he reached Loch Dhu. He was between the hills when he lost it. The valley filled with the dusk, whilst the hill-tops still kept the sun. Then there was twilight everywhere.

A motor-cyclist passed him about half an hour later, coming up with extraordinarily little noise, slowing as he passed and then shooting away. The road became rougher and rougher. The last ten miles was merely a track, with at least two bends that were dangerous in daylight and an adventure in the dark.

About half a mile from the loch the hill had been quarried. There was a flattish space by the side of the road. Charles drove his car on to it and stopped the engine. It would be better to wait till to-morrow before trying to see Ann, but quite definitely and certainly Charles knew that he was not going to wait—not till to-morrow anyhow. There would be a moon in an hour or two. He would wait till then and no longer. How, in the middle of the night, he was going to get hold of Ann he really did not stop to think. Fortune had been kind to him before, and might be kind again. Once on the island, it would go hard if he could not contrive a way to Ann.

He switched on a small electric lamp and proceeded to a picnic meal. When it was done and everything neatly put away, he hefted the collapsible boat, which weighed exactly fifty-six pounds, and went down to the shore of the loch to wait for the moon.

The motor-cyclist had been there before him, but he was not there now. In response to his hail a boat had put off and fetched him over to the island. Jimmy Halliday rowed the boat, and he seemed to expect his visitor.

The motor-cycle was pushed under the lee of the ruined house and covered with a tarpaulin. Charles found it there and stood a moment staring at it by the light of a carefully shielded torch. He had been wandering aimlessly round the ruined house wondering who had lived there and why it had been allowed to tumble down, when he came on the motor-cycle.

Presently he went on round the house and found something else. On the side farthest from the track the roof had been roughly repaired, and what might have been the kitchen looked now uncommonly like a garage. Rough wooden doors had been fitted, and a padlock fastened them. Charles made a complete circuit of the house and then sat down on a bit of broken wall. The moon ought not to be long now.

Ann met Mary in the dark of the upper landing with a candle. She looked more wraith-like than ever. She came close and pressed Ann's arm.

"Ma man's hame."

"Your husband?"

"Ay."

Ann was faintly startled. They were so cut off, it seemed strange that anyone should come to them from the outside world.

"Are you glad, Mary?"

There was no gladness in Mary's tone, nor in the way she threw out her hands at the question.

"Glad?" Then, coming very close, she said with her lips at Ann's ear, "Mind yersel, lassie," and slipped away.

No one else mentioned Mary's husband.

Ann went to bed and slept. She left the blind up so that if she woke she would see the moon go up the sky. There were stars when she leaned from the window after blowing out her candle. They were not very bright, because the sky was still so full of light. It would not be really dark all night in those reaches of the upper air. The hills were dark, and the trees were dark, but the sky would not be dark all night.

Ann left the blind up, and fell asleep with her face to the window.

She didn't know how long she had been asleep, when she began to dream that it was raining—heavy, plopping rain that hit the ground like hail. It wasn't rain at all; it was hail—gold and silver hail, coming down out of a clear sky and bouncing all round her. She woke up and found herself in the moonlight with the sound of the hail in her ears, and as she sat up and shook back her hair, it came again—the plop of something falling just inside the window.

She threw off the clothes and stared at the window. The thought of hail was still in her mind, but the sky was clear in the moonlight.

Plop. Something fell again, as a pebble falls.

Ann slipped out of bed and felt on the floor. She found a small dark pebble and, picking it up, she went to the window and looked out. The moon was just above the trees. The moonlight shone on her. It made her feel pale and unsubstantial, and as if it would be quite easy to float away out of the window and disappear into a dream. Anything in the world might happen on such a night as this. She leaned out over the sill, and Charles Anstruther said,

"Ann—"

For a moment she really did wonder if she was dreaming. And then she remembered that in a dream she would not have wondered, because nothing is too strange to happen in a dream. She looked down and saw Charles on the near edge of the lawn looking up.

"Ssh! Ann—"

"Charles—ssh!"

"Come out!" said Charles in a penetrating whisper.

Ann's heart began to beat wildly. Anyone might hear, anyone might come—and Charles was right in the eye of the moon. She made a vehement sign in the direction of the trees, nodded her head, and put a warning finger to her lips.

As Charles ran across the lawn, she turned back into the room and groped for her clothes. Suppose someone waked. Suppose someone heard her. Well, suppose they did—they couldn't *do* anything, could they? There wasn't anything criminal about landing on an island at night, even if it was a private island. She remembered with comfort that trespassers couldn't be prosecuted unless they damaged something. Mrs. Halliday's sense of propriety was the only thing that was in danger of being damaged.

Ann went down the stairs, carrying her shoes as she had done before, but this time she got out of the parlour window. She ran across the lawn with a breathless sense of adventure. The shadow was very black under the trees. She blinked at it, and had begun to say, "Where are you?" when Charles' arms came round her and she was lifted up and kissed.

"Oh, Charles!"

"Ann, darling!"

"Oh, Charles—you mustn't!"

"Why mustn't I? Ann—kiss me! You're letting me do it all."

"I'm not letting you!"

"Liar!"

"You're just doing it."

"Do it too! *Ann!*"

Ann kissed him, and then she pushed him away.

"Come farther under the trees—come where we were before. This isn't safe. If anyone came down to the boat-house—"

"They'd find my boat," said Charles coolly.

"Oh, they mustn't!"

"I don't suppose they will—I don't care a damn if they do. Look here, darling—"

"Ssh! Come down here."

She guided him as she had done before. The path was too narrow for them to go abreast, but when they came to the clearing which showed the moonlit sky above, Ann stopped.

"How did you come? Did you say you had a boat? How did you get it here? Did you come all round by sea? They all say it's fearfully dangerous."

"It's a collapsible boat," said Charles with pride. "I went to Glasgow and got it."

"Glasgow?"

Charles kissed her.

"I'm the world's non-stop speed merchant. I've got simply loads to tell you. Do you know that you're an heiress, and that I'm going to marry you for your money?"

"Am I—are you?"

"I am—you are. And if I was the sort of noble-minded hero you read about in books, I should say, 'Woman, unhand me! I am but a poor broken-down land-owner with a blighted ancestral property which will probably land us all in the workhouse some day. Who am I to ask a rich heiress to join her fate to mine? Tempt me not, but let me go my way—*alone!*'"

"Charles, if you make me laugh, someone will hear us."

"You—not us," said Charles. "You've got one of those ringing laughs—pleasing to the ear but noticeable. *I* am not laughing—I'm telling you the sort of bilge I'd talk if I had a heroic nature. I haven't. I'm going to marry you even if you turn out to have a million. Only don't get all buoyed up, darling, because shipping isn't what it was. Anyhow, whatever it is, you're bound to marry me, because I've compromised you like anything, luring you out to a secret assignation by throwing gravel in at your window. I say, darling, I thought you were never going to wake up. You must have a frightfully good conscience to sleep like that."

"I've got a lovely conscience—pure as the driven snow. Charles, how did you know it was my window you were throwing gravel through? Just suppose it had been Mrs. Halliday you had lured to a secret assignation. You'd have been strewed all over the lawn in bits by now. It was marvellous of you to guess right the very first time. How did you do it?"

"There was only one open window. Oh, my sainted aunt—only one in the whole blessed house, on a night like this! I plumped for you as the fresh air fiend." His arms tightened round her. "Ann—what are we going to do? How soon will you marry me?"

"I haven't said I'll marry you," said Ann with a quiver in her voice that was only half a laugh.

Charles shook her.

"I do wish you wouldn't keep on saying the same thing over and over again! It's just like a gramophone record. You ought to be encouraging me like anything. You told me to look out for an heiress—you know you did."

Ann put a hand across his lips.

"Don't, Charles!... No, let me speak—*please*. Do you mean I'm really going to have some money? I heard them say something about it here."

"Who?" said Charles sharply; and then, "What did they say?"

Ann pinched his arm rather hard.

"It was little bits and no names—something about a will, and a girl, and a lot of money, and its being a pity that Gale Anderson couldn't marry her, and perhaps she'd have a boating accident, and things like that."

"What?"

"I don't like it," said Ann. "I—I hate it—it's rather frightening. And now you come and say I'm an heiress. Was it a joke? Because I don't feel like joking."

"No—it wasn't a joke," said Charles in rather an odd tone of voice. He was remembering that Hilda Paulett had said that she wouldn't go into mourning if Ann had an accident.

"Ann," he said—"one minute. Who said all those things about the boating accident, and the money, and the will?"

"It was Gale Anderson and Jimmy Halliday."

"They didn't know that you could hear what they were saying?"

"No. Please tell me what you know about it."

"You remember you told me you had an uncle called Elias Paulett, and I said I knew a girl called Hilda Paulett. Do you remember?"

"Yes."

"Well, I ran into her in a tea-shop in Glasgow yesterday afternoon. I had tea at her table, and she started talking. She's the most awful babbler, and before I knew where I was she was telling me she was secretly married to her uncle's secretary. She called the fellow Gale."

"Gale Anderson," said Ann quickly.

"It might be. Is he here?"

"Yes."

"Staying in the house?"

"Yes."

"I see.... Well, Hilda went rambling on about not knowing what to do, and Gale being fed to the teeth because they'd found out that Uncle Elias had left all his money to another great-niece, and I was most awfully bored, and wondering how I could stem the tide and get away, when all of a sudden out came your name. My jaw dropped about a foot and a half, and if Hilda ever thought about anything except herself she'd have noticed it. As it was, she just went on babbling. I gathered that she'd had a peep at the old man's will—saw he'd left everything to his great-niece and hadn't time to turn the page. If she had, she'd have found out that the name on the other side was Ann Vernon and not Hilda Paulett. She went off as bright as a button and told this Gale fellow she'd seen the will, and that she was sole heiress. I gather that Gale said, 'Righto—how soon can we get married?' After which the gump Hilda fell into his arms, and everything in the garden was lovely until they found out that she wasn't the right great-niece, and that you were. Gale cut up rough, and Hilda doesn't quite know whether he's going to kill her off and marry you, or do you in so that she will have the money."

"Charles, I don't *like* it," said Ann. Her voice sounded as if she was cold and she shivered a little.

"Nor do I," said Charles. "Ann darling, don't shake like that—you're all right. I say, you did hear them talking about a boating accident— you're sure of that?"

"I think so. It was all bits and scraps. Oh, I don't know—I thought he said—"

"Gale Anderson?"

"Gale Anderson. I thought it was his voice. I couldn't see either of them. I heard the voices coming up through a sort of cleft in the rock. I think they must have been in a cave underneath—" She broke off suddenly. "You see, Charles, it's all 'I *think*,' and 'I *thought*.' I can't be certain about anything."

"What did you think you heard?"

"I thought I heard Gale Anderson say, 'You ought to encourage her to learn to swim,' and something about 'Now it will have to be a boating accident.'"

A sharp involuntary exclamation came from Charles.

"You're sure?"

"No—that's just it. It goes round and round in my head and I can't be sure about anything. Only I think that's what he said, and I made up my mind that nothing on earth would make me go in a boat with him."

"Has he asked you to?" said Charles quickly.

"They both have," said Ann. She gave a little shivery laugh. "Jimmy Halliday's begun to make love to me. He's frightfully funny over it."

Charles said something about Mr. Halliday.

Ann laughed again.

"You needn't. He's like a great lump of a schoolboy and desperately proper and respectful. And Mrs. Halliday told me how she'd saved him from all the girls who had wanted to marry him. It was very, very funny indeed."

Charles was silent. Ann *thought* she had heard Gale Anderson say that it would have to be a boating accident ... Hilda Paulett said she was frightened because Gale talked in his sleep about a boating accident ... And Hilda was such a babbling fool that nothing she said ought to have the slightest weight with any reasoning human being ... And Ann wasn't sure of what she had heard.... He said abruptly,

"You've got to get out of this. I'd like you to come away with me now."

"Now?"

"Now."

"Oh, I couldn't!"

"Why couldn't you?"

Ann caught about her for reasons. She must find some, and they must be good, strong, sensible ones that Charles would listen to, because the real reason was one that she couldn't possibly tell him. If she ran away with Charles like this in the middle of the night, she would simply have to marry him whether she had any money or not—Charles would see to that. Even now-a-days it would make it difficult to get another job if she eloped with Charles and didn't marry him. And she wanted to be quite sure about the money before she allowed Charles to marry her. She caught at Mrs. Halliday and played her with an air of virtue.

"Oh, Charles—how could I? The poor old lady would have a fit. I couldn't go off like that in the middle of the night. She'd say I was a hussy, and a great deal worse than that. No, honestly, I couldn't do it.

And there isn't the slightest need—nothing's going to happen to me tonight. My room is next to Mrs. Halliday's, and Riddle's just across the passage. It's as safe as a Young Women's Christian."

"I won't have you staying here!" said Charles in a furious tone.

"Darling Charles, I don't want to stay here. Do be soothed. I've got a much better plan. Eloping's too Gretna Greenish—and just think of your relations and the breath of scandal. No—you shall come along in the morning bright and early after breakfast, and we'll both say we're awfully sorry and we hope we're not putting them out, but I've got urgent private affairs that make it absolutely necessary for me to leave at once. After all, they can't stop me—can they?"

Charles stood there frowning in the dark. The shadow of the trees was over them both, a warm pine-scented shadow with the moonlight bright beyond it. What Ann said was entirely reasonable. He had been driving all day over bad roads, and except as a necessity he wouldn't choose to drive back over those same roads all night. Both for Ann's sake and for his own he didn't want to run away with her in the middle of the night. He wanted to marry her with as little delay as possible, and he wanted his relations to accept her and be pleasant about it. The most influential of his aunts was also one of the most strait-laced women in England. His eldest sister was married to a bishop. It would certainly not help Ann's future relations with them if Charles and she eloped. In about seven or eight hours he could present himself openly and remove Ann with the most perfect decorum. Neither aunt nor bishop's wife could censure a day's run in a car. It was all superlatively reasonable and sensible—*but* he wanted to pick Ann up and carry her off, turn the car towards civilization, and step on the gas.

"Ann—come now!"

"No," said Ann.

"*Ann!*"

"No, no, no, no, no!"

"Ann—*darling!*"

Ann snuggled up to him.

"I won't. And you're wasting time. It's such a lovely, perfect, heavenly dream of a night. Wouldn't you like to make love to me?"

Charles made love to her.

Chapter Twenty-Two

AT THE MOMENT when Charles Anstruther stepped out of his boat and pulled it up on to the sandy beach of the island, the man who had passed him a few hours before on a motor-cycle was lying out on the heather of the headland which overlooked the strait. It was the same headland from which Ann had watched the night before and had seen something move in the water and leave a foaming wake behind it.

As soon as Charles had landed, the man got up and made his way noiselessly to where the path went up to the house. He moved at the loping trot of the Highlander—a small, spare, wiry man with a forward thrust of the head and shoulders. Charles had already passed when he came to the path. He followed him, and stood in the bushes at the edge of the lawn until Ann and Charles went down the path and turned off it amongst the trees. Then he went round by the back of the house and in by the kitchen. He knocked on the dining-room door and went in without waiting for an answer.

Gale Anderson was playing patience. Jimmy Halliday did not appear to be doing anything at all. His pipe had gone out and his glass was empty. He may have been asleep. He looked up as the man came in, and said,

"What do you want, Hector?"

Gale Anderson looked over his shoulder. He had the knave of clubs in his hand. When Hector said, "He's come," he turned back to his game and laid the knave on the queen of diamonds.

"Who's come?" said Jimmy Halliday. He blinked, stretched, and ran his hands through his hair.

"Him," said Hector.

In the light he showed a swarthy skin and the high cheek-bones which give a look of savagery to the face. His black eyes were restless and wary as an animal's. His right hand fidgeted at his hip as if it expected to find the hilt of a knife there.

Jimmy stretched again.

"He's landed?"

Hector nodded.

"How did he come?"

"He had a boat."

Jimmy whistled. Gale Anderson turned up the seven of spades.

"A boat, has he? One of those canvas affairs it'll be. That's what he went away for. What's he doing now?"

"Talking with the girl among the trees."

Jimmy swore.

"How did she know he was coming? I'd like to know that."

"He was throwing stones up at her window."

"And they're in among the trees?"

Hector nodded.

Gale Anderson turned up the queen of hearts.

"Then you'd better get back and watch them. He's not to get away till you've heard my whistle. I don't know how you'll stop him, but you're as full of tricks as a monkey—you must think of something."

Hector snapped his fingers.

"I will not have to think of anything. The girl will keep him. It is you that will have to wait." He smiled a little.

Jimmy scowled at him.

"Get along and watch them! And speak properly about that young lady, because I'm going to marry her! Get along with you and keep an eye on them! A nice time of night to come sneaking round a man's house and getting a young lady out of bed—by gum it is! Get along with you!" He put a hand upon Gale's shoulder and shook the cards from his hand. "Are you coming or are you staying? You can please yourself, but if you want to come you've got to look lively, because I'm not waiting for you. Do you hear?"

"Oh, I'm coming," said Gale Anderson. He pushed the cards together and got up without haste.

"Then look sharp and stir those lazy stumps of yours, for I'm not waiting for you nor for nobody—by gum I'm not!" said Jimmy Halliday. He struck the table a blow which made the glasses jump and went off down the passage to the old part of the house, swearing in a vehement undertone at all skulking blackguards in general and at Charles Anstruther in particular.

Gale Anderson followed him.

About half an hour later under the trees in the pine-scented dusk Charles Anstruther said,

"I must go."

Ann said "Yes," but she did not lift her head from his shoulder. Perhaps it would never be there again. The world can change in a night. This was their enchanted hour. Perhaps when they had come back to civilisation, and ordered ways, and what the world would think—perhaps then she would find that she mustn't marry Charles however much she loved him or however hard he pleaded with her. Those early days of being on sufferance in someone else's house had left their ineffaceable mark.

Charles tightened his hold.

"I must go."

Ann said "Yes" again. The enchanted hour was over. The dawn waited cold and grey on the other side of it. A little shiver went over her.

"How I hate this money business!" she said with something piteous in her voice. "I don't want that wicked old man's money. He let my mother kill herself with work. She might have been alive now if he had helped her. I hate his money, and I hate the feeling that we are waiting for him to die. It's horrible!"

"But, Ann—"

"It's horrible!"

"But, Ann, my blessed darling child, we're no doing anything of the sort. I don't care whether you've got twopence-halfpenny or a million."

Ann pulled back as far as she could and stood there straining against his arm.

"Don't you care if you have to sell Bewley?"

His clasp did not exactly relax, but something happened to it. Ann did not have to strain against it any more.

He spoke soberly.

"I shall keep Bewley if I can."

"And if you can't—if you have to sell, and if I let you marry me with twopence-halfpenny only I haven't even got that, you *will* have to sell. Are you going to say you don't care?"

"No, I won't say that," said Charles.

"He mustn't marry me—he *mustn't*! I mustn't let him!" Ann said this desperately to herself.

Charles gave her a sudden shake.

"What's the matter? Are you planning to be noble and give me up? Look here, let's have this out once and for all. I can't keep Bewley unless I can keep it up. I'd rather sell the place than see it go to pieces. If this money comes to you, we'll be able to keep it up. If it doesn't, we'll have enough to live on, and I'm going to have an experimental fruit farm. What I am not going to do is go round cadging for an heiress. Now say, 'Charles, I love you enormously, and I'll marry you as soon as we can get a licence'—or whatever it is you do get in Scotland—we shall have to find out. Say it—say it quickly! Because I ought to be going."

"I can't," said Ann in a mournful whisper.

Charles picked her up, kissed her, and set her down again.

"It doesn't really matter whether you say it or not—you're going to do it all right. Now I'm going, and I want to see you back into the house first."

"I thought I'd come down to the beach to see you over the strait."

"Nothing doing. I want to see you safe indoors before I go. There aren't going to be any accidents in this scene. You go in, and I'll wait on the edge of the lawn till I see you wave out of the window. And in about seven or eight hours I'll be back here to take you away, so you'd better pack before you go to sleep."

As they stood on the edge of the lawn, there came upon the air the strange booming sound which Ann had heard before. It shook the silence and was gone again. Ann caught at Charles' arm.

"Listen!"

"What is it?"

"I don't know. I heard it last night, and afterwards—there was something—swimming in the loch."

"How do you mean, something swimming in the loch?"

"I don't know. I didn't see it—not really—only a sort of foamy track. And Mary said, 'It comes—swimming—in the water.' She said I must keep away from the water. And oh, Charles darling, I hate your going over in that little boat!"

By the time that Charles had convinced her that she might have seen a seal, and that seals were of all creatures in the world the most peaceable and harmless, Hector had become impatient. He, no less than Charles, had had a long day's run, and, unlike Charles, he had nothing to compensate him for the loss of his night's rest.

At last he saw Ann cross the lawn. She got in by the parlour window, and presently she leaned from her own window and waved. Charles at once turned on his heel and went down to the beach. Instead of following him, Hector ran out along the face of the slope and so back to his old look-out place upon the headland.

Charles pushed off his boat and rowed out upon the strait. The moon was high overhead and the air a little thickened by a light haze which veiled the hills and gave to the water a blurred and softened look The far reaches of the loch were of a ghostly whiteness, and as his oars rose and fell, they dipped into a hands-breadth of mist and came up through it again.

He was only a third of the way across the strait, when he heard the booming sound again. It reminded him of something. A bittern? He wondered if there were bittern as far north as this. And then there was a swirl in the water ahead of him, and out of the mist there rose up a long black serpentine head and neck. The water dripped from it. The moon shone on it. It reared up and came at him in a roar of sound, the water boiling before it and rushing past in foam. Charles pulled violently upon his left-hand oar, but failed to get the boat clear. He had no time to do more than throw all his strength into that one desperate stroke, for in the same moment he was caught by the full force of the onset and plunged into the water. His head was struck, and he went down and for an instant lost himself. Time and his sense of direction were gone. When they returned, he felt that he was drowning and struck out for the surface.

He came up by the boat, which had capsized. One of the oars floated near, the other at some distance. He caught a glimpse of it as the haze closed down. There was nothing else to be seen. He discovered a hole in the boat, so wasted no time in trying to right it. He got it to the farther shore without incident and then went back for the oars.

It must be confessed that he disliked doing this as much as he had ever disliked doing anything in all his life. Things out of nature shake the nature in us. That snaky head and neck coming up dripping out of unknown depths and rushing upon him with horrid force had certainly shaken Charles. But if he didn't get the oars, he wouldn't be able to go back for Ann to-morrow. He thanked heaven that he had not persuaded her to come away with him to-night.

When he had retrieved the oars, he hefted them and the boat and made his way back to the car. He was, of course, wet through. He was also shaken and puzzled. And he was afraid, because Ann was still on the island.

Chapter Twenty-Three

THE MORNING CAME UP in a mist that shrouded everything. Ann waked to find it curtaining her window, and was considerably dashed in spirits. If the fog was very thick, would Charles be able to find the landing-place? This was really a very frightening thought, because the little sandy bay was the only place on this side of the island where it was at all possible to land. There was one narrow inlet on the other side, but everywhere else the coast was defended by humped and pointed rocks which might be terribly dangerous in a fog.

She went and stood by the window and leaned out. The mist was white, dazzling, and impenetrable. She could not see the trees on the farther side of the lawn. It was just as if they did not exist. Yet she and Charles had stood under them last night, and Charles had held her close and kissed her. A most desolate, cold feeling swept over Ann. The fog seemed to have blotted everything out.

She shook herself impatiently. "Don't be such a gump! At your age! Doing lost dog just because there's a mist, which probably means that it's going to be an absolutely topping day!"

She went down to breakfast and sat there straining for the sound of Charles' step. The fog was certainly lifting. The faint wraith-like spectres of the trees could be discerned across the lawn.

"Nothing I 'ates like a fog," said Mrs. Halliday. "Let me see what's happening, I say, and bad or good you know where you are. But a fog gives me the creeps. You don't know where you are, nor you don't know what's alongside of you, and if it's something that shouldn't be, you'll likely find it out too late. There was my own grandmother's nephew by 'er first husband, Abram Sidebotham by name, come home in a fog on the Tarriton turnpike with a girl as he was friendly with and wishing that he was something more. They wasn't engaged nor they wasn't walking out, but he'd tried to snatch a kiss and got 'is face smacked for him, and he was wishful for 'er better acquaintance. Annie was the girl's name, and some said she was 'andsome, but I couldn't see it myself—bit of a chit of a little thing and as quick as an adder, with a great fuzz-bush of hair a-hanging down her back. Well, Abram and she they walked a piece together, and it was frosty and a thick fog, and I won't say as he hadn't had 'is glass, nor I won't say as he hadn't had a glass too much. Anyhow it seems he tried to kiss 'er, and Annie she dodged away from him, so there they was, 'er a-dodging 'im, and 'im grabbing at 'er all over the highway, and the fog that thick you couldn't see your 'and before your face. Albert Larkin he come up with them in 'is gig driving very slow and careful acause of not being able to see, and he hears Annie give a screech, and he hears Abram yell out, 'I've got yer!' And the language he used after that was what Albert couldn't bring 'isself to repeat, being Methody-reared. And all of a sudden the fog shifted the way it do, and by the light of Albert's gig-lamps there was Abram with his arm round the neck of Eli Todd's old donkey, cuddling its mane and saying, 'I got yer, and I'm going to keep yer!' And a couple of yards away there was that piece Annie with 'er great bush of 'air that Abram thought he'd got hold of 'er by laughing and making game of him. Albert didn't hold 'is tongue neither, and pore Abram got so laughed at that he went and turned teetotal. Annie she took up with Albert Larkin, that was born to be poll-pecked if ever a young man was, and rule him she did good and proper, and all 'er eleven children likewise. So I don't 'old with fogs."

"It's lifting," said Jimmy Halliday. He had his own reasons for wanting it to lift and to stay lifted. He had a cargo to run and he wanted fair weather for the trip. A light mist was one thing—he wouldn't object to a mist, in fact it would make things all the safer—but a fog like this would be the devil.

It was lifting all right. The trees were not spectres any longer but trees seen through a haze. A little faint sunlight began to filter through.

Ann sat down to read a five-days-old paper to Mrs. Halliday, and found it very difficult to keep her mind on what she was reading. The old lady's remarks about car-bandits, vigorous though they were, hardly reached her—"A paperful of pepper right in the eyes—that's what they want. An uncle of mine he always made his girls carry pepper travelling lonely roads."

The front door shut, and Ann jumped in her chair. She saw Jimmy Halliday go round the house and went back to her paper with a sigh. Mrs. Halliday shot her an angry, suspicious glance.

"Who was that went by?"

"Mr. Halliday," said Ann.

"Then I'll thank you to keep your eyes for what you're supposed to be reading and not go looking out of the window after my son!"

The bright furious colour rushed into Ann's face. She bit her lip hard enough to draw blood and read in a muffled voice: "An unknown man who jumped from the running-board of the car and made off down Green Street is requested to communicate with the police."

"And a lot of good it is asking him to do that!" said Mrs. Halliday. "And let me tell you, Miss Vernon, that if I hadn't thought as how you were a young lady that knew how to behave 'erself, I wouldn't have 'ad you in my house."

Ann put down the paper.

"I'm leaving here to-day, Mrs. Halliday," she said.

"And may I ask *how*?" said Mrs. Halliday with a tremendous aspirate.

Ann hesitated. Suppose Charles didn't come. Suppose he had lost his way in the fog. Suppose a hundred different things…. She did not dare to burn her boats. The angry tears were stinging her eyes. They made an iridescent halo about Mrs. Halliday's morning cap.

"Miss Vernon!"

Ann ran out of the room and banged the door.

The morning went on, slowly, draggingly, and in a rising mist of fear. The fog outside lifted, but the fear gathered thicker and thicker about Ann. Charles did not come, and every hour dragged by more slowly than the last.

She went up into her own room and sat there thinking of reasons which might have prevented Charles from coming. He might have overslept. He might have found a puncture. For the matter of that, he might have had almost any kind of mechanical breakdown. By twelve o'clock none of the reasons seemed to have any life in them. They faded out and left Ann alone in the fog.

She could not have said just at what point "Charles hasn't come" became "Charles isn't coming," but by lunch-time she had given him up. Something had happened, and he wasn't coming. A verse from an old German folk-song came ringing in her head:

"Mein lieb is auf die wanderschaft hin.
Ich weiss nicht warum Ich so traurig bin.
Vielleicht ist er falsch, vielleicht ist er tot.
Darum wein' ich die lieblichen äuglein rot."

It went on ringing there, sometimes in German and sometimes in English.

"My love he is wandering far and near,
I know not why, but my heart it is drear.
Perhaps he is false, perhaps he is dead,
And so I weep and my eyes are red."

It was a song of the most uncomfortable melancholy. Another of the verses said:

"Oh thistles and thorns they prick full sore,
But a false, false tongue hurts a heart far more.
No fire on earth so burns and glows
As a secret love that no man knows."

In the last verse of all the poor forsaken damsel begs the wandering lover to return and shed one tear upon her grave.

"Dieweil ich dich so treulich geliebet hab."

The sweet, melancholy cadence fell on Ann's heart, and for a moment there was a faint reaction. Charles loved her, and he hadn't gone away and left her. He wouldn't—he never would. She was just letting herself be mesmerized by a sad old song.

"Oh love of my heart, one thing I crave,
That you will stand by my lonely grave,
That you will drop one tear for me,
Because I so truly have lovéd thee."

Ann reacted a little more vigorously. "Sloppy, sentimental idiot—you're just wallowing! You're being a coward and a fool, when you know perfectly well that Charles cares a lot more for you than you deserve! You know perfectly well he does!" The part of her that Ann was scolding struck back, and suddenly. "That's just it—he *wouldn't* go. Where is he? What's happened to him? Something's happened to him."

She was so pale at lunch that Gale Anderson frowned above the cold suspicious glance he gave her. Jimmy Halliday pressed food upon her until she could have screamed. And Mrs. Halliday retailed a selection of anecdotes on the text of *Wilful waste makes woeful want.* "And leaving of food on plates is what I don't hold with and won't 'ave in my house. There was my cousin Sarah Rankin as reared 'er children on the outside crust of the loaf all hot from the baker, they having a fancy that way—and what they done with the crumb 'eaven knows, but I reckon it went to the pigs. And what come of it?" She fixed Ann's pallor with an accusing glare. "There was the eldest, Samson—he drunk 'is wife and children out of house and home. And Delilah that there was such a fuss over the christening of, parson holding it wasn't no Christian name and Sarah saying as it was in the Book and that was good enough for 'er and threatening to go over to the Methodies—Delilah, she had six children by 'er first 'usband, and married a widower with ten for 'er second, and lived like pigs, the lot of them, so as the whole village cried shame. And the third, Annie Amelia, she come on the parish, and none of the rest of them was any credit to the family. And what can you expect, with them brought up to waste good food?"

It was a most trying meal.

As soon as it was possible, Ann escaped from the house and went up on to the heather knoll at the top of the island. She could see the hills, and the loch, and the strait, and the bend of the road coming down to the waterside. If Charles came, she would see him come. She had still a little faint hope that he would come. Just when it seemed most dead it would spring up again. For he must come—he *must.* He couldn't leave her here—he wouldn't—not *Charles.* There was an answer to this stammering hope—a final, dreadful answer. Ann tried to prevent herself from hearing it, but it was getting harder and harder. Soon it would be impossible, and then she would have to hear it, and it would say:

"Charles won't come, because he can't."

"He can't come, because something has happened."

"He can't come, because he's hurt."

"He can't come, because he's dead."

Ann sat on a stone at the top of the knoll and stared at the strait. The mist had thinned and lifted, but the sky was not clear. There was a milky veil across the blue. The sun came through it, faintly warm and faintly golden. There were shreds and wreaths of mist in the clefts and hollows of the hills, and all their colours were faint, like colours remembered from a long time ago. The surface of the loch was dim, like bright glass that has been breathed upon. The outlet to the sea was lost in a thick haze. The air and the water were alike still and without movement.

Ann sat with her hands in her lap and looked at the road by which Charles must come.

She did not know how long she had sat there, when she heard a sound that was very far away. It jarred the edge of the silence. When it came again, it was louder. Ann strained towards it, listening. All at once her heart began to beat with a loud and joyful relief, because the sound was the throb of a motor. And it was coming nearer. Charles was coming. What a perfect, absolute fool she was to have been afraid! She wouldn't dare tell Charles what a fool she had been. Yes, she would—she *would*. It would be lovely to tell him, and to hear him say, "Oh, Ann—you blessed little idiot!" Great stupid tears brimmed up in her eyes and ran over. She dashed them away and jumped up, leaning forward so as to see the car the minute it came round the bend. Perhaps he would stop behind the hill and walk down to the waterside. Perhaps—

The sound was louder. Ann's hand came up to her breast and pressed down hard upon it.

Round the bend there came a motor-cycle.

The shock and the disappointment were so great that she felt quite numb. She watched the motorcyclist come down to the edge of the water, lean his machine against an angle of the ruined house, and cover it carefully with a tarpaulin. She saw him remove his cap and goggles. She recognized the little dark man who was Mary's husband. They called him Hector. He stood above the water and hailed the island, and presently Jimmy Halliday put over in a boat and fetched him off.

Behind the numbness, Ann's mind struggled with all this. Hector had been here the night before. Mary had told her that he had come, and she had passed him in the hall when she went down to supper—a dark man, small and strong, with eyes that looked aside as she passed. Mary was afraid of him. He was here last night, but he had come back from over the hills just now. He had come back ...

When had he gone?

Why had he gone?

The two questions went on saying themselves in Ann's mind. As the numbness grew less, they became more insistent. She felt suddenly as if she could not bear them any more, or to be still, or to watch the strait for Charles.

She turned, and, looking down, she saw something move on the slope below. The undergrowth stirred, and between the branches of the trees she could see that someone was passing along the face of the hill. She could not see who it was, and a desire to avoid either Gale Anderson or Jimmy Halliday made her crouch down so as to be as much out of sight as possible. Whoever it was moved fast.

Ann watched and listened with a queer feeling of expectation. She could see a long distance from where she was. The person moving in the undergrowth was going away from her towards the sea. Presently there was a bare space where the bushes ceased and stones and heather clumps took their place, with a few pine-trees thinning away to a bare slope. She watched this space and saw come out upon it the last person she had expected to see—not Gale Anderson, or Jimmy Halliday, or Hector; not a man at all, but Mary, with a grey homespun shawl about her and something hugged up under it. The shawl came over her head and crossed her breast. She held it close about her and went hurrying on among the trees.

Ann jumped up, scrambled down the slope, and followed her. It was a relief to move after that long waiting. She wanted to ask Mary where Hector had been. She lost sight of her as soon as she came among the undergrowth herself. There was a track here, too rude and undefined to be called a path, but quite easy to follow. She hurried along it until she came out upon the bare space under the trees. She could not see Mary.

She went on down over the slope towards the sea. On this side the island was bare and rugged. It ended in a tumbled wall of rock which went down steeply into the water. When Ann came to this place she stood still and looked about her. She couldn't see Mary, but she could hear a voice speaking, and that not so far away. It seemed to come from the cliff. Climbing and scrambling, she got to the edge and looked over. The loch stretched away before her into the haze. The voice came from so close that it startled her.

She looked down and to her left, and saw Mary standing against the face of the cliff. There was a ledge of rock under her feet and a tall boulder upon either side of her, so that she stood like a saint in a niche. A cleft in the rocky wall behind her showed how she had reached this position. Upon the ledge beside her there was a basket full of fish. The shawl had dropped back from her head, leaving her grey hair ruffled. Her eyes were fixed and blind-looking. She was speaking in a strange high voice that reminded Ann of a sea-bird's cry. She said,

"Hungry are ye, and roarin' after yer prey? What ails ye, deil? Is there no meat eneuch for ye in the Almighty's sea that ye maun seek it here? And if ye're the muckle deil that gaes seekin' his ain, then tak yer ain and let the lave o' us gae free!" She stopped, groaned, put her hands before her eyes, and said in a more human tone, "Gude save us—we're in the tents o' wickedness!"

Ann felt a cold trickle down her back. The mist was thickening. There was still a faint shine on the water, but the sun looked like a pale moon above the shoulder of a high shrouded hill. She felt as if she were looking over the edge of the world.

Mary flung out her hands with a sudden loud cry.

"Haud off, deil, and tak yer ain—or tak what I gie ye!"

She plunged her hands into the basket and flung a large fish out over the water. It described a gleaming arc and fell with a splash. Her voice dropped again to that lower tone.

"If I bow down in the house o' Rimmon, Gude forgie it me!" She stooped and flung another fish. "Hey, deil! And may it choke ye! Tak yer ain and gae yer ways to him that sent ye—*and ye ken wha that is*—Gude keep us!" She flung the last and largest fish, and as the drops sprang up where it met the sea, she began to recite in an even, monotonous way and with much less than her usual accent:

'Thou wilt be the friend o' God,
And God will be thy friend.
Iron will be yer twa soles.
And twelve hands shall clasp yer heid.
Thy affliction be in tree or holly
Or rock at sea or earth on land,
A protecting shield be aboot thee,
To protect thee from elfin bolts,
And from the enclosures o' pain,
From the troubles o' this world
And o' the ither world."

She said "Amen" and drew a long sobbing breath. Then she wrapped herself in her shawl and went back through the cleft between the boulders.

Ann ran after her. Not for all the world would she be left behind in the mist. She ran, and called Mary and caught her by the shawled arm.

"Oh, Mary—wait for me!"

There was a startled jerk, and then Mary turned. She pushed back her hair under the shawl and shivered.

"Ay. Is't you, lassie?"

"Yes. Mary—what were you doing? What was that thing you were saying? I couldn't help hearing it—about being the friend of God." She felt the need to speak, and this was the nearest she dared come to the strange things that she had heard.

Mary pulled her shawl about her with a jerk that twitched her arm away from Ann.

"Yon? Yon's a Hieland charm Hector's mither taught me. She was aye kind tae me—but Hector's an ill man."

"He's come back," said Ann. "Mary, when did he go? He was here last night. *Why* did he go?"

"Back is he?" said Mary. "Ay—trouble's nae far when Hector's near. I tell't ye he was an ill man."

"When did he go?" said Ann.

"In the nicht."

"And why did he go?"

"Ask them that sent him," said Mary. She had begun to hurry. Ann had hard work to keep up with her.

"Mary—wait! I want to talk to you. I've no one to talk to, and I'm afraid—"

Mary looked back at her over her shoulder, her features white and sharp, with the grey line of the shawl cutting straight across her cheek.

"Ay—ye dae weel tae be feared, lassie." And then, "Ye mauna keep me, or it'll be the waur for the baith o' us."

Chapter Twenty-Four

BEFORE THEY WERE half-way back to the house Ann had fallen far behind. It was not only that Mary moved with an extraordinary quickness, but the impulse which had made Ann hurry soon failed her. She didn't want to ask Mary any more questions about the queer things that she had said. The questions frightened her, and she had a dreadful feeling that the answers might frighten her a great deal more. Her feet lagged, and she saw Mary disappear amongst the green bushes and the over-arching trees.

Why should she hurry to go back into the house which held an old woman who had turned bitter to her, and three men of whom she was afraid? She began to think whether she really was afraid of Jimmy Halliday.... Not yet—and not in the same way that she was afraid of Gale Anderson and of Hector. It was strange that of the three she feared Hector the most—a man whom she had hardly seen and who had not spoken a single word to her. There was something about him that gave her a cold, sick feeling of dread.

She found herself wandering off the track and not sure where she was going. She kept pushing her way through the undergrowth and expecting to find the track again. Instead, she came out suddenly upon a bare, narrow place above the sea. The bushes had been so thick that she had had no idea of where she was. There was only just room to stand safely between them and the edge where the rock fell away to the water. There was something like a path going on in the direction where she guessed the house must be. It wound along the cliff with trees and bushes on the one side and scattered boulders on the other.

Sometimes it dipped very sharply and then climbed again. She came in a few minutes to a dip which took her almost to the level of the loch. The climb on the other side was a very steep one. There were signs here of a made path which ran in zig-zag up the cliff.

Ann was nearly at the top, when she heard a sound—a heavy scraping sound. It seemed to come from overhead. She looked up and saw immediately above her one of the grey boulders—tilting. She saw it move, and heard it grate as it moved. And then she knew that it would fall, and that she was right in its track. It moved, hung on the verge above her, and came crashing down. As it fell, Ann jumped, and went slipping and clutching over the edge of the path and down the cliff. Her hands caught at a bush which tore them. She could not hold it, but that desperate clutch had checked her fall. She fetched up in a kind of cleft, her skirt caught on a point of rock and her feet with a bare standing space and no more. The world span dizzily. The crash of the boulder which had just missed her reverberated in her ears. Some fifteen feet below, the waters of the loch were waiting, smooth, and grey, and deep.

The world stopped spinning. The noise in her ears grew less. Then it ceased. She looked down in a dazed sort of way and saw the loch—and her hands which were bleeding. There seemed to be some connection in her mind between her hands and the water. She looked at the blood with a frown. Water—and her hands were bleeding.... That was it—she wanted to wash off the blood. She made a movement, but it was checked. Something was holding her.

All at once her head cleared and she realized why it was that she had not been able to move. Her skirt was caught on a rough point of rock, and as long as it held she could not move and she would not fall. If it gave way, there was nothing to stop her from pitching down into the water. If it hadn't been foggy to-day, she would have been dead by now, because if it had been fine like yesterday, she would have had on her blue cotton frock, and it would have torn like paper. It couldn't have held her weight for a moment. It wouldn't even have broken her fall. This old tweed skirt was strong. It would hold her here till somebody came.

She called out as loudly as she could, looked up, and saw Gale Anderson looking down at her. He was a little to the left on one of the zigzags of the path from which she had fallen. He looked down at her with a blank expression on his face, and as she called again, he moved up the path and out of sight.

Ann's heart began to beat, and all at once she was horribly, sickeningly afraid. The words she had heard him use came into her mind—*"It will have to be a boating accident."*

"No, it won't—not now. A fall from the cliff will do just as well. He's going to make me fall. He's going to kill me. He pushed that stone over."

"Oh *no!*" said Ann in a vehement fervour protest. "He can't—he couldn't! I'm not going to *die!*"

She didn't know whether she said the words out loud or not, she didn't know that she gave one high agonized scream, because the shock of what happened next blotted out the memory of what had gone before.

It was a repetition of the grinding which made her scream. The next moment, with a horrible rending sound, a second mass of rock crashed past her into the loch. The spray flew up and wetted her. It stung her eyes and was salt upon her lips. It stung her bleeding hands. The booming echo ran along the cliff.

It died away. She was still there. The noise and the violence had passed her by. The rock had missed her by no more than a foot. She looked up shaking, and saw why it had missed her. Just above her a great rounded boulder jutted out. A rock pushed from above would be deflected and fall a little to one side or the other.

This had hardly passed through her mind before another stone fell, a smaller piece this time; but because it was smaller it came nearer, actually passing within a few inches of her shoulder.

Ann screamed again, this time with a conscious purpose. She did not know how far she was from the house, but someone might hear her, or Gale Anderson might be afraid that someone would hear her. She screamed as loudly as she could and went on screaming. No more rock fell, and a little hope was springing up, when, to her despair, she saw Gale Anderson climbing towards her along the cliff. He had left the path and was edging his way across a steep rocky place which afforded only the slightest of hand and foothold. In the midst of her terror Ann felt a last stab of fear, because he still looked so entirely calm and ordinary. He was risking his life to take hers, and he looked like a bored young man at a picnic. Ann's scream had all the terror in the world behind it.

Gale Anderson went on edging his way along the rock, feeling carefully for the least crevice or projection that would help him.

And then suddenly from the sea Ann's last long scream was answered by a hail. A boat came into view round the point. Jimmy Halliday bent vigorously to his oars and hailed again.

"Where are you? Miss Vernon!"

And with that he saw her and began to pull in under the cliff.

Gale Anderson looked down for a brief instant. In another minute he would be clear of this difficult place. He could reach her before Jimmy did. And then, as he came within view of the drop between Ann and the loch, he smiled a little. Nobody could climb fifteen feet of sheer, smooth water-worn rock. Jimmy certainly couldn't. At the moment that he reached this gratifying conclusion Jimmy Halliday was staring up at Ann.

"However did you get there?"

"Mr. Halliday, he's coming! He's trying to kill me!" Ann's voice was choked with terror. She looked sideways and saw Gale Anderson smile. Not a bored young man any longer, but a pleased young man with something he desired just within his grasp. Her voice rose to a shriek. "Save me! He's coming! *Mr. Halliday!*"

It was at this moment that Jimmy saw Gale Anderson. He roared out,

"Let her be, Gale! Give over!"

And then, as he realized that he was wasting his breath, he shouted to Ann.

"Jump! The water's deep—it won't hurt you."

"My skirt's caught!" Ann's voice shook in an extremity of terror. She had never thought to admire Jimmy Halliday, but her heart gave a jump of hope and gratitude as he dived into a capacious pocket, produced a clasp knife and a ball of twine, fastened the end of the twine to the knife, and with a brief "Catch!" tossed it up to her. She missed it, and it went down into the water with a splash.

Gale Anderson was clear of his bad place and was swinging himself round a jutting boulder. She looked down and saw the knife in Jimmy's hand. He said "Catch!" again and threw it up, and this time she caught not the knife, but the string.

Gale Anderson was round the boulder and out of sight, but she could hear him. She could hear him coming, his boots grinding and slipping on the rock. And she couldn't open the knife. Her wet, bleeding fingers fumbled with it. She felt the blade move. She dragged at it with breaking nails and got it open. She had to reach up and slash at her skirt, and as she did so, Gale Anderson came into view again, not two yards away on her left with a great stone poised in his hand. Something like a mist came between them. She felt her skirt give way and the knife drop from her nerveless hand. She heard Jimmy bellow, "Jump!" and felt herself falling blindly down, and down, and down.

Chapter Twenty-Five

WHEN CHARLES ANSTRUTHER had got out of his dripping clothes and into some dry ones he went over his boat with an electric torch and found that the canvas was split and the wooden framework damaged. He gave a whistle of dismay. The damage could be put right, but not here. A patch on the canvas and a splint to strengthen the frame, and he could get over the strait and back again with Ann. But to put on the patch he would want some canvas and a sail-maker's needle. He whistled again. There was no possibility of keeping his appointment. He would have to run out to Ardgair, get the boat mended, and come back again.

He stood there with the bright ray of the torch making a dazzle of light on the stones at his feet and considered. A couple of hours to Ardgair, an hour there, and two more to come back. And it would be no good starting until five or so. He supposed that Ardgair would be awake at seven. Well, even allowing a couple of hours in Ardgair, he ought to be back here by eleven. That wasn't so bad. He wished he could have let Ann know, but since he couldn't, it was no good bothering about it, and he had better get some sleep whilst he could.

He did not, however, immediately get on with the business of going to sleep. Up to now he had not let himself think of anything except the practical needs of the moment, and of the immediate future. You can stop yourself thinking when you are doing things all the time, or when you are actively considering what must next be done, but when all this is over, thoughts which have been forbidden come out and have their say. Charles switched off his torch and frowned at his own shadow on the moonlit road. The fold of the hill hid the loch, but it lay there under the moon only just out of sight. If he were to walk a few hundred yards down the track, he could stand there and look at it.

He didn't think he would. He felt as if he had had enough of the loch. He had a horribly clear picture in his mind of the Thing that had risen out of it and run him down. He had had only an instant's sight of it, but he had seen it quite clearly—a serpentine head and neck coming up dripping out of the hands-breadth of mist which covered the water. He thought there was not much more than four or five feet of the neck, perhaps not so much. The head was horrible—shapeless, and uncouth—a snake's head monstrously enlarged.

His frown deepened. He couldn't reconcile that head and neck with the force that had knocked him spinning. He supposed a great snake would strike a tremendous blow, but it would surely strike with its head—and he felt certain that it was not the head that had struck him.

Or was he certain? Was he certain about any of it?

All at once he wasn't certain. The thing was a sheer impossibility. He was dog-tired and he didn't want to think about it, but his brain went on thinking.

Impossibilities don't happen. Suppose he had run on a rock, bust his boat, concussed himself, and imagined that serpentine head and neck. Sea-serpents don't exist. Officers of British warships who report having seen a sea-serpent are laughed out of court. Fellows of the Royal Society who describe a sea-serpent are told in scientific language that they are lying. Who was Charles Anstruther that he should think he had seen what he *had* seen?

"*Eppur si muove*," as the late Galileo remarked.

If he couldn't explain what he had seen, he was hanged if he'd explain it away.

He got into the car, and within five minutes was soundly and dreamlessly asleep.

It was some little time after this that the man called Hector came round the turn of the road behind the car. How he had reached this point was his own affair. It must certainly have involved some climbing. He came silently up to the Morris and stood in a crouched attitude, listening. After a while he straightened up and looked over the back of the hood at Charles, who lay peacefully asleep in the moonlight with his head on a cushion and his feet on an assortment of suit-cases.

Hector's features twisted in an expression of savage contempt. With a shrug of the shoulders he went past the car to where the canvas boat was lying. He squatted down beside it and examined the damage which it had sustained. It ought to have been smashed, and he ought to have been drowned—a thousand devils fly away with him! It would be easy to make the damage worse. He slipped his hand into his pocket and got out a large, serviceable knife. With the blade bare in the moonlight and his left hand grasping the edge of the boat, he hesitated. His brows drew together in a frowning line. Then all at once he pursed up his lips, nodded as if in satisfaction, and with a muttered word or two of Gaelic put the knife away, got up, and made off down the track. As soon as he was round the bend he left the road, climbed a little way up the side of the hill, and sat down to wait.

Charles woke with the first of the light. It came late because of the fog. He frowned with annoyance, because it would take him a good bit more than two hours to get to Ardgair if it was going to be as thick as this all the way. He boiled a kettle and a couple of eggs, made tea, and consumed a quantity of well-buttered scones. Then he loaded the boat into the car—an untidy job, as it refused to fold up—and took the road for Ardgair.

Hector got up and stretched himself. Unlike Charles, he was quite pleased with the fog. He went briskly down to the loch, collected his motor-bicycle, and followed the car.

At some fifteen miles from Loch Dhu the rough track emerged upon something which more nearly resembled a road. Twenty miles farther on this road divided, the right-hand branch bearing back to the coast and so to Ardgair. As Charles approached the fork, going slow because he was on the look-out for it and afraid that he might take the wrong turn in the fog, he heard the chug-chug of a motor-cycle coming up behind him. To his surprise, it came to within a certain distance and then no nearer. The fellow must be playing the same game as himself, going slow and looking for the fork. He concluded that he was right when, as soon as he had passed the turn, the motor-cycle shot ahead and went away out of sight.

Hector, who had only been making sure that the car was really going to Ardgair, now desired to arrive there before it. He had people to see and arrangements to make. It suited him very well indeed that Charles should go to Ardgair, since he had very good friends there and could rely on their help. When, therefore, Charles in due course arrived and made inquiries as to the repair of his boat, he found himself directed to the same black-haired and black-browed Donald McLean whom he had before approached with a view to hiring. He had not on that occasion received any encouragement, but to-day Donald was a good deal more forthcoming. He could mend the boat easily enough. It would take a little time, but—

"What do you mean by time? How much time? I'm in a hurry."

Well then, it appeared that Donald couldn't just say. He would have to get a piece of canvas. His sister's husband had some that might do, but he was out with the boat.

"In this fog?"

The fog was lifting—it was going to be a grand day. But besides his brother-in-law there was his brother James—he might have a piece of canvas that would do—he would very likely have a piece. If Mr. Anstruther would go up to the hotel, Donald would report to him there.

It was then about ten o'clock. The drive had been slow and wearisome in the extreme, but the exasperations of the road were as nothing to the exasperations of Ardgair. The business of getting the boat mended was dragged out until it resembled a slow-motion picture. Donald's brother James had no canvas, but suggested that his cousin Ewan might have some. Ewan in his turn suggested someone else. When, at long last, a piece of canvas had been produced, Donald McLean drew Charles' attention to the fact that the damage was much greater than he had supposed. Besides the original split there was a second long jagged tear at which Charles stared incredulously.

"I swear that wasn't there last night."

"It might have been done getting her into the car," suggested Donald.

"Well, it wasn't!" Charles' temper was getting short.

"There is no way that it could have been done here," said Donald sullenly. And then," I'll need some more canvas."

The day wore on. The mist drew up. A pale clouded sun looked down upon a pale clouded sea. Ardgair appeared to have run out of canvas altogether. Donald's manner suggested that the boat might be ready by Christmas. It was, in fact, ready by six o'clock.

Charles drove away from Ardgair hoping fervently that he would never see it or any of its inhabitants again. He had his first puncture when he had gone about five miles. There was a flat-headed nail in the tyre—he supposed a parting souvenir of that blighted place. He put on a spare wheel, and had run another two miles, when he had a second puncture. This one seemed to be due to a nasty gash in the outer cover. Broken glass would make a cut like this, *or a knife*. He thanked heaven he had a second spare wheel. When, about four miles farther on, a third tyre went flat, he had no words, but he had some very serious thoughts. This time he found that the valve was loose. If someone had unscrewed it slightly, it would have produced a slow leak like this. Looking back, Charles remembered Ardgair's reluctance to help him on his way to Loch Dhu by water. It began to look as if someone was interested in preventing his getting there by road. He screwed up the valve and pumped the tyre. It was now past seven o'clock, and the fog was coming down. He would be lucky if he reached the loch by daylight.

Hector did not pass him on the return journey. After a pleasant day amongst old cronies, he had started for home some hours before. When Ann saw him come to the shores of the loch and row across with Jimmy Halliday, he had just put the finishing touches to a most satisfactory day's work.

"Full of tricks as a monkey—aren't you?" was Jimmy's comment. And then, "Suppose someone else comes along first."

Hector snapped his fingers.

"Who else would be coming?"

"You never can tell," said Jimmy gloomily. He bent to his oars, and had a last word. "You'll be getting wind in the head if you don't look out, and then you'll be sorry, my lad. I'm captain here, and don't you forget it."

When they had landed, Hector put a hand in his pocket and produced a slightly crumpled orange envelope.

"There was this for him at Ardgair—I was to ask for it. He will be expecting it," he said.

The envelope bore the name of Gale Anderson. Jimmy breathed on the flap until the melted gum permitted him to raise it, pulled out the telegram which the envelope contained, unfolded it, and read:

Uncle sinking. Doctors say not more than twenty-four hours. Please come. Hilda.

Jimmy read this through twice. Then he folded the message, put it back in its envelope, and stuck down the flap.

"I'll give it him," he said shortly.

The fog was really bad by the time Charles came to the long steep hill that led down to the loch. It would have been a nasty hill on a made road in daylight; on the roughest of tracks, in a perfectly horrible mixture of fog and dusk, it was a nerve-racking business. Charles had done it by night before, but it had been clear, and he had not then any idea of what it was going to be like. He had therefore been spared the pleasures of anticipation. He knew now that there were two hair-pin bends, and that the second and steeper sloped to an undefended drop where the rocky hill-side went down a sheer forty feet or so.

He managed the first bend, and then racked his memory for the distance between that and the other. It was no distance from the loch; he was sure of that. The next turn had brought him to the quarry where he had parked his car. But whether the distance between the two hair-pins was two hundred yards or four, he couldn't for the life of him remember. He proceeded with caution, crawling along with his headlights dipped and hugging the inner side of the track. The fog threw the light back at him, and he had to strain to make out where he was on the road.

After what seemed like an interminable period of strain he came on the bend. As he slowed the car to take it, his near front wheel rose with a bump and stubbed itself against rock. Under the impression that he had run into the bank he pulled the steering-wheel over, bumped sharply over another of the rocks which Hector had thoughtfully disposed in a pile round the inner side of the bend, and before he realized what was happening the off front wheel was over the edge. He wrenched at the steering, but too late. He felt the car tilt to the fall, hang for a sickening second, and then plunge down. After which he felt nothing for quite a long time.

Chapter Twenty-Six

ANN CAME TO HERSELF gasping and shivering in the bottom of Jimmy Halliday's boat. Jimmy was holding her head over the side, thumping her on the back, and adjuring her to "cough it up." Her first emotion was one of unnatural anger towards her preserver. She said,

"Don't do that!" choked in the middle of saying so, and over her head heard Jimmy address an encouraging remark to her, and all in the same breath, a volley of objurgations which she found startling until she realized that they were addressed to Gale Anderson. She pushed Jimmy away and sat up.

Gale Anderson had disappeared. She hoped that if out of sight, he was not out of ear-shot. It would have been a pity if he had missed any of Jimmy's remarks. They contained so many words which Ann had never heard before that she felt sure that they must be very abusive.

Her anger against Jimmy died. She pushed back her hair and said between chattering teeth,

"Thanks most awfully for saving my life. He was trying to kill me."

Jimmy said, "Murdering scum!" and then begged her pardon with a return to his drawing-room manner. After which he took up the oars and rowed her round to the landing-beach in silence.

Mrs. Halliday had judged the day to be too foggy for her to leave the house. At all times a little suspicious of fresh air, the moment it contained even the faintest trace of mist she considered it to be definitely dangerous. She attributed her excellent health in no small measure to the fact that she had never give in to the crazy new-fangled practice of sleeping with her window open.

She was sitting at the parlour window—closed of course—when she saw Ann emerge dripping upon the lawn, closely followed by her son. She stared in unmixed surprise for a moment, and then made her way into the passage to find out what had happened.

Jimmy told her what he thought good and no more, whilst Ann dripped and said nothing.

Mrs. Halliday's reactions were of an extremely complicated nature. She gathered that Ann had fallen from the cliff and had been nobly rescued by her Jimmy. This naturally inflated her maternal pride and at the same time roused her maternal suspicions. There was the case of Fanny Lintott who sprained her ankle right in front of the shop where her cousin Jane Selby's William was apprenticed, and the even more sinister affair by which Rose Tappit induced old Mr. Moggridge to offer her marriage by pretending that he had run over her on his way back from Shepperton market—"And him so drunk he wouldn't have known if he'd run over a steer let alone a young woman." On the other hand, Ann did ought to be in bed with a warm drink inside of her and a hot brick to the feet. A confusing business being a proud mother, a jealous mother, and a decent old woman—"all under one," as she herself would have put it.

She sent Ann to bed, with Riddle to see that she was rolled in blankets and Mary to take her a hot drink, and then, bursting into tears, asked Jimmy whether he intended to break her heart, yes or no, because if he did, the sooner she was laid in her grave the better for all concerned.

It took Jimmy quite a long time to pacify her. He had to listen to the story of William Treddle—"And him not so old as you by a twelvemonth, that married a good-for-nothing 'ussy, which Lottie Dibbs was 'er name, and getting on for thirty years younger than him. And what happened?"

Jimmy patted her shoulder.

"There, old lady—don't take on."

"What *happened*?" said Mrs. Halliday on a rising note and with an aspirate that fairly blew the word out of her mouth.

"I don't know, I'm sure," said Jimmy, who knew very well.

Mrs. Halliday twitched her shoulder away.

"I'm a-telling you, aren't I? And a shame it is that I've got to, and a worse shame for William Treddle and that good-for-nothing Lottie of his—as turned his mother out of doors and let 'er go to the workhouse infirmary, and the 'ole parish talking about it!"

"Come, come, old lady!" said Jimmy.

Mrs. Halliday gave one of her most intimidating snorts.

"It's 'Come, come' now, but by-and-bye it'll be 'Go and we don't want you back again,' when you've married a slip of a bit of a thing that'll think 'erself a sight too grand for your pore old mother!"

Jimmy put in another half hour's soothing and then went away to have a heart-to-heart talk with Mr. Gale Anderson. Life wasn't any too easy at the moment.

Ann lay in bed between blankets and watched the fog thicken against the window, which Riddle had carefully shut. She was none the worse for her dip in the loch. She didn't in the least want to lie in bed and drink the queer strong-tasting stuff which Mary had brought. Goodness knew what was in it. Whisky and peppermint on a foundation of milk, with a dash of something really horrible which was like a blend of candle-grease and camphor. She was soon so hot that she felt as if she would choke. In any other circumstances she would have dressed and gone down, but bed, even with blankets and a camphor brew, was preferable to a meal at the same board as Gale Anderson. Of course he mightn't be there. Jimmy and he were bound to have a row, simply bound to. But on the other hand, in a place like this, you couldn't just push a man out and tell him to go to blazes. Or could you? Ann had a shrewd suspicion that Jimmy's affairs might be so far entangled with those of Gale Anderson as to make a complete rupture a difficult and perhaps dangerous matter.

Anyhow, if she'd got to stay in bed, it should be a decent human bed with sheets. She had had enough of these sticky, pricky blankets. She threw them off, opened the window, washed her face and hands, and remade the bed.

Presently Mary looked in.

"What'll ye tak?" she said. "The auld leddy's speirin'."

"What is there?" said Ann.

"There's guid broth, and fush."

Ann gave a little shiver. The thought of fish took her back to the scene on the cliff—Mary throwing three big silver fish out into the loch and saying, "Haud aff, deil!"

"I don't want any fish. I'd like some soup," she said. And then, "I'm quite well, you know. I could get up and come down, but—I think I won't."

Mary nodded.

"Ye're safer in yer bed," she said, and went away again.

The time dragged most dreadfully. Ann had her broth, and then Riddle came and asked her if she was all right, and when Mrs. Halliday came up to bed she paid Ann a state visit, sitting bolt upright on a hard wooden chair and narrating several cheering stories of people who had caught their deaths through a sudden immersion in cold water. This led her to one of her favourite subjects—the present generation's wanton indulgence in baths.

"Clean's one thing, and taking off all your clothes and setting in hot water constant is another and what I don't hold with, nor my mother didn't before me, and a cleaner woman never stepped. I'd like some of these young 'ussies to see how she kep' 'er brass—see your face in it you could, and 'er copper pans as bright as a new penny. And a bath on Saturday night we all 'ad, in a wooden tub in front of the kitchen fire, and the rest of the week we washed our faces and our 'ands and made do with that. My grandfather he didn't hold with 'aving baths at all. He said he hadn't never had a bath in his life and wasn't going to. He said so much washing was right down hurtful, and I'm not so sure as he wasn't right, seeing as how he lived to be getting on for a hundred and never had nothing the matter with 'im that ever I heard tell about."

She presently bade Miss Vernon a majestic goodnight and swept out of the room, returning half way through Ann's sigh of relief to stand in the doorway and lecture her upon the immodesty of scrambling up and down cliffs and falling off them under the eyes of a steady, respectable, hard-working man.

"Not," said Mrs. Halliday, "as he's one as 'ud take any notice if a score of girls was to throw themselves at his 'ead. If he was that sort, he wouldn't be single to-day, Miss Vernon, so don't you go 'aving your hopes raised nor thinking that he means anything—*which he don't*. And I'll wish you good night, and don't you go opening that window again or it's a funeral you'll be 'aving and not a husband."

"Golly!" said Ann when she had gone.

She waited five minutes, and then leapt out of bed and opened the window which Mrs. Halliday with many ejaculations of horror had closed immediately upon entering the room. She stood there in her nightdress looking out. It was not very cold, but the fog was thick and clammy. The air was dead still. There was no sound from land or sea. The thought of Charles which had lain at her heart like a cold lump of fear became suddenly a sharp stabbing pain. He was somewhere on the other side of that curtain of fog and silence. *Or was he?* She was shaken by a most dreadful terror. Suppose he wasn't anywhere any longer. Suppose he had gone out of the living world and left her ...

She caught her breath, and immediately upon that sound of her own making she heard another sound. Very, very faintly there came to her through the deadening fog the sound of oars. There is no other sound quite like it. Lip, lap, splash—lip, lap, splash, with a regular rhythm that was quite unmistakeable.

She wondered who could have gone out in the boat on a night like this. A most comforting answer presented itself. It was Gale Anderson going away after such a frightful row with Jimmy that, fog or no fog, he simply couldn't stay in the house any longer. Ann frowned in the dark. It was a beautiful explanation, but there were too many holes in it. There had been hours of daylight for Jimmy and Gale to have their row in. If Gale had been going to shake the dust of the island off his feet, he wouldn't have waited for the fog to thicken and the dark to come down. He was a knave and a would-be murderer, but he wasn't a fool.

There were other answers. The boat might be returning, not going. Gale Anderson might have been put across some time ago. Or Jimmy might have taken him out and dropped him in the loch.

No—the boat wasn't coming back, it was going away. The lip, lap, splash was growing fainter all the time.

Ann gave it up and went back to bed. After all, what did it matter who came or went, since Charles did neither? She buried her face in her pillow and wept scalding tears of anguish. Then suddenly slipped away from it all into sleep.

Chapter Twenty-Seven

ANN WOKE with the moonlight on her face. She started up and stared at the window. The fog was gone, and the moon, very clear and bright, stared back at her. There was a sound of wind in the trees. Mary had been right after all when she said that the wind was getting up and the fog would lift before morning. She had said it when she brought that horrible hot drink and stood there waiting for Ann to finish it—"The fog'll lift afore mornin'. There's wind comin'—I ken the sound o't." There had been no sound of it then for any ears except Mary's, but anyone could hear it now. The trees of the island made a queer hushing sound which came, and went, and came again a little louder.

It was in one of the pauses when the wind seemed to be holding its breath that Ann heard another sound—the tramp of feet on grass. In a moment she was out of bed crouching down beside the window. There were three men coming across the lawn. The moon shone down on them, and she could see quite clearly enough to recognize Jimmy, and Hector, and Gale Anderson. They came out of the shadow of the trees with Jimmy going ahead and the other two carrying something between them—some thing or some one.

Ann's heart began to knock against her side. She couldn't see what they were carrying, and she *must* see. Two of them, a man's length apart—carrying something. She must see what it was that they were carrying. She pressed her hands down hard upon her breast, as if the pressure would stop that heavy knocking. If it was a man they were carrying, why couldn't she see his face? There was something dark thrown over what they were carrying—a dark covering that fell down almost to the ground on either side—*like a pall.* The three words dropped heavily into her mind. A dead man's face would be covered like that. For a moment she was so cold with fear that she could not move. Then, as she made a convulsive effort to lean out of the window and look down, she heard the door below her open and saw the men and what they carried pass out of sight.

She got to her feet and crossed the room, she hardly knew how. At the top of the stairs she stood to listen, and heard the sound of feet going past and down into the kitchen. A light flickered and was gone again. She could see nothing, and now that the door into the old part of the house was shut, she could not hear anything either. She stood in darkness and silence and was wrenched by terrible thoughts. It was Charles whom they were carrying, and he was dead. Perhaps they had killed him. Or perhaps Gale Anderson had killed him and the others were helping to cover it up. If he wasn't dead, then why had they covered his face?

By this time she had no doubt at all that it was Charles whom she had seen carried up from the loch. There had been no drip of water on the ground, so he had not been drowned. But if he wasn't dead, then why had they covered his face? This thought kept coming back and back, and every time it came it hurt a little more.

She sat down on the top step of the stair and laid her head upon her knees. She was giddy with grief and pain.

She might have sat there for a long time if it had not been for her torn hands. She had them clutched together, and the pain startled her out of her giddiness. For a moment she couldn't remember why they should hurt her so, and then her head was clear again. She got to her feet and began to think what she must do. If she were sure that Charles was there in the kitchen hurt or dead, she would be brave enough to go down the stairs, and along the old dark passage, and through the door, and so come in upon them. It wouldn't matter what happened to her if Charles was dead.

Was it Charles?

Just now she had been sure, and now she wasn't sure. After the shock and certainty of grief there was a faint reaction. The voice that says, *"This is too dreadful to be true,"* spoke in her now: "It can't be Charles. He can't be dead—not just when everything was coming right." And low and very insistent the voice of her own inmost self: *"This can't happen to me."*

It was here that she remembered the old stair which ran down to the kitchen. If she went down that way, she might see without being seen. The prospect of being able to do something steadied her.

She went back to her room and put on her dressing-gown. It was of a deep shade of blue and would hide her light nightgown. She fastened it round her waist with a cord and, leaving her feet bare, began to feel her way across the landing and down the passage to the back part of the house.

The stair came up into a little room like a cupboard that was next to Mary's room. The space was so small that it seemed as if it was just a slice taken off the passage to enclose the stair head. Perhaps in the old three-bottle days the laird had taken this precaution against falling down into the kitchen after his potations.

The stair was the old stair of the house, winding with steep, uneven steps about a central pillar. Ann had never been down it until she came down bare-foot in the dark, feeling for each crumbling step and holding to the wall. She went down into silence. The walls were too thick to let in the sound of the wind.

The door at the foot of the stair was shut. There was no line of light beneath it, and no mutter of voices from the farther side. She leaned against the rough panelling and held her breath to listen, but there was no sound at all. Very slowly and with cold, stiff fingers she lifted the latch.

The door opened outwards into the kitchen. She got the latch clear and felt the door begin to move away from her of its own weight. She held it with both hands, letting it go a very little at a time, with her heart beating so hard that she was afraid someone would hear it. If there was a light in the kitchen, she ought to be able to see it now.

The door slipped from her hands and swung out with a creak.

The kitchen was dark and empty.

Ann stood on the threshold looking into the darkness and listening. There was no sound at all except the sound of the wind passing high up over the house. After a minute or two she came out from the shelter of the door. She could see a least faint glow from the embers on the hearth, and moonlight on the hill beyond the dark yard. Now that her eyes were accustomed to it, the kitchen was not quite dark after all. The moonlight showed the window and the corner of the kitchen table, and the glimmering embers gave her the position of the hearth.

She went to the back door, tried it, and found it fast, the key in the lock. With the cold iron against her palm, she thought, "Charles—what have they done to him—where is he—where are they?" The key hurt her hand and she let go of it. One thing was certain—they were not here. The kitchen held no one but herself, and the door was locked on the inside. Yet only a very few minutes ago she had stood at the top of the stairs and had seen a light flicker past and heard men's feet go down the old passage to the kitchen. It was just as if they had walked into the darkness and vanished there.

With a long-drawn breath of relief she remembered the wash-house. The door was there on her right. It was open, for she could see it as a black oblong in the shadowed wall. If they were there, they were very still. If they were there, she would have heard them. She felt suddenly very much afraid. But there was the black doorway, and she must go through it. "Not without a light! I won't—I just *won't*!" There must be matches somewhere—there are always matches in a kitchen. She went over to the hearth and felt along the narrow shelf above it. There was a box there, but it was a very light one, only three matches left in it, so that she had to decide whether she could risk one of them on the chance of finding a candle. She wouldn't dare to light the lamp, because it would betray her if anyone were to come. You can snuff out a candle in a moment, but a lamp is another matter. She thought she would look into the wash-house first. Even a match would show her whether Charles was there, and if he wasn't there, she had no need of any more light.

She crossed to the dark doorway with the stone flags cold under her feet, stepped over the threshold, and struck a match. It went up with a little flare that dazzled her and then tried to go out. She had to hold it head downwards, and twist it about until the flame got hold of the soft wood. Such a small, brief flame. She looked about her by the light of it and saw the copper, and the wash-tubs, and a soft black rush of shadows. Blackest of all, a yawning pit of shadow in the corner with something standing over it.

The flame burnt her fingers and she dropped the match. Her hand shook a little as she struck another. It fizzed like a tiny rocket. The burning head flew off and the useless stump went to join it on the floor. There was only just the one more match. She struck it carefully, shielding it with her hand till it burned with a steady yellow flame. It showed her a tall barrel pushed aside from the corner and, where it had stood, a black hole in the floor. Then with a splutter the match burned blue and went out. Ann let the box fall from her hand. The hand was trembling violently.

She had been in the wash-house before. The barrel always stood in the corner. Now it had been moved, and in the place where it had stood there was a square black hole as if one of the flagstones had been taken away—no, not taken away, tilted up. The match-light had shown it tilted back against the wall. It left that square black hole like the mouth of a pit, and the men had gone down into it with the thing which they were carrying.

It couldn't be Charles—taken down into some unimaginable black vault for burial—or to be left there hurt, alive. Ann could have cried out in the extremity of her fear, but before the sound could leave her lips it froze and died. The black hole in the corner was not black any longer. It showed against the darkness of the room as a lighted window shows against a dark house, and as she stared at it with a fixed and terrified gaze, the sound of voices came to her. She looked wildly round her. The men were coming back. She might gain the stair by which she had come, but she would not have time to reach the top, and Hector would be more likely to come up that way than not. If she went the other way, she could not be sure of any safety. The other two might make for the dining-room, the parlour, or the stairs. There was no time to get back to her bedroom.

She might have stood there numb with fright until the light of the advancing lantern discovered her if it had not been for the thought of Charles. She had to find out where Charles was. She had to know whether he was alive. And if he was alive, she had to help him. A rush of courage came to her. It swept away the numb, icy feeling, and in a moment she knew what she must do. The copper—if only it was empty she could hide there.

She pushed aside the rough wooden lid and thrust down her hand as far as it would go. The copper was dry. She scrambled up by the help of the wash-tubs and got over the edge. The voices came echoing up to her, and the light made a bright dusk in the little room. She had only just time to pull the wooden cover over her before a hand thrust the lantern up out of the hole and stood it on the floor.

Chapter Twenty-Eight

ANN SAT CROUCHED down in the bottom of the copper and heard the clatter of the lantern on the floor and the footsteps of the men coming up into the wash-house. They were coming up out of that hole in the floor. Where had they been, and what had they been doing down there? She tried to think how long they had been away. It is very difficult to measure time in the dark. She didn't really know how long she had sat at the top of the stairs, because when you think that the person whom you love most in the world is dead, time goes by and you don't notice it. After that she had gone into her room, put on her dressing-gown, and gone down the old stair to the kitchen. That would only have taken a very few minutes—perhaps two or three, because she had had to feel her way and go slowly. After that there was another break in her reckoning, because she didn't know how long she had been lost in her fear when she found the back door locked.

These thoughts went through her mind like flashes whilst the men were coming up out of the hole. She heard them swing the flagstone into its place and roll the barrel back into the corner. Then she heard Jimmy Halliday's voice, speaking so close to her that she very nearly cried out. He must be standing right over the copper for his voice to sound so loud. And as she thought that, there was a bang on the wooden lid. Jimmy had set the lantern down upon it, because she could see the light coming through a crack in the wood. It looked like a gold line drawn on the dark.

Jimmy was speaking to Hector, sending him off.

"I'll keep the light. You can find your way to your bed without it. And take off your boots, for I don't want anyone waked. Take them off here, and then get along with you!"

Ann heard Gale Anderson yawn.

"I'm off too," he said. "What are you going to do down here, Halliday—have a quiet wash?"

"I'm having a quiet talk with you—that's what I'm having, Gale. Look lively, Hector! And you can leave this door open and shut t'other one."

The latch of the staircase door clicked. Hector's bare feet made no more noise on the kitchen floor than Ann's had done.

Jimmy leaned against the copper, shifting the lid slightly, and said,

"Now, Gale—you've got to listen to me. I told Hector this afternoon that I was captain here, and I'm telling you the same thing—and there can't be two captains. Do you hear me say that?"

"I should think everyone in the house will hear you," said Gale Anderson.

His voice gave Ann the impression of a lounging, careless attitude. He was, as a matter of fact, leaning up against one of the fixed wash-tubs with his hands in his pockets. The lantern left the floor in darkness and threw black shadows up to the ceiling.

Jimmy dropped his voice.

"I'm not wanting any of your lip, my lad! I'm captain, and you'll take your orders from me same as Hector does! And if I've any more trouble with you, you'll get something you won't like!"

"Sez you," said Gale Anderson affably.

Jimmy brought his fist down with a thump on the copper lid. The lantern jumped, and the shadows made a wild leap and then fell again.

"Now you look here, Gale—I've had enough of this! If you'd killed that girl this afternoon like you tried to, where 'ud we be? I was a fool to give you the telegram to say the old man was dying, but I did think you'd got enough sense not to try on any silly game like that. Why, that telegram was sent off last night, and as like as not old Paulett was dead before you got it. Well, if he was dead, your wife was out of the running."

"You said all this this afternoon," said Gale Anderson.

Jimmy thumped again.

"And I'll go on saying it till I've got it into your head! If the old man was dead, it wasn't a mite of use your killing that girl."

Gale Anderson laughed.

"It was a sporting chance."

Jimmy's tone became a shade more conciliatory.

"Now look here, Gale, talk sense! A hundred thousand pounds or so ain't a thing you can afford to take chances over. And once and for all, there's better ways of using a pretty girl than knocking her on the head. I've said that before, and I mean it. I'm going to marry her, and you'll get your share if you behave. And if you don't, you won't get a penny, so put that in your pipe and smoke it!"

"Well, you're wrong about the period of residence," said Gale Anderson, "I told you so all along."

"I've got a Scotch domicile, haven't I?"

Gale Anderson laughed.

"Are you setting up to be a Scot? Why, man, you haven't a drop in your veins that isn't dirty English!"

Ann hardly recognized Jimmy's voice in the growl that said,

"Take that back!"

"Clean English then!" said Gale Anderson with a mocking inflection. "I don't think you'll get much out of your domicile—and I'm sure it's three months before you can get married, under Scots law."

"And I say it's three weeks! And I say I don't care which it is! She's going to stand up and take me for her husband in front of you, and the old lady, and Miss Riddle, and Hector, and Mary—and she's going to live here with me as my wife, and if it takes three months we'll live here three months. Do you think she'd go back on it after that, a young lady like her, even if she could—and I tell you she couldn't. It'll be a good enough marriage by Scotch law before I'm through with it—I can promise you that. Besides"—Jimmy's voice changed and took on a tone of self-satisfaction—"long before three months are up she won't want to get out of it. There's something about me that takes the women's fancy—you ask the old lady if there isn't. You wouldn't believe how I've been run after. And only for her keeping them off I wouldn't be free to marry Miss Vernon now."

Ann's flesh crept with horror. His fatuous voice—the picture she had of his sandy hair, light lashes, and coarse stubby hands—coarse, strong hands.... She realised with a shudder how strong they were.... The prim London room in which he had sat and made stilted conversation seemed a thousand years away—a thousand years, and a hundred thousand miles.

Gale Anderson said coolly over her head, "And suppose she won't. Suppose your fatal beauty leaves her cold."

"What's that?" said Jimmy. "I'll thank you to mind your manners and talk respectful about a young lady that's going to be my wife!"

"I said suppose she won't," said Gale Anderson.

His voice had come much nearer. He and Jimmy were, in fact, facing each other across the copper lid.

Jimmy picked up the lantern and swung it out of the way.

"That's where the young man comes in," he said in a tone of satisfaction.

Ann's heart gave a sudden leap. A terrible feeling of faintness had been creeping over her. And she mustn't faint. She must hear what they were saying. She mustn't miss a single word. She heard Jimmy say, "That's where the young man comes in," and then the darkness round her filled with fiery sparks. Jimmy's voice seemed to come from a long way off. It said, "She'll do it fast enough to get him off." And with that the sparks went out and she lost consciousness.

Chapter Twenty-Nine

ANN CAME TO HERSELF with a long sigh. It was quite dark, and she was very stiff and cramped. She moved, felt the cold side of the copper against her cheek, and remembered where she was. She had fainted, and just before she fainted Jimmy Halliday and Gale Anderson had been arguing over her head and the lantern-light had showed through a crack in the boards that covered her. Now everything was dark and silent. She wondered how long she had been here alone, and whether it would be safe for her to push the cover aside and climb out.

She knelt up and listened. She was very stiff indeed, so she thought that she must have been there some time. Her mind felt stiff too, and her thoughts wouldn't move. Jimmy and Gale Anderson had been talking when she fainted, but she couldn't remember what they were saying or why it should have made her faint. Then, in a flash, there it all was, quite sharp and clear—Jimmy talking about marrying her, and Gale Anderson saying, "Suppose she won't." And then Jimmy had said, "That's where the young man comes in," and, "She'll do it fast enough to get him off." She had heard the words in a sort of fog of faintness; now they stood out clear. And they meant that Charles was alive—they couldn't mean anything else. They meant that Charles was alive, because you couldn't use a dead man to bargain with. If Jimmy said she would marry him to get Charles out of wherever they had put him, it meant that Charles was alive, and likely to stay alive.

Ann's heart filled with such a glow of blessed happiness that for a minute or two she forgot all about everything else. After being cold and hungry and afraid, she was all warm and comforted and lifted up. For the moment nothing else mattered. But the moment passed. Charles was alive, but she didn't know where he was, and she couldn't get to him. Or could she? That was what she had got to find out without an instant's delay.

She got to her feet, pushed the lid of the copper to one side, and climbed out. When she had pulled the lid back again she tried to get her bearings. As she stood facing the copper like this, the wash-tubs were on her right, the door of the kitchen behind her, and the corner with the barrel on her left. If she could move the barrel and raise the flagstone which it hid, she might be able to find Charles. No, *must* was right word, not might. She *must* find Charles, because they must get away out of this place before something dreadful happened.

She felt her way to the barrel and tried to move it. It was Mary's water-barrel, which Hector kept filled for her. She wouldn't be able to move it if it was full or even half full. She strained at it with all her might, and found she might just as well have tried to shift the copper.

Ann leaned against the barrel in despair. If she were twice as strong, she couldn't move it. Then what was she to do? Somewhere down under her feet was the way to Charles. And he might be hurt. They would never have got him there like that if he hadn't been hurt. She found herself trembling at the thought of Charles shut up in some horrible dark place—hurt. Then with a violent effort she steadied herself and tried to think clearly. The water in the barrel was used for drinking and cooking. When Hector was away Jimmy filled it. They pumped the water in the yard and carried it in buckets. There was a spigot a little more than half-way down, and when Mary wanted water she set a jug or a bucket under the spigot and turned the tap.

That was it. That was what she must do. She must run the water off until the barrel was light enough to move. She began to feel for the spigot. Her hands went up and down over the staves—up and down, and then sideways, and then up and down again. And there wasn't any spigot.

Ann put up a hand and pushed back her hair. It was *nonsense*— there *must* be a spigot—she had seen it. She had seen Mary stand the water-jug under it and turn the tap. She could hear her own voice saying, "What do you do when the water gets below the tap? Doesn't it get stale?" And Mary's answering, "We just tilt the barrel, and it does fine to wash the floor."

So there was a spigot.... She felt for it again and found nothing but the smooth staves hooped with iron. There wasn't any spigot.

Then it came to her. The men had pushed the barrel back in a hurry and in the half light of the lantern. In pushing it they had turned the spigot to the wall.

Ann beat with her bare foot on the stone. She wondered whether she could bale the barrel out. It would take a long time. And suddenly she became aware that it was not quite dark any more. A square of grey sky showed through the window of the wash-house, and when she looked over her shoulder she could see through the open door into the kitchen. It was not morning yet, but the night was thinning away. And Hector would be up with the dawn. She must have been unconscious a long time, or unconsciousness must have passed into cramped, uneasy sleep. She remembered that she really did not know at what hour she had waked, to see the men come up from the loch.

It was getting a little lighter every moment. She couldn't do anything more to-night. It wouldn't help Charles if she were caught down here. The fact that she knew about the hole in the floor was her one advantage. If anyone found out that she knew, it would cease to be an advantage, because they would see to it that she didn't use her knowledge.

She came into the kitchen on cold, unsteady feet. If she went up the old stairs, she would have to pass the room where Hector was. She turned the other way and groped along the passage. It was still dark here, and dark on the stairs and the upper landing, but her own window showed a brightening sky above the black mass of the hills.

She crept into bed and covered herself to the chin. For the moment all the strength and courage had gone out of her. She had come to the end of both thinking and doing If it were to save her life, or Charles' life, she could neither think nor do any more. She fell asleep.

Chapter Thirty

ANN WOKE WITH A START to find a watery sun looking in on her. She sat up—remembering.

Yesterday seemed like a hundred years ago. Looking back at it was like looking through a black tunnel. It came to her in pictures. Jimmy crossing the lawn with a lantern in his hand. The lantern swinging. The other two men behind him carrying something long and dark—which was Charles. That was the first picture.

And then the empty dusk of the kitchen.

And then the gaping hole in the wash-house floor.

There wasn't a hole there now. The flagstone lay over it, and the barrel stood upon the stone. And somewhere underneath the stone there was Charles.

Ann jumped up and dressed herself. Her hands moved quickly, and her thoughts more quickly still. They raced through her mind like leaves in the wind, moving all the time, here and gone again. She must get Charles out. She could get him out by marrying Jimmy Halliday.

There was no fog this morning, and no wind. The sky was heavy with cloud, but every now and then the sun looked through. It was not at all cold, so why should she be shivering? There would be some other way of saving Charles—she needn't shiver at the thought of marrying Jimmy Halliday. It was silly to shiver about something that couldn't possibly happen.

She went down to breakfast without having been able to think of any plan for helping Charles. Even if she had a plan, she could do nothing by daylight.... Unless Mary helped her.

She found Gale Anderson and Jimmy Halliday in the dining-room. There were grilled herrings on the table, and a pile of fresh-baked oatcakes. Jimmy bade her good morning in the politest voice and, rising from his chair, indicated Gale Anderson with a wave of the hand.

"Good morning, Miss Vernon. Mr. Anderson has something to say to you."

Mr. Anderson, who had been looking out of the window, advanced with a look of concern upon his face.

"Miss Vernon, I owe you a most sincere apology. I do hope that you are none the worse for your fall."

Ann's eyebrows went up. She really couldn't help it. She said, "Thank you, Mr. Anderson," and waited for more.

It came.

"Halliday tells me that I startled you. I need hardly say how sorry I am, but you know, you startled me quite horribly. When that stone fell and you slipped, I thought you were gone. When I found you were on the ledge, I did my best to reach you."

Ann looked at him for a moment.

"I'm quite sure you did."

Their eyes met, hers steady and indignant, his cool and smiling.

"That's very nice of you, Miss Vernon. You can imagine my horror when I saw you fall into the sea."

"I don't like imagining things," said Ann gravely. She took a chair and sat down by the table. "I should like half a herring, please, Mr. Halliday."

Mrs. Halliday did not come down. Breakfast was not a very comfortable meal. Ann said, "Yes" or "No" when asked a direct question. Jimmy Halliday devoted himself to the consumption of herrings and oatcake.

As soon as breakfast was over he addressed Ann.

"Might I have a word with you, Miss Vernon, in the parlour?"

Ann's heart jumped. What was he going to say? Whatever it was, it was better for her to hear it. She followed him to the parlour, refused a chair, and stood by the window fingering the cord of the blind. It was some slight solace to see that Jimmy was not finding it easy to begin. He took a box of matches out of his pocket, rattled it, and put it back again. After which he wandered round the room clearing his throat and fingering any book or knick-knack within reach.

Ann watched him with a growing feeling of encouragement. If she embarrassed him like this, she could surely manage him. He picked up a photograph album, said "Miss Vernon—" and let it slip with a crash that shook the table.

"Yes, Mr. Halliday?"

"Miss Vernon—"

"Yes?"

Jimmy took out a handkerchief and mopped his brow.

"It's a right down sultry morning—isn't it?"

"I thought it was rather chilly."

Jimmy bent all his attention upon fastening the photograph album. It had a pointed gilt hasp upon one side and a round gilt stud upon the other. When the hasp had clicked home, he looked up with a reddened face, cleared his throat noisily, and again said,

"Miss Vernon—"

This time Ann decided to help him out. If there was anything she could do for Charles, she wanted to get on with it. She said in a small quiet voice,

"What do you want to say to me, Mr. Halliday?"

Jimmy mopped his brow again.

"That's where we come down to brass tacks. There's things I'm wishful to say to you, and things it'll be to your advantage to hear, but it isn't just as easy as you'd think to get them out, if you see what I mean."

Ann twisted the cord of the blind rather tight about one of her fingers. She was paler than she knew, but her eyes looked steadily at Jimmy as she said,

"What do you want to say?"

Jimmy undid the gilt hasp again with a sharp jerk.

"You remember what I said to you yesterday about its being time an unprotected young lady like you was settled in life?"

"Did you say that?"

Jimmy banged the lid of the album.

"By gum I did! And a sensible young lady would have been thinking it over. A man that's come to my time of life don't say that kind of thing to a young lady unless he's got intentions, and a young lady that's had those expressions used towards her ought to have been thinking them over careful."

Ann looked down at the little acorn which finished the cord of the blind. It lay in her palm and moved when she moved her hand. She felt a most desperate desire to laugh, or to cry. It would be quite easy to do both.

Jimmy Halliday cleared his throat. He was feeling better pleased with himself. He had got started. That was the main thing— to get started. He approved Ann's downcast eyes as an evidence of maidenly modesty. Her pallor pleased him too. He continued in a more assured voice.

"I'm not the man to say more than I mean. Rather less than more has been my motto, and not to go raising hopes. I won't say I haven't had my laugh and my joke here and there, and nothing serious meant, but I wouldn't have used the expressions I did to a young lady that I've a respect for if I hadn't meant what I said and a bit over."

Ann would by this time have been considerably bewildered if she had not last night heard Jimmy Halliday announce his intention of marrying her. These preliminaries, therefore, did not obscure the issue. It remained bitterly clear in her mind, whilst above it there came and went like the wash of waves those impulses of laughter and tears. The tears were for Charles, the laughter for Jimmy Halliday's stumbling courtship, and the bitter fear for herself, because in the last resort she might have to buy Charles' freedom.

Jimmy was saying, "There's a time when a man feels he ought to settle down, and that's a thing he don't feel drawn to do by himself."

"I'm sure Mrs. Halliday wouldn't dream of leaving you," said Ann innocently.

It pleased her to see how red Jimmy got. His ears positively glowed.

"Well," he said, "that's not just what I meant—not but what the old lady won't be always kindly welcome. But I was thinking more about marrying, if you take my meaning."

To Ann's rage, she blushed. Jimmy, much heartened by her colour, went on.

"Everybody'll tell you I've been a good son, and a good son makes a good husband. So, as I'm saying, I'm wanting to settle down. I've been in a way of trade that's a bit risky, and I'm wishful to cut loose from it and settle down quiet and happy." He paused, as if for a reply. When none came, he cleared his throat and said, "How does that strike you?"

Ann felt the approach of panic. She said hastily,

"Mr. Halliday, I think you're making a mistake."

Jimmy shook his head.

"I wouldn't have spoken if I hadn't felt clear about it. There's no mistake about it. I've never got as far as asking a young lady to marry me before, but that's what I'm doing now, and there's no mistake about it. I'm asking you to marry me, Miss Vernon, and you needn't be afraid I won't make a good husband."

Ann went back a step until she touched the window. Now they were coming to it. There had to be a struggle between them, and she didn't know how it was going to end. She drew a long breath and said,

"Mr. Halliday—why do you want to marry me?"

Something in her tone gave Jimmy pause. He looked at her, and looked away.

"You're a young lady that I've got a great respect for."

Ann nodded.

"I hope so. But that doesn't explain why you want to marry me. As a matter of fact, you don't really want to marry me at all."

Jimmy Halliday's expression changed.

"Oh, I don't, don't I? Then why do you suppose I'm asking you? I don't do that sort of thing for fun—by gum, I don't! There's been girls and plenty that'd have been only too pleased to hear me say what I've been saying to you—and they'd have given me a pleasant answer too. A young lady that is a young lady don't tell a man he's made a mistake when he asks her to marry him—she gives him a proper civil answer, that's what she does."

Ann caught her hands together and stood up straight.

"Then thank you very much, Mr. Halliday—and the answer is no."

Jimmy gazed admiringly at the brightness of her eyes and the burning colour in her cheeks. She reminded him of a squirrel he had tamed, and how it had bitten his finger before he had trained it to eat out of his hand. He had no fear but that he could tame Ann too. If, like the squirrel, she bit him first, it would all add zest to the game. He had got over his bashfulness and was beginning to enjoy himself. He came a step nearer.

"Come, come now—you don't expect me to take an answer like that, do you? Why, if it wasn't for nothing else, didn't I save your life no further back than yesterday? And look here, my dear, haven't you still got a life to be saved? And wouldn't you rather be my wife than what Gale would make of you if he had his way?"

Ann could not go any farther back. She could feel the cold glass of the window against her shoulder-blades. She said,

"Are you threatening me, Mr. Halliday?"

Jimmy came closer. He dropped his voice.

"I'm not—but Gale is. You needn't let him know I told you. I could see you didn't swallow what he said just now, but don't you be afraid, my dear—you'll be all right with me to look after you."

Ann made a desperate throw.

"He wants to kill me—and I know why. Do you understand? I know why. I know about my uncle's money, and I know why Mr. Anderson wants to kill me, and why you want to marry me. No, listen to this! I *know*. And I want to tell you something. I suppose Mr. Anderson can kill me, but if my uncle is dead, it won't do him any good—will it? I suppose he can kill me—but you can't make me marry you, so it's no good trying."

Jimmy smiled pleasantly.

"Well now—just to think of that!" He slid an arm round her. "Come, come, my dear, give us a kiss, and we'll see about it."

Ann put both hands against his chest and pushed. It was like pushing against stone. She said in a hard whisper,

"Your mother's upstairs. I'm going to scream."

"Are you now? What for?"

"Let go of me at once, or I *will* scream!"

He patted her shoulder and withdrew a pace.

"Now, now—easy does it! You're being foolish. Say you scream and the old lady comes down—do you think she'll be pleased when she finds out I've been asking you to marry me? I tell you she'll be fit to scratch your eyes out. And when she hears you've said no—do you think that's going to please her? Not much!" He slapped his leg. "No, by gum! She'll be fit to tear your hair out for not appreciating me!"

"It's quite useless, Mr. Halliday. Please let me go."

He withdrew a little.

"You can go if you like—I'm not stopping you. I thought maybe you'd like news of your friend."

Ann stiffened herself. He had come to the point at last. All that had gone before was only a preparation for this.

She said, "What do you mean?" and was thankful that she had not to meet his answer unprepared. If she had not waked in the night and looked out of the window—

Jimmy's voice cut across her thought.

"Well now, I'm afraid I've got to give you a bit of a shock—about that friend of yours that I was mentioning just now."

Ann turned and faced him. Now that it had come, she felt strong. It was the waiting that had made her feel as if her knees might give way under her at any moment—the waiting, and his horrible love-making. In a battle of wits she felt more sure of herself. And yet she mustn't make the mistake of under-rating Jimmy Halliday. He looked stupid, but he wasn't so stupid as he looked.

She said, "A friend of mine?" in as incredulous a voice as she could manage.

Jimmy stood about a yard away from her with his hands in his pockets.

"Isn't Mr. Anstruther a friend of yours?"

"Charles? Yes."

There was something comforting about being able to say his name. It seemed to bring him nearer and set up a defence between her and Jimmy Halliday.

"Oh yes, by gum! Well, my dear, your friend Mr. Anstruther—he's had a nasty accident, and we've had to bring him here to get over it."

"Charles—here! Is he hurt?" She did not have to act the anxiety which shook her voice.

"Hurt? Well, nothing to speak of. You know those bends in the road up there?" He jerked an elbow towards the hills. "No—you'd hardly have noticed them coming down in the dark. Well, it seems he didn't notice them either, or not enough, for he'd gone clear over the cliff at the second one, and we found him pinned down under his car not able to move."

Ann's blood ran cold. She saw the foggy night, the sharp bend, and Charles going over the edge, with the heavy car falling on him, pinning him down. Perhaps he was dead. She said with dry lips,

"Mr. Halliday—is he hurt—*please?*"

She had taken an involuntary step forward. Jimmy patted her familiarly on the shoulder.

"Now, now—there's no need for you to take on. The car had turned clear over on him, and if he'd had an arm or a leg in the way, they wouldn't have be much use to him again, to say nothing of his head. But as it turned out, there he was, sweet and sound like the kernel in a nut, except maybe for a bit of bruise or two."

Jimmy pulled himself up and stepped back. He oughtn't to have said that last bit—no, by gum, he oughtn't! He'd let himself get carried away. He made haste to get back to his book.

"Of course he was knocked right out when we found him. Why, out there in the fog and all we didn't know but what he was dead, so we took him up and brought him along to a sort of store-house I've got for business purposes, and—well, you see, that's just where it gets a bit awkward."

Ann's eyes opened to their widest.

"Why?"

Jimmy scratched his head and looked sheepish.

"Well, the fact is—well, see here, I told you my business was a bit risky. That's why I want to get out of it and settle down. Well, the fact is"—he came closer and dropped his voice to a confidential tone—"well, the fact is, Mr. Anstruther not being dead after all, he's in a position to make things a bit awkward."

"He *wouldn't*," said Ann. "Oh, Mr. Halliday, he *wouldn't*—not if you let us go."

Jimmy's light eyebrows drew together. From under them he looked at her with shrewd suspicion.

"Here, here, here!" he said.

"We'll both promise not to tell," said Ann—"we will really."

Jimmy dropped a heavy hand on her shoulder.

"Here, what's all this?" he said roughly. "What is this you could tell? Seems to me you've been listening at doors or something! D'you know what happens to folks that pry into what don't concern them?"

"Mr. Halliday—"

His hand closed on her in a hard grip.

"What d'you know?"

"Mr. Halliday—

He shook her a little.

"Don't you go on saying that! You answer me when I speak to you, and listen when I want you to listen! And now I want you to listen. Your friend Charles has got to know more than is good for him, and my friend Gale he wants to out him. I'm not mincing any words with you, because you're going to be my wife, and I believe in plain speaking between man and wife. Gale wants to put this Charles of yours out of the way, and up to the present I'm standing between them. I don't want Anstruther killed if he can be made safe without. To my thinking there's only one way he can be made safe. Once you're my wife, I'll take his word that he won't do anything to get your husband into trouble. If he's fond of you, he won't want to bring trouble on you—and once we're married, he can't bring trouble on me without bringing it on you."

Ann was suddenly, coldly afraid. Every word that Jimmy said had the ring of truth, and every word was alive. If she hadn't known the truth, she would have believed him without question. She had under-valued Jimmy's intelligence, and it was the knowledge of this that frightened her. She must be very careful. She must have time to think and plan. Jimmy mustn't know that she didn't believe him. His story about Charles was a very clever one. If she hadn't known that she was to be married for Elias Paulett's money, and that Charles was being used as a lever to make her consent, she would certainly have believed Jimmy. She must have time to think. She looked up at him and said in a low, shaken voice,

"Please let me go—*please!* I must think. I must—oh, *please*, Mr. Halliday!"

Jimmy released her. He was very well pleased with himself. He thought it would be as well to let his words sink in, and he didn't want the old lady to come down and find him here with Ann. All the same, he meant to have a kiss before she went. Nothing like a good hearty kiss to bring a girl round.

Ann had her hand on the door when his arms came round her, pinning hers. She could not move at all, and had therefore to endure Jimmy's hearty kiss, which alighted upon her averted cheek. They stood like that for a moment, Ann tense with fury, crushed between him and the door, her face pressed to the panelling. And then there came the sound of Mrs. Halliday's voice upon the stairs. Jimmy sprang back. Ann wrenched the door open and ran down into the kitchen.

Mrs. Halliday continued to descend the stairs.

Chapter Thirty-One

ANN RAN AS FAR as the kitchen door and then stopped to listen. The door was ajar. She must see Mary, but she must see her alone. She was trembling from head to foot with anger and disgust. She wanted to tear off her body and fling it away. She hated being a girl, and she was sick with fear about Charles. She pushed the door a little and looked round it. Mary was standing by the fire stirring something in a saucepan.

In an instant Ann was in the room and across the floor with the door shut behind her. In a whispering, hurrying voice she said,

"I must speak to you! Which is the safest place?"

Mary looked back over her shoulder with a face of fear. The lines showed that it was an old fear horribly quickened. The corners of her mouth twitched as she pointed to the back door.

"Rin oot tae the byre. I'll be wi' ye."

'Ann slipped into the yard, and felt safer. There was the back of the house and the hill that faced it, and to right and left cow-house and hen-houses. She ran into the byre and stood behind the door with her feet in rustling straw, hearing the slow contented champing of the little black cows and listening for Mary's step. It came at last, slow and reluctant. The door did not move, but Mary passed the narrow opening and put a hand on Ann's arm.

"What is't, lassie? Ye frichted me."

Ann shuddered. Her own fear was as much as she could bear.

"Mary—will you help me? Please—*please*. They've got him here—Charles—and I think he's hurt. They say he has had an accident, but I think they made him have it. I saw them carrying him into the house last night, but when I got down to the kitchen there wasn't anyone there." She brought her lips close to Mary's ear and whispered, "There was a hole in the wash-house floor. They've taken him down there. I hid in the copper and heard them come up. Oh, Mary, help me! He's down there under the stone, and I can't move the barrel—and he's *hurt*! Mary—you'll help me?"

Mary's clasp on Ann's arm became rigid. She said,

"Gude save us!"

"You'll help me?"

"I'm a deid woman if I do."

Ann's heart gave a great jump. Then Mary *could* help her—and if she could, she must.

"Mary, please, *please* help me!"

Mary went on as if she had not heard.

"I'm no feared o' being deid, but I'm gey feared o' deein'—and ye've got tae dee afore ye're deid. Ay—I'm gey feared o' deein'."

"He's down there, and he's hurt," said Ann in a most piteous tone.

"If I were deid, there'd be nae mair o't," said Mary, still as if she had not heard.

Ann took her by the shoulders and shook her desperately.

"It's not for me—it's for Charles. He's *hurt*!"

Mary's gaze came back from the shadows in the corner of the byre and dwelt upon Ann.

"He's your lad?"

"Yes."

"Ye're tae be married tae him?"

"Yes," said Ann with a sob.

Mary nodded solemnly.

"Ay, lassie, I'll help ye."

Something in her voice and look stayed Ann from speaking.

"I'll help ye," said Mary again. Her voice had a strange, absent sound. She moved as if to go, but Ann held her.

"Will you help me to move the barrel?"

Mary shook her head.

"There's ither ways."

"What ways?"

"Ye maun bide till they're gane oot."

Ann ran out at the yard gate and round the house. Hope came easily to her. If Mary would help her, everything would be all right. They would get Charles out, and he wouldn't be *really* hurt—he would be able to row a boat. Perhaps they would have to wait till after dark. Then they would take the boat and row across the strait. Lovely to get away from the island! Lovely to be eloping with Charles! If his car was smashed, they would take Jimmy Halliday's and kill two birds with one stone, because if they had Jimmy's car he couldn't come after them. It would be very amusing. As for Charles' relations, they had ceased to exist. They mattered so little that she couldn't even remember why they had ever seemed to matter at all.

She came to the front door rather breathless, and was met by Riddle, plaintive and genteel.

"I'm sure I've been looking for you everywhere, Miss Vernon. I'm sure if Mrs. Halliday's asked for you once—"

As she stood aside for Ann to pass, Jimmy Halliday came out of the dining-room.

"My mother's in the parlour asking for you, but if I might have a word with you first—"

"I think I'll go to Mrs. Halliday."

"Not till I've had a word with you. Miss Riddle, you go and tell the old lady she's coming—and you needn't say nothing about me, good nor bad."

He pulled Ann inside the dining-room and shut the door.

"Now, my dear, you needn't look at me like that. I won't kiss you again until we're a bit more private than we are here—and I'm in a hurry, because I don't want to put the old lady in a tantrum. I've only got one thing to say, and that's this—if you've any notion of upsetting Mrs. Halliday by telling her any silly trumped-up stories about me, or my business, or Mr. Gale Anderson, or your friend that's met with an accident, well, I'll just tell you two things quite plain. One is, she won't believe you, not on your Bible oath—she'd only think you'd gone batty in the head. That's one. And this is the other. Anything you thought of saying like that 'ud make things very unpleasant and dangerous for your friend. And now you'd better go to the old lady."

Mrs. Halliday received Ann with an air of extreme offence. She inquired very distantly how she found herself this morning, and produced a hopeful anecdote of one Fanny Stokes who, having been caught in a heavy shower of rain of a Monday, was took ill Tuesday and given up Wednesday.

"Did she die?" said Ann after an awful pause.

Mrs. Halliday sniffed her loudest sniff.

"Not she, and more's the pity! Why, there was 'er mother's sister come from Wales, and 'er brother come down from London, and 'er aunt that lived at Tiverton went so far as to buy 'er black, she taking a out-size and seeing something that would just do 'er in a shop near the station where she'd the best part of an hour to wait at the junction. And after putting of them all out like that she took and got well, and married a grocer's assistant with carroty 'air. 'Ad twins the first year and triplets eighteen months later, and serve 'er right. And if you've quite finished all you want to do this morning, Miss Vernon, I'd be glad if you'd read me the paper."

The paper was a week old, a new batch being due next day. Ann began to read hastily:

"MISSING TYPIST. DIAMOND RING CLUE."

"And who give it 'er?" said Mrs. Halliday suddenly and loudly. "Diamond rings indeed! Girls that take suchlike presents is asking for trouble! Keep yourself to yourself and mind your manners—that's how my mother brought me up. But once a girl begins running after the men, she's running after 'er ruin—and it'll be a good thing if you'll remember that. What else did he give 'er beside the diamond ring?"

Ann bit her lip till it bled and went on reading.

The morning was a very long one. After lunch she thought that the men would go out, but they sat on in the dining-room. Presently she heard them call Hector in, and in a flash she ran down the old stair into the kitchen.

Mary was washing up the lunch things, her figure bowed, her hands moving mechanically, her face drawn and grey. Ann stood in the doorway and called to her under her breath.

"Mary—come here!" And, as she looked round with a start, "I can't wait any longer. They're just sticking there in the dining-room. Show me how to get to him."

"Lassie, it's no safe."

"It won't ever be safe! I can't wait!"

"Lassie!"

"You promised!"

Mary made a hopeless gesture.

"Rin out intae the byre then an' bide till I come!"

She was there almost as soon as Ann was, with hurry in her steps and fear in her eyes. She thrust a lantern into Anne's hand and a box of matches.

"Dinna licht it till I shut the stane," she said, and began to pull away the straw in the far corner of the byre.

There was an iron ring set there, very old and rusty. Mary pulled on it, and all of a sudden a flagstone tilted and left a gaping hole. Ann stood above it and looked down. She could see the beginning of a rude stair. Her heart quaked at the blackness and the cold, damp smell.

"What is it?" she said in a choking whisper.

"There's cellars aneath the hoose. They were for hidin' in the auld times. There was ae way in and anither way oot, so that they shouldna be trappit. For Gude's sake gae doon if yer gaun, or we're a' deid thegither!" Her tone was sharp and thin with terror.

Ann put her foot on the topmost step. The place smelt of old, dreadful things. If Charles was down there, she must go and find him. She took two more steps down, and felt as if she were going down into black evil-smelling water. Perhaps there wouldn't be any air to breathe and she would be choked when Mary shut the stone.

"Haste ye, lassie!"

Ann turned up an agonized face.

"You won't shut it so that I can't get out?"

"There's a ring aneath the stane. Ye'll need tae pull on't. It's no hard tae move."

She pressed Ann's shoulder and sent her stumbling down the next two or three steps. As she brought herself up gasping, the stone fell back into its place and all the light was gone. She stood there clutching at the damp wall, and realized that the lantern had slipped from her hand. The noise that it made bounding from step to step bewildered and terrified her. She waited for the noise to stop, and then the silence was more terrifying still.

It was a minute or two before she remembered that she still had the matches. She had slipped them into the pocket of her jumper—one of those silly little pockets that aren't really meant to hold anything, but it had held the box of matches and it held it still. She got it out, struck a match, and saw dark slimy steps going down into what looked like a black pit.

She made herself go down five steps before she struck another match. This time the light brought her a little comfort. There were three more steps, and then a passage ran off in what she judged to be the direction of the house. The match flared and went out, but before it died she had seen the lantern lying against the passage wall. The worst of her terror left her then. It was the dark that was so dreadful. If she had a light she could bear it. And to find Charles she must have a light.

She groped her way to the lantern, set it on end, and lighted the inch or two of candle which it contained. That feeble yellow flame seemed to her the most beautiful thing that she had ever seen. She closed the glass of the lantern and, holding it up, began to make her way along the passage. It was of rock, and she guessed that it was in part a natural fissure enlarged and shaped by man. In some places the roof and sides were rough and untouched by any tool. In others the surface had been cut, and where this was the case the roof was very low. At the end she had to go down on her hands and knees. When she straightened herself up after this, she thought she must be under the house.

She had come out into a place like a cellar. In one corner a stair ran up to the stone roof. Quite illogically, Ann felt safer here. She thought the stair must lead up to the wash-house. She held the lantern up and looked all round. The place out of which she had crawled showed a black arch about three feet from the floor. Beyond it was another arch, a little higher. And on the same side as the steps there was a bolted door.

Ann's heart gave a jump. If the door was bolted, it was to keep someone in—and someone meant Charles. There must be a cellar under the kitchen, and Charles was there.

She ran to the door, set down her lantern, and tugged with both hands at the bolt. It was a huge rusty thing as thick as her wrist, and so stiff that she could not move it. But someone had been oiling it. She could feel the oil on her hands. She strained and pulled, and suddenly the bolt gave way—so suddenly that she went stumbling back against the lantern and knocked it over. The light went out. The swing of the cellar door caught her shoulder, and with a rush someone sprang upon her from the darkness and brought her down.

Chapter Thirty-Two

IT WAS LIKE the most dreadful nightmare in the world. Darkness, and a slippery floor where her feet went from under her. The blow that made her dizzy. Arms that held her in a cruel grip. Heavy breathing close above her head. She thought she screamed, but she wasn't sure—and oh, what use to scream in this dreadful buried place?

She made a small weak sound scarcely louder than a sob, and almost before she made it the grip which held her changed; she was up against Charles' breast, and his voice was murmuring in her ear.

"Ann! My darling! My little darling! Did I hurt you? I thought it was those swine. They left me roped up, and I've just got my hands free. Ann, are you hurt? Darling—darling—do say something!"

Ann said, "Oh!... It's *you!*"

"Of course it's me. Who did you think it was?"

"A n-nightmare."

"Thanks, darling! I say, let's get up, shall we? Ugh! I'm stiff! They left me roped up, and I've only just got my hands free. I'm still hobbled, so you'd better stand clear while I get up."

Instead of standing clear Ann gave him both her hands. She pulled, Charles pulled, and with a floundering jerk he was on his feet again. She heard him laugh, and was pulled up close.

"I say, darling, did I give you a most awful scare? When I heard someone at the bolt, I was bound to give whoever it was the fright of his life."

Ann nuzzled her face into his neck and said, "Beast!" And then, with a sob, "Oh, Charles darling—you nearly killed me!"

Charles hugged her.

"Yes, I know, darling—but I couldn't tell it was going to be you. I didn't really hurt you, did I?"

"You b-bashed my shoulder."

Charles kissed the shoulder.

"Anything else?"

"My f-feelings." This time the tremor in Ann's voice was nearer laughter than tears.

Charles assuaged the feelings.

"What did you think I was? An underground monster, or the ghost of a Highland prisoner who'd been left here to starve two or three hundred years ago?"

"Ouf!" said Ann. "*Don't!* I'm not feeling brave enough for ghosts."

"I think it was frightfully brave of you to come and look for me. I suppose you were looking for me?"

"Yes, I was."

"Well, if you got in, we can both get out, and we oughtn't to waste any time about it. By the way, what *is* the time?"

Ann tried to remember. Everything seemed such a long time ago.

"It's early afternoon—somewhere between two and three."

"It would be easier to get away after dark. I suppose they're all three here still?"

"Yes, they are."

"Well, I've got to get my ankles untied before I do anything else. I had to shuffle to the door and then jump. I thought if I fell on the feller and then beat his head on the floor I might be able to make him see reason. I say, darling, you didn't come here in the dark, did you?"

"I've got a lantern, but you knocked it out."

"Good! I've got a torch, but I want to save it."

They found the lantern, lighted it, and set to work on the rope which tied Charles' ankles together. There wasn't much that Jimmy Halliday didn't know about knots, and it wasn't going to be a very quick business.

"What did you think when I didn't come?" said Charles over the knots.

"I thought you were dead," said Ann, and the lantern shook in her hand.

"I say, steady with that light, darling! What a little owl! Why should I be dead?"

The lantern shook again.

"You nearly were, weren't you? Charles, tell me about it. What happened? You're not hurt, are you?"

"Only my feelings—same like yours, darling." He began to laugh. "You *are* an owl! Did I feel as if I was hurt when I jumped on you? There goes one of the blighted knots! Well, this is what happened. You know when I left you—well, going across the strait I met a sea-serpent, and it rammed me."

"Charles!"

"Honest it did—and smashed my boat. I say, darling, you'll be prepared to swear I was sober—won't you?"

Ann shivered.

"Charles—what is it? I saw it too—in the moonlight. And then a cloud went over the moon, but I could hear it—swimming. And, Charles, Mary says it's a devil, and she told me to keep away from the water or it would get me. That was why I was so afraid when you didn't come, because I knew you wouldn't go away and just leave me."

Charles spared a hand from the knots to pat her shoulder and then went on again.

"Whatever it is, it rammed me good and hard. I've got some ideas about it, but I shan't tell you what they are. When we get out of here I'm going to get to the bottom of it whatever it is. Well, I had to go to Ardgair to get my boat mended. They took all day over it, and coming back there was a beast of a fog, and I took a toss on one of those damned hairpin bends and went over the cliff. I gather that the toss was arranged by a bloke called Hector, because I heard your Mr. Halliday telling him to make sure he'd cleared the track again. I think he'd banked it up on the inside with some good selections of the local boulder. There are several places where it wouldn't take much to send you over."

"You're sure you weren't hurt?"

"I told you I wasn't." He patted her again. "I don't mind telling you I was like you for a bit—I thought I was dead. And when I came round there was about a ton of car between me and the outside world. She'd turned turtle and boxed me in, and there I might have been till now if your kind friends hadn't come along and got me out. I should say they'd been waiting for Hector's little smash and blew in to pick up the bits. Hector and that prize swab Anderson seemed a good deal peeved that I wasn't dead, but your Mr. Halliday seemed to think it was all right as it was. I'm afraid I made rather a poor show, but they hauled me out from under the car, and just as I was getting ready to say thank you, the swine Hector sat on my head and the other two tied me up. I landed a couple of good kicks, but I'm afraid they didn't do much damage. When they'd tied me up, they shoved a gag in my mouth, slung a blanket over me, and carried home the corpse."

"I saw them out of my window," said Ann—"and that's when I really did think you were dead. I saw them carry you in."

"How did you know it was me?"

"I *knew* it was. And I went down and found out about this place."

"Only one more knot," said Charles. "Yes, there we come to it—what is this place?"

"Cellars under the house. They're awfully old. There's one way in through the wash-house floor, and another through the cow-shed. That's how I came. Mary showed me."

Charles frowned over the last knot.

"Then that's the way we'll be going as soon as I've got this undone."

"They won't let us go."

Charles looked up with a set, frowning face.

"Look here, my dear, what *is* this show? What are they after, and how far will they go? Is it old Paulett's money, or is there something else as well?"

Ann's voice came back in a slow whisper.

"It's the money—and it's me—like you said. If I'm dead, Gale Anderson's wife gets the lot, so Gale Anderson wants me to be dead. He tried to kill me yesterday afternoon.'

"Ann!"

"It's all right—he didn't. But it was a most frightfully near thing. You say, how far will they go? Well, Gale Anderson will go as far as murder, and he'll rather enjoy doing it. He pushed down boulders on me, and I had to jump off the cliff into the loch. Hilda would be getting the money all right if Jimmy Halliday hadn't fished me out."

"Halliday?"

Ann gave a little shaky laugh.

"Jimmy is my noble preserver. My skirt was caught up on a rock, and he threw me a knife to cut it away. I only did it just in time, because that beast Gale was crawling along the cliff to get at me."

"Halliday saved you?"

Ann nodded.

"He's my noble preserver. He doesn't want me to be dead, because he wants to marry me. You see, Hilda having the money isn't as much fun for him as it is for Gale. Besides, if Uncle Elias has died by now, Hilda's out of it. This is where you come in."

"Where do I come in?"

"Well, Jimmy does think he's awfully fascinating, but still I don't think even he was quite sure that I'd marry him all in a hurry like that. You come in as the turn of the screw. Jimmy put it very nicely. He said that if I married him, he could be sure you'd hold your tongue because you wouldn't want to hurt my husband, but that otherwise he was afraid things would be very dangerous and unpleasant for you. He seemed quite sorry about it. I don't think Jimmy cares about murdering people. He's not cold-blooded like Gale Anderson or blood-thirsty like Hector, but all the same I don't think he'd stick at killing someone if it was a choice between that and his own safety."

"His safety?" said Charles. "What's he been up to? There's something besides this, isn't there? Do you know what it is?"

"N-no. But there's something. He as good as told me that. He said he wanted to settle down and get married because his business was a risky one and he wanted to get out of it before anything happened to upset the old lady. He is a good son, you know."

"Damn his being a good son! What's he been doing? Smuggling dope?"

"I don't know. Do you think it might be that?"

"Well, it would be an awfully good place for it. I expect the old lady goes down with her bonnet-boxes full of cocaine."

"Oh no, she wouldn't! She's frightfully respectable."

"Well, I know how I'd do it," said Charles. "I'd have a minion who delivered groceries once a week or so—tinned food and all that sort of thing—bottles—plenty of bottles—things with screw tops. And the returned empties wouldn't be empty at all—they'd be neatly packed with dope. I say, darling, that's one way out—we can make him an offer for the goodwill of the business and set up in the dope-running line."

"Charles, do be serious!"

"Darling, when I'm serious I can't see any way out at all. I'm afraid I was a bit optimistic when I spoke as if we could just walk out through the cowshed. I don't quite know how I'm going to get you off the island. And even if we had a boat, we wouldn't be much forrader, because my poor old bus is quite definitely a wreck."

"Jimmy's got a car."

"I hoped he had. I thought I'd found a garage in the ruins the other night, but it was too dark to make sure. Well, that's that—and we might steal a boat after dark, but I'm awfully afraid there's nothing to be done by daylight, and that means you'll have to go back now and come down again at night."

"Charles, I *can't!*"

Ann's heart quailed within her. To have to do it all over again, to have to go back—she just didn't feel that she could do it.

Charles put his arms round her.

"Darling, I simply don't see any other way. And it will be the last lap. You've been so awfully brave."

"Oh, Charles—don't make me!"

"Darling, what else can we do? Steady on, and just think. That brute Anderson's got a revolver—he shoved it up against my ear before they started to tie me up. I don't know if the others are armed, but I should think it's practically a dead cert that they are. Hector would have a knife if he hadn't got anything else, but I should think they've all got firearms. We simply haven't got an earthly chance of getting away in daylight. You'll have to bolt me in and go back. If one of them comes down alone, I can make sure of laying him out. If they come two together, I'd still have a pretty good chance, because they'd be expecting me to be tied up. Well then, if they didn't come back, the third man would probably come and look for them, so with a bit of luck I might lay them all out and go off with you in style. And failing that, you'll have to come down when the house is asleep and let me out. You see you must bolt me in, or I won't get a chance of springing a surprise on them."

Ann shocked back from that. To push the bolt between her and Charles was to cut herself off from her only helper. She was to do that and then go back to Mrs. Halliday, who had turned against her, to Jimmy, who had made her feel his brute strength, to Gale Anderson, who had tried to kill her. She said these names to herself, but she did not say Hector's name. Just why she feared him so much she could not have said, but she did fear him—more than Jimmy, who meant to force her into marrying him—more than Gale, who had come within an ace of murdering her.

She looked at Charles in a dumb misery of fear.

"What is it, darling? Ann, what is it?"

"I *can't* lock you in!"

"Darling, you must. Don't you see, if the bolt's drawn back, they'll know someone's been down here, and I won't get a chance of surprising them. Do go on being brave for just a little bit longer. I know it's beastly for you, but I've got a plan. As soon as you've got away I shall kick up the devil's own row here—shout and yell, and bang with my heels, and all that sort of thing. There are some packing-cases over there that I can have a go at. By the way, that's where I got my idea about the dope from—there's some fairly suspicious looking stuff in them. I was having a look at it with my torch when you started in on the bolt. Well, if it is dope, and they think I'm kicking the stuff about, someone's pretty well bound to come down and see what's happening."

"What's that?" said Ann in a sudden strained whisper.

"What's what?"

She caught his arm and held it convulsively.

"That noise. Listen!"

Chapter Thirty-Three

THEY LISTENED. There was no sound.

"What did you hear?" said Charles on a whispered breath.

"Someone moved the barrel—I'm sure they did."

Charles reached silently over to the lantern and put it out. He pushed it into Ann's hand in the dark.

"Get a little bit up the passage you came by, and don't come out whatever happens. I'll catch them coming down. Hop it, darling!"

He had her out of the cellar and into the open space as he spoke. There was one gleam from his torch to show the low arch through which she must go, and then she was down on her hands and knees crawling into the passage.

Charles felt an immense relief. This was going to be rather fun, only Ann had got to keep out of it. He risked his torch again for a moment, had a passing wonder as to where the other arched passage went to, and located the steps going up to the roof. If they had moved the barrel, they had not raised the stone yet. The steps went straight up without an atom of cover. Better get back to the cellar, and make a rush before they had time to notice the bolt.

He had taken the first step towards the door, when panting, and stumbling to her feet, Ann caught at him. Her hands shook, her breath hurried. She whispered against his ear,

"Someone's coming down that way! Hector! I saw the light! *Charles!*"

As she spoke his name, and before he had time to do anything at all, the flagstone at the top of the steps was tilted up and a bright shaft of light shone through the opening. Jimmy Halliday's voice said,

"He should be through by now."

And with that Charles remembered the second archway. He made for it, his arm round Ann. The torch showed a rough passage about four feet high with a sudden turn to the right a few feet in. He stooped to it, pulling her with him, and got round the bend, with a sound of voices in the cellar behind him. There were three of them all right. If he had been alone, he would have waited for them at the bend and trusted to luck, but Gale Anderson's revolver stuck in his mind. This narrow space, and Ann, and a man who had tried to kill her only yesterday—it wasn't good enough.

He hurried her along, throwing the beam of the torch in front and praying for another bend. If it didn't come soon, they'd be done. Gale Anderson would be able to pot them as they ran. He put Ann in front, and felt a coldness between his shoulder-blades. The roof had risen and they could stand upright, and suddenly there came, not one bend, but two. Charles felt an extreme relief.

The passage went on turning and twisting. It got rougher and rougher till all trace of a made path was gone and they climbed and slipped in a rocky fissure which began to take a sharp downward slope.

They came suddenly into the cave. One moment the torch shone back on them from black dripping walls which almost touched, and the next its long beam travelled far across a place of shadows and strange echoing sounds.

Charles caught Ann by the arm and swung the torch about.

"Careful—it's awfully steep here. We're down to the loch. Better let me go first."

They were on the edge of a fifteen-foot cliff. The path went down it in zigzags, with stanchions set here and there to hold to. At the foot of it the waters of the loch lapped against a pebbly beach. On the far side there were boulders piled in fantastic heaps. Charles hurried Ann across the beach and behind the rocks. He had no plan. The whole thing had come so suddenly. He thought now that he ought to have got her round the bends and gone back. There wasn't much chance for them here in this open place. If he had been alone, he would have tried swimming for it.... Was it just possible that Jimmy Halliday kept a boat here? That was a handy little beach, and private. It might suit Jimmy pretty well to have a private landing-place. Now that he had put his torch out, he could see a faint glimmer as of reflected daylight in the direction of the loch. That meant that there was an exit above water— probably not so very much above water.

He stared across the cave in the direction from which they had come. There was no light to show where the passage was—no light, and no sound—no sound anywhere, except the lapping of the water and Ann's soft troubled breathing. She had sunk down on the stones, and crouched there, pressed close to him with her cheek against his shoulder. He said to himself, "I'll count twenty. If I don't see or hear anything by then, I'll chance it. There might be a boat."

He counted twenty slowly, resisting the temptation to hurry towards the end.... Seventeen—eighteen—nineteen—twenty.... No sound, and no light. He turned on his torch and sent the ray across the water. It came to rest about twenty feet away.

Charles' hand stiffened, his arm stiffened, his whole body stiffened. Ann made a little choking sound against his shoulder. From the black water of the loch there rose a serpentine head and neck. It swayed a little in the ray. In a half open jaw there were teeth—there was the green gleam of an eye—there was a tangle of mane.

There was no sound but the sound of the water moving against the rock and upon itself, as if the loch were breathing—lip, lap, lip, with a smooth continual motion. And with this motion the head and neck moved too. It seemed to have no movement of its own. It rose and fell with the rising and falling of the water.

With an effort Charles controlled the rigidity of his hand. He made it move, and the ray of light moved with it. The green eye went out in the dark. The beam slid down the long neck and rested upon the water.

There was something there—a long floating body with the water washing on it. And all of a sudden Charles was shaking with excitement. His arm went round Ann and hugged her.

"Ann! Ann! It's a submarine!"

Ann lifted the face that had been pressed against his shoulder.

"Charles!"

"It isn't a sea-serpent—it's a submarine!" He ran the light up and down the long shape and came back to the monstrous head and neck. "Leery devils! They've rigged up the periscope that way to frighten off anyone who happened to be about when they came up. I thought the thing that rammed me was uncommon hard for a reptile! I say, just think of the fun they must have had! An ugly devil—isn't it?" He brought the beam back to the staring eye and then shut it off in a hurry.

"Charles, can we get away in it? If you're *sure* it's not a creature?"

Charles laughed.

"I'm sure all right. That eye is good green glass. But I don't think we'll meddle with it. I don't know the first beginnings of anything about a submarine. I expect it would be a damn sight more dangerous than staying where we are."

"We can't stay where we are! Charles—they must have been in this cave when I heard them talking! There was a crack that ran through to the cliff. We might find a place where we could get out. Quick—before they come! Look and see if there isn't some way out!"

Charles swung the torch to and fro. The beam made the shadows move and shake and run together like black quicksilver. Beyond the rocks where they crouched there was something which could hardly be called a track. It went up and up to the very roof of the cave and lost itself there.

"Wait, and I'll go and look."

"Charles, I won't be left!"

"But, darling—"

"I simply won't!"

They scrambled up the track together. Ann's spine crept as if a cold finger were touching it. It was all very well for Charles to say that the Thing wasn't alive, but supposing it *was*.... He couldn't *know*—he hadn't *touched* it. Here she shuddered violently and nearly fell. Suppose it was alive—suppose it was slithering up the rocks after them at this very moment....

"Good Lord, darling—what a sprinter you are!" said Charles, and with that they were at the top.

A narrow rift split the rock wall just where it joined the cavern roof. Charles shone the light into it, and stopped. The rift seemed to dwindle to a mere gash. A place where one might be trapped and find no way out.

Ann looked back over her shoulder and choked on a cry.

"They're coming! Oh, Charles—go on!"

"Suppose it doesn't go on—"

He too looked back. A bright electric lamp shone from the top of the cliff down which they had come. The mouth of the passage gaped behind it. Two men were on the cliff face. The third, Gale Anderson, held up the lamp to light them. The cause of the delay in their pursuit was plain. They had gone back for this powerful lamp.

With a leaden sinking of the heart Charles realized what this implied. If there had been any way out of this place, the pursuers would not have risked delay. They had gone back because they knew that they had all the time they wanted. And he, Charles, had been mug enough to play into their hands by leaving the passage, where they could only come at him one at a time. He looked on into the narrow rift.

Ann tugged at his arm.

"Charles—Charles!"

Jimmy Halliday had reached the foot of the cliff. Gale Anderson set down the electric lamp on a rock at a level with his shoulder, drew a revolver, took careful aim, and fired. The bullet struck a jutting rock an inch or two from Ann. The sudden noise, the sound of the impact, and the shattering echoes which followed the shot seemed for the moment to render her incapable of moving. Noise—bewildering, stunning noise. She took in no more than that, and the next thing she knew was that Charles was thrusting her before him through the rift. There was just room and no more. The width would not take Charles' shoulders, and he had to move sideways like a crab. There was only about a dozen feet of this, and then Ann cried out and, turning, clutched him. The ray went into emptiness. Charles looked over her shoulder and turned the light this way and that.

The rift had come to an end. They looked down into another cave. It had no beach, no floor but the waters of the loch which filled it from end to end. Far away to the right the faintest thread of daylight showed that it had an exit. The air had a heavy, musty smell.

Charles thrust the light over the brink and looked down. They were some twenty-five feet above the water-level. Six feet below them there was a ledge. He turned the light here and there. The ledge ran away to the left and sloped towards the water. About twenty feet away there was one of those tumbled piles of great water-worn rocks. They must make for that and put up the best show they could. Impossible to stay here, where a shot or a blow would send them head down into deep water.

He wedged the torch in a crack, took Ann by the wrists, and lowered her until her feet were on the ledge. Then he gave her the torch and dropped down beside her.

So far, so good.

The ledge was about two feet wide, and there was plenty of handhold. It went down sharply to within six feet of the water and ended at the pile of rocks. They were slippery and hard to climb—a low clutter of them sprawling on the edge of the pool, with one great boulder thrusting up like some huge monolith. It leaned against the cliff, and might have been the doorpost of some great unhewn door.

They had reached this and were skirting it, when the torch showed them the ledge again, running on round the cave. In the past it might have marked some higher level of the loch. Now, here in the present, it might mean a path to safety. It ran away to a sharp turn at the head of the cave. He was not sure whether there was a break at the turn, the shadows were so heavy.

If it ran all the way round the cave—if they could reach the faint gleam of daylight—if—

Chapter Thirty-Four

JIMMY HALLIDAY'S bright electric lamp thrust out of the rift above their heads.

Charles switched off his torch, pushed Ann behind the boulder, and stood covering her. This new light seemed extraordinarily brilliant after the meagre ray which had lighted them.

Jimmy Halliday dropped to the ledge and came along it, holding up the lamp and calling out,

"Miss Vernon! Mr. Anstruther! I'm not armed, and I want to talk to you. You can't get away out of here, you know—there's no way out. Let's see if we can't do a deal. And by gum, let's do it quickly, for if you've a fancy for this place, I haven't, and that's flat."

He stopped where the ledge met the rocks, held up his light, and looked all round the cave. The roof ran up in tumbled arches and broken groins. The ledge followed its uneven way above the water. The pool slept its eternal sunless sleep. Under the bright light it had the black, still look of water which is very deep.

"The waters that are under the earth—" The words went through Ann's mind, and then Jimmy Halliday was saying,

"Miss Vernon—are you there? I know you are, because there isn't anywhere else you can be, but I'd like to hear your voice. Oh, come along now and be a sensible young lady! Would you rather do business with me or with Gale? That's what it comes to. I'd choose me if I was you. Gale's a bit too handy with his shooting-iron for a young lady to do business with. And he wants you dead, and I want you alive—so you speak up pretty, and we'll see if we can't do a deal that'll be satisfactory to all parties."

"You can address your remarks to me, Halliday," said Charles.

Jimmy heaved a sigh of relief. He was standing where the boulders began, the ledge at this point being no more than six feet above the water-level. He spoke in a hearty voice.

"Well, I won't say I wouldn't rather. I've done business with men all my life, and I know where I am with them. Now, Mr. Anstruther, you come out from behind that rock and we'll have a talk. I'm not armed, and I don't want to hurt either you or Miss Vernon. That's why I've got rid of Gale. I don't like shooting, and I don't like violence. All I want is a straight business deal, and I don't see why things can't be arranged so as to satisfy everyone."

"Don't go!" said Ann in Charles' ear. "Please, *please* don't!"

Charles gave her a little shake.

"Be quiet, darling! All right, Halliday, go ahead. We can talk very nicely as we are, I think."

The position was indeed all to their advantage. The huge monolith stood guard over them, its bulk screening them from the light and from Jimmy Halliday, but by moving the least shade Charles could see Jimmy whilst remaining himself unseen.

Jimmy set down the lamp on a smooth-topped stone. A pool beneath it reflected the light.

"Well," he said, "it's this way. You've put me in an awkward position. I've no ill feelings towards you, but you can't deny that you've butted in on my private business—now, can you?"

"Miss Vernon happens to be my private business," said Charles.

"Now—now—*now!*" Jimmy's manner was that of one who soothes a froward child. "What's the good of talking like that? You know as well as I do that I wasn't meaning Miss Vernon. What's the good of pretending you don't know what I mean? I may as well tell you I don't take you for all that stupid, Mr. Anstruther. You'd got your hands loose, and you'd got the lid off one of those packing-cases in the cellar, and if you don't know what my business is after that, you're just a natural born fool—and I don't think that of you."

"Thanks!" said Charles. "Then we'll take it as agreed that you've been running dope.

Jimmy nodded emphatically.

"And never been caught once! You saw my little craft in there, I take it. Pretty little bit of goods—isn't she? Smallest submarine in the world, and a two-man job. I'd like to show you over her. Perhaps I may if we bring this deal off." His tone was easy and conversational. "Nice little job that periscope of hers—isn't it? And that was my idea. When I came here first there was all manner of silly stories about some kind of a sea-serpent in this loch. I tell you I've talked to men as sober as you and me that said they'd seen it—and that's why I didn't like it when Miss Vernon said she'd seen something in the loch at a time when it couldn't have been my little craft. She was only kidding of course, but it gave me a bit of a turn. The only time I ever saw anything myself I'd been celebrating the old lady's birthday. It was in this very cave we're in, and I've never rightly fancied the place since, but it gave me the idea, and I got a periscope rigged up as near what I'd had described to me as I could get it. I can tell you it worked like a charm. Anyone that saw us—well, they didn't wait to see no more than they could help!" He laughed a genial laugh.

Charles' thoughts ran rapidly—"Why is he telling us all this? It's a very bad sign. He can't let us go after this. What's he playing at?" He said aloud,

"What's the deal you're offering us, Halliday?"

Jimmy put his foot up on a step in the rock and leaned his elbow on his knee. In this confidential attitude he proceeded.

"Well now, Mr. Anstruther, there we come to it. I take it that you're fond of Miss Vernon. You'd like to get her out of this mess, and you wouldn't do anything that'd upset her or get her into trouble. You'll agree with that, I suppose?"

"Don't!" said Ann in a fluttering whisper. "Don't agree to anything—because I *won't*!"

She had edged forward, and stood pressed between Charles and the great boulder. The light of Jimmy's lamp lit up the cavern, but where she and Charles were there was a deep patch of shadow. She had the queerest feeling that this shadow was their safety. She held Charles tight lest he should step beyond it.

Charles shook her again and answered Jimmy.

"I don't mind going as far as that."

"That's good!" said Jimmy heartily. "Well then, the way for Miss Vernon to get out of the mess is for her to marry me right here and now. And then, taking into account that you wouldn't want to hurt her, and that you couldn't hurt me without hurting her, I'd consider taking your word that you wouldn't do anything to stir up trouble. And on my side I'd be willing to give an undertaking that I'd retire from business. I've seen a lot of men going on too long and getting caught out, and I wouldn't like that to happen to me, because of the old lady. All I want is to settle down respectable and live quiet. Miss Vernon'll tell you that's the proposition I put to her this morning. It's a good sound proposition, and the more you look at it, the better you'll like it. You get your life, and as soon as my wife and me have settled down together, and I think it's safe, you'll get your liberty. Miss Vernon'll get a good husband, though I say it as shouldn't, and there's no reason why things shouldn't be pleasant all round."

"Are you off your head, Halliday?" said Charles.

"*Me?*" said Jimmy in a tone of offence. "*Off my head?* Why, I'm offering you a plain business deal! I grant you it couldn't be done in England where there's a lot of red tape about getting married, but I've got what they call a Scotch domicile here, and that means I can get married by Scotch law—and it's good Scotch law that if two people stand up and take each other for man and wife in front of witnesses, man and wife they are, and all the lawyers in the world can't make it any different. I hope you don't think, Mr. Anstruther, that I'm the sort of man that'd trifle with a young lady like Miss Vernon."

"I'm quite sure you want to marry Miss Vernon, if that's what you mean. And I'm quite sure Miss Vernon won't marry you. Come on, Halliday, talk sense! What will you take in cold cash to get us out of this—we undertaking to keep our mouths shut?"

Jimmy took on a tone of reproof.

"*Now*, Mr. Anstruther—that's not the sort of thing I'd have expected from a gentleman like yourself! I put it to you now that when a man makes a young lady an offer of marriage, does he expect an answer or doesn't he?"

"Ann," said Charles in a pleasantly detached tone—"Mr. Halliday wants an answer to his proposal of marriage. Perhaps you'd better let him have one."

In his mind the thoughts raced—"Why does he go on talking? Where are the others? He's marking time for them. We oughtn't to have stopped—we ought to have kept right on round the cave. He's been keeping us here. We ought to have gone on. But if he's got a revolver, he could have picked us off the ledge as easy as shelling peas. I wonder if he's armed. I wonder if it's too late to make a sprint for it now. There's no more cover after this."

He heard Ann speaking from behind him clearly and steadily.

"Thank you, Mr. Halliday, but I'm sure you know that I can't marry you."

Jimmy took up the electric lamp and held it high above his head. The light lapped round the corner of their boulder. Charles swung Ann back into the shadow. As he did so, she cried out.

"They're coming—the others! Oh, Charles!"

He said, "Where?" but as he spoke he knew, and cursed himself for a fool. Away to the left where the path had seemed to break, where the cliff wall turned so sharply and the shadows were so heavy, there were two dark figures on the ledge. Plainly, among the shadows there must be an opening. He could have laughed. It was all plain enough. Jimmy was to delay them whilst the others came round and cut off their rear.

The men were only some fifty feet away, but they came slowly, Hector first, with a knife in his teeth, and then Gale Anderson, hugging the rock, for the ledge was broken and for some twenty feet gave only the barest foothold.

Jimmy shouted, and the cavern rang with the echoes. He held the light up high, and it shone on the wet glistening rock, on the steel of Hector's knife and on the fierce pleased face above it, on Gale Anderson's slow purposeful advance, and on the black untroubled pool.

Ann looked once at Hector's face and shuddered away from its raw cruelty. She looked at the pool and wondered if he would kill them, and whether it would hurt very much, and whether she would be able to help screaming. She mustn't scream, because of Charles. It would be much worse for Charles if she screamed. She tried to fix her eyes and her thoughts upon the blackness of the pool, and suddenly there slid into her consciousness the knowledge that the blackness at which she was staring was not quite black any more. It was changing, as the colour of shoaling water changes. She said, "Charles!" in a startled, urgent whisper, and Charles looked down at her for a moment and said, *"Ann,"* with something in his voice which she never forgot. She had not been aware of any movement on his part, but he must have moved, for he had a big stone in his hand. After that one look his eyes went back to Hector. He must wait till he couldn't possibly miss and then get him with the stone between the eyes.

Ann's whisper came again, sharper, more urgent.

"Charles—the pool! *What is it?*"

He looked then where she was looking, and saw what she had seen—that shoaling colour in the water under the bright light. For a moment they both had the illusion that the water was draining away, and then to both at the same time there came the realization that it was not the water that was sinking, but that something was rising up towards them through the water.

A moment later it was not they alone who realized it. On their right Jimmy stiffened with the lamp in his hand, and to the left Hector, crouching on the narrow ledge, let out a screaming Gaelic oath. The knife dropped from his teeth and went clattering down into the water. It threw up a tiny fountain of spray and was gone. Gale Anderson, clinging to the rock, looked back across his shoulder. Charles saw his face for a moment, white and sweating. And then they were all looking at the pool.

Something was rising up through it. From moment to moment the water changed, black merging into green, and green into livid grey. It was like seeing a fish rise—but it seemed to fill the pool. They stared, and did not know for how long they had been staring. If it was many moments, they ran together and made one moment. If it was one moment, it was a moment endlessly prolonged. Then the livid colour touched the surface of the pool and broke through it. There were folds of wrinkled skin, fold upon wrinkled fold, like rock come alive, scabbed and scarred and humped, with the water washing off it. The humps showed, moved, and sank down again, leaving a curd of foam. They stretched an unbelievable distance. The livid colour of them lay under the surface and stopped the light.

Ann drew in her breath. It was the first movement that any of them had made. She had time to draw it in and to let it out again. And then, between them and the ledge where Hector and Gale Anderson were frozen, there came up a head and neck. Ten feet—fifteen feet—and it went on rising. It was so monstrous as to be unbelievable, yet they all saw it. It was like the mockery which Jimmy had made of it to mask the periscope of the submarine—like, and most dreadfully unlike. For a rigid figure-head, here was a sentient, malignant Thing, swaying and undulating with horrid, eager life. It brought with it an awful musky stench which filled the cave.

As the head swayed to and fro on a level with the ledge, Charles wrenched his eyes away. He caught Ann up under her arms and pushed her up the side of the great boulder where it joined the cliff.

"There's foothold, and you've got to find it! Don't look round—I'll see you're all right. That's right, get your feet on my shoulders and up you go. Cling—crawl—scramble! You can do it, and you've got to!"

Ann's very mind felt stiff. She did not think that she could move. It is certain that left to herself she would not have moved, but would have gone on staring until the dreadful end. It was the rough vigour of Charles' words which made her move. And then, when she had got her first foothold and was reaching for another, panic came on her and she climbed with a desperate strength. She gained a place where she could stand and look down.

Charles was following. He called,

"Don't stop! Don't look! Go on!"

But, having looked, she could not turn her eyes away. All across the pool the humped body showed. Over the ledge and the two men the head hung poised, like a snake's head ready to strike. There was a dark mane that made it most horrible. The water ran dripping down it. And the head began to move, bending on the neck, coming up against the rock, lipping it with a wet snout as if to feel its way.

"Go on!" said Charles. "Don't look! Go on climbing!"

He had reached the place where she stood. He thrust her on. A series of natural steps led up to the top of the boulder. There was just room for the two of them to stand pressed together with the rocky wall of the cavern at their backs.

Charles put his arm round her, and they looked down.

Gale Anderson was gone. The humps of the monster's body were gone. The head was rising. It was nearer. Jimmy Halliday still stood with the lamp in his hand and an expression of stony terror on his face. Charles called sharply down to him.

"For the Lord's sake, Halliday, put out that light! It's attracting it. Haven't you ever poached salmon with a flare? Put out that light, I say!"

Jimmy turned irresolutely towards the voice. He seemed quite stupid with terror. The monstrous head rose high over the ledge and hung above Hector, who crouched there motionless. Charles' hand came down hard over Ann's eyes. She felt his heart beat against her own. There was an awful scream, and after that a gurgling splash. She heard Charles call again.

"Halliday! Wake up, man! Run for it—back to the rift! You've a sporting chance! But hurry, man—hurry! And put out that damned lamp!"

The pool lay empty under the light. And then the surface broke again and the head came up not half a dozen yards from where Jimmy stood at the edge of the water. It rose up and hung there swaying as it had done before, and for the first time they saw the eyes—not the green glass eyes of Jimmy's make-believe, but the eyes of a reptile, horn-lidded, bright, and blank—blind bright eyes, staring at the light which blinded them.

"Halliday!" cried Charles. And with that Jimmy dropped the lantern and ran, not up the ledge to the rift, but towards the voice which had called to him.

He came slipping and plunging over the slimy rocks, his head thrown back, his eyes straining upwards, his breath coming in great thumping jerks. It wasn't like seeing a live man run. It was as if his body was galvanized into an unnatural energy by sheer terror. He did not seem to look where he was going, but though he slipped, he did not fall. With a final bound he reached the deep shadow where Charles and Ann had crouched. They could hear him below them, labouring for breath and clawing at the rock. Charles called down to him.

"Right in the corner against the cliff, Halliday! There's foothold all the way up Hurry, man—hurry!"

The monstrous head was rising. The humped outline of the body broke the water. Ann gazed with wide, horrified eyes. The humped protuberances moved under the watery film that covered them, as a muscle moves under the skin, knotting and flexing with an easy strength. The water from the mane ran down the neck. The skin was a livid grey shading into yellowish brown. It was all seamed and corrugated. In these seams and corrugations the water ran and glistened, and whilst the head swayed to and fro the blank blind eyes watched the light.

Jimmy Halliday was about half-way up the great boulder, when without the slightest warning the head struck downwards at the lamp. It struck as a snake strikes, with a darting swiftness that the eye could not follow. Ann cried our faintly, and felt Charles hold her close. The lamp rolled over and fell amongst the wet rocks with a clatter that waked all the cavern echoes. The light still burned, but it no longer illumined the cave. It lay half in and half out of a pool whose steep sides shut it in. There was a half light with heavy shadows, and one white beam shining up from between the rocks like a searchlight. The head was poised about ten feet above the water. They could see it—a black shadow hanging over the black pool, a featureless, eyeless thing, the more horrible because only half seen.

Ann went on staring, and had a double image in her mind—this shadowy, hovering blackness, and behind it a picture of the dripping mane, the darting head, the bright blank eyes. Gale Anderson was gone, and Hector was gone, and the lamp was gone, and Jimmy Halliday had climbed his frantic way to where she could feel his clutching hands against her foot. He called in a hoarse, choked voice.

"Let me come up, Mr. Anstruther! Let me come up!"

"There's no room."

Ann's head was on his breast, but Charles' voice sounded to her as if it came from a very long way off. Perhaps that was because it had the sound of the world they had left behind—a sane, ordered world where the sun shone. Charles spoke as if he was still in that world, quietly and plainly.

"Can't you hold on there, Halliday?"

Jimmy looked back over his shoulder and saw the Shadow move. It seemed to rise. It seemed to sway towards them. His voice broke from him in the extreme of fear.

"It's coming—take me up—Mr. Anstruther, for the Lord's sake!" He beat and tore at the rock with his hands. "Let me up—I saved her life! It'll have me!"

Ann saw the shadowy neck bend. She saw the head sway down until it seemed to touch the boulder on which they stood. They were looking right down upon it now, and as they looked, they could hear it lipping the stone as it had lipped the ledge to which Hector and Gale had clung. It must be at least fifteen feet below them—but the neck was bent in a curve. Charles edged Ann back until she was pressed against the cliff wall. The top of the boulder on which they stood was not much more than a couple of feet across. If it had not touched the cliff, they could not have kept their footing.

Charles spoke.

"We've got to take him up. Lean back and shut your eyes. I'll have to give him a hand."

That moment when Charles let go of her was the worst of all for Ann. If Charles were to fall—if Jimmy pulled him over—if she were left here alone.... She began to pray that she might not be left alone. Then she heard Charles say in that quiet, steady voice,

"I'm going to help you up, Halliday. Pull yourself together and do as I tell you!"

And then after a long intolerable minute there were three of them on the place that had been narrow for two, and she and Jimmy and Charles were standing pressed together, such desperate hunted things that it no longer mattered to any of them that Jimmy's arm should be round her. The sickening musky smell came up to them in waves. No more than a tall man's height below them the Thing was lipping the stone on which they stood.

And it was then that the light went out. The battery may have been injured by its fall, or the water may have reached it, but suddenly it failed and the dark came down on them.

It was as if they were buried alive. It was like the darkness of a place where no light has ever been or ever will be. And in the darkness, coming nearer, was that soft sucking sound against the rock.

For a dreadful minute it was the only sound. Breath had stopped. The thudding pulses of terror were frozen. And then Jimmy Halliday broke into a half choked mutter, his head bowed down upon Ann's shoulder and his tongue stumbling over words learned long ago at his mother's knee. It was a little boy's prayers gasped out in broken phrases by lips that had used none since. "Make me a good boy—forgive us our trespasses—bless Mother and Dad—f'r ever and ever amen." Even at that moment it came to Ann how pitiful it was—the hot convulsed face against her shoulder; the strong clutching hands; and the words which a little boy had learned half a century ago. At least the sound of them drowned that other horrible sound.

She looked down and saw staring out of the dark two fixed, unwavering eyes. They were luminous, not with the jewel glint of a cat's eyes or a wolf's, but with a pale phosphorescent shining. She could see nothing but the eyes. And they were quite near—and they were coming nearer.

"Stop that noise, Halliday!" said Charles very low and stern, and at the sound of his voice Ann was able to move, to drag her eyes from those pale shining eyes and hide them against him. She pressed her face into the cloth of his coat and said his name over, and over, and over again:

"Charles—Charles—Charles!"

And another minute went by.

Charles held her and braced himself against the sheer cliff. How long would it last? Would Halliday pull them both over? Could the Thing reach them where they were? He had the faintest hope in the world that it could not, because if it could, why did it still delay? And the stare of the eyes was upwards. He had seen it strike three times. It had reared above the two men and dashed them from the ledge with a blow like that of a striking snake. It had hung poised over the lamp and then darted down on it. But now the eyes looked upwards.... They were very faintly green. They were pale and yet they dazzled him. He began to see a faint movement in their phosphorescence, as if its multitudinous atoms were in a state of flux, and all at once he felt the strangest prompting to loose his hold of Ann and lean forward—over the edge of the stone.

And Ann, with her face against his breast, said, "Charles—Charles—Charles!"

With a most violent effort Charles bent his head. It took every bit of his strength to do it. He could no longer see the eyes. He looked at the darkness which hid Ann's hair and set his lips against the hidden curls.

Jimmy Halliday still gasped and muttered his broken prayers.

Chapter Thirty-Five

TIME HAD STOPPED. And then, strangely and giddily, it began again.

"F'r ever and ever amen," said Jimmy Halliday.

And Charles said, "Dry up, Halliday! I want to listen."

They all listened then. Jimmy Halliday caught his breath with a gulp. He raised his working face from Ann's shoulder. They strained against the silence and listened.

There was no sound, and there was nothing to break the darkness. Silence and darkness filled the cave. The pale phosphorescent eyes which had watched them were gone. The soft sucking sound had ceased. All sounds had ceased. There was nothing but empty silence and the even featureless dark.

Charles said very quietly, "It's gone, darling."

Jimmy let go his pent-up breath in a convulsive sob. Charles had lifted his head and was staring into the dark. Ann put up a hand and touched his cheek.

"Really?" she said in a small whispering voice.

"I think so. Lean back against the rock—I've got to get at my torch."

Its thin ray went out into the dark. He turned it downwards, and it showed the boulders beneath them, and the black edge of the pool, and the hole into which the lamp had fallen. He sent it farther, and all that black water lay still as death.

He switched off the light.

"It's gone," he said. "It was that damned light of Halliday's that attracted it. Now we've got to get away as quick as we can. I'm going back by the way we came—it's the nearest and we know it. I'm going down first—then you, Ann—Halliday last. I want you to hold the torch and light me. Halliday—have you got any string in those pockets of yours? You've got enough of them. Come along, man, pull yourself together!

Have you got any string?... Oh, you have. Well then, get it ready, and as soon as I'm down, lower the torch to me and I'll light you both."

Ann came down the boulder with the feeling that about a hundred years had passed since that frantic upward climb. Suppose the Thing came back—suppose it was only waiting for them to leave their place of safety.... She shut that resolutely away. She had got to do what Charles told her. She mustn't let herself think—or remember.

She reached the bottom and saw Jimmy come sliding down behind her. They had to skirt the pool before they could reach the ledge. Charles took her by the arm.

"Don't look, and don't think. We'll be out of this in a moment.... There—that's the worst part over."

Their feet were on the ledge. Every step took them farther from the pool. Ann was lifted up to the mouth of the rift, and the two men scrambled after her, helping one another.

To come through into the other cave was like coming into another world—fresh air to breathe after that musky stench, and a plain track for their feet. Jimmy Halliday was recovering himself. He regretted the electric lamp, and dwelt brokenly upon its usefulness and its cost. Its loss seemed to affect him a good deal. He also deplored the fate of Hector, but had no tears for Gale Anderson, with regard to whom he was disposed to take a high moral tone. By the time they had reached the cellar he had begun to cock a wary eye in the direction of his own immediate future.

The barrel had been removed, and the flagstone stood open at the top of the cellar stair. They came through the wash-house into the kitchen and saw the daylight which they had never thought to see again. It was just the plain grey light of a cloudy day. It showed them to each other torn and dishevelled, streaked with dirt and slime, but it had an almost unbearable beauty. The common air, the common light, the common day were just for one enchanted moment something rare and strange. They were safety and release.

Mary stood in the middle of the kitchen and watched them come, her face grey and her eyes fixed. Then, before any of them could speak, she said in a strained whisper,

"Is he deid? Is Hector deid?"

It was Ann who answered her, clinging to Charles' arm. She said, "Oh, Mary!" but it was enough.

Mary lifted her head and said with dry lips,

"The Lord be thankit! He was an ill man."

Ann ran to her, and suddenly she cast her apron over her head and broke into bitter weeping.

"Mary! Mary—dear! Don't cry! Don't cry like that!"

"And wha'll greet for him if I dinna?" The voice broke with sobs. "An ill man—and his mither's deid! Let me be, lassie, for there's naebody tae greet for him but me!"

Jimmy coughed in an embarrassed manner.

"I'd like a word with you, Mr. Anstruther," he said.

Between the two doors, which led on the left to the parlour and on the right to the dining-room, he paused, scratched his head, and listened. The silence of a summer afternoon filled the house. Charles, listening too, thought of the silence of the cave. His mind shuddered away from the thought. This silence in the house was a comfortable, restful thing, not a dead weight to crush out courage and endurance.

Jimmy opened the parlour door a handsbreadth and looked in. Mrs. Halliday and Riddle slept each in a stiff armchair on either side of the hearth. The fire had been lighted after lunch. It had burned away to a bed of red ashes. The windows were tightly shut. The room was very stuffy. The old ladies looked very comfortable.

Jimmy shut the door without a sound and tiptoed over to the dining-room.

"This way, Mr. Anstruther, if you don't mind. I don't want to wake the old lady—and you'll be ready for a drink."

His hand was quite steady as he produced a bottle and glasses. He drank off about half a tumbler of rum, after which he got out his handkerchief and gave his face what he called a bit of a polish up. Charles watched him with interest. As he had been invited to a conference, he thought he would wait for Jimmy to begin. He took down his own drink, refused the offer of another, and continued to wait.

Jimmy stuffed the handkerchief back into his pocket and began.

"Well, Mr. Anstruther, I thought we'd better have a bit of a talk—man to man, as you may say. But take a seat, won't you?"

Charles sat down on one of the neat Victorian chairs.

"Well?" he said briefly.

Jimmy scratched his head. His efforts with the handkerchief had not really improved his appearance. His pale freckled skin was horribly smeared, and his sandy hair was patched with greenish slime.

"Well," he said—"well, as man to man, Mr. Anstruther—what about it?"

Charles leaned an elbow on the table and smiled a little.

"What about what?"

"Oh, come, Mr. Anstruther!" Jimmy's tone was reproachful.

Charles continued to smile.

"Oh, *come*, Mr. Anstruther!"

"Very well," said Charles, "what shall we take first—your attempt to murder me, or your attempt to murder Miss Vernon?"

Jimmy Halliday looked genuinely pained.

"If I hadn't thought you were a gentleman, Mr. Anstruther, I wouldn't have wanted to talk to you. Murder Miss Vernon? Now why should I want to murder her—a young lady that I admire and respect? Why, I wanted to marry her—you heard me ask her yourself."

"Well, do you know, Halliday, I think on the whole she'd rather have been murdered."

Jimmy decided to treat that as a pleasantry.

"Ah!" he said. "You're a young gentleman that will have your joke. But to talk of me hurting Miss Vernon—why, I saved her life only yesterday! I suppose she hasn't had time to tell you about that."

"Yes," said Charles, "she told me. And I don't mind saying that it's precious lucky for you. I notice you don't say anything about trying to murder me."

Jimmy was all outraged innocence.

"Me, Mr. Anstruther? Now you know that's carrying a joke too far!"

"Halliday," said Charles, "when we were in that damned cave, you were kind enough to tell me that I wasn't such a fool as I looked, or words to that effect. Now, as man to man—I think that's how you put it just now—what's the good of talking like that?"

"Mr. Anstruther—"

"Look here, Halliday—I went over that cliff because someone had banked up the bend with rocks, but I'm going to let that go. You did save Miss Vernon's life, so I'm prepared to call quits. Then there's the matter of your having tried to force Miss Vernon into marrying you so that you might have the handling of Mr. Paulett's money. Well, we are prepared to let that go too. A prosecution would be unpleasant for Miss Vernon."

Jimmy poured himself out some more rum.

"Now, Mr. Anstruther—*now!* You can't prosecute a man for asking a young lady to marry him!"

"Then there's the dope-running," said Charles. "I give you fair warning that I shall report that to the Procurator Fiscal—isn't that what they call him in these parts? And they don't have coroners in Scotland, do they? I shall have to see someone like that about the deaths of those two men."

Jimmy leaned forward with his glass in his hand.

"Now that's what I wanted to talk to you about," he said earnestly. "If you go into a police-station, or an office, or a court, and say you saw two men killed by a sea-serpent, what's going to happen? Why, you'll be laughed at, Mr. Anstruther. There'll be policemen trying to keep their faces straight, and clerks"—he pronounced it *clurks*—"sniggering behind their hands, and maybe before you know where you are a couple of loony-doctors trying to get you put away. No, no, you take my advice—those two chaps were drowned along of their boat getting upset when they were out fishing. If all three of us say that and stick to it, who's going to say anything different?"

Charles stood up.

"Save your breath, Halliday," he said. "I'm not telling any lies—they've a particularly nasty way of coming home to roost. Besides, did you ever hear of three people keeping a secret? You wouldn't like to be hanged for someone you didn't really murder—would you? That would be rotten luck. Now look here—I'm leaving with Miss Vernon as soon as she has changed and had something to eat and drink. We're going in your car—the one you keep locked up in the ruin over there. I'll leave the car in Glasgow at any garage you like to name—I expect you've got a friend who can fetch it away. I suppose you'll do a bunk on the motor-bike. I don't want to ask any questions about that, but if there's anything we can do about getting your mother away from here, we shall be quite willing to do it."

Jimmy got up rather dejectedly.

"Well," he said, "I won't trouble you. I've a cousin that I can get word to about the old lady. He's in the family hotel business, and he won't like it right in the season and all, but he'll just have to come along and fetch her away. He owes me a good turn, for I set him going. And Mary'll be wanting to go back to her own people, I expect. He'll have to see about that for her." He had the serious air of a family man considering the welfare of those for whom he was responsible, and it was all quite genuine. Charles simply couldn't see him in the dock. A respectable man—a very respectable man.

"I suppose you wouldn't shake hands, Mr. Anstruther?" Jimmy's tone was modest and deprecating.

Charles shook hands.

Chapter Thirty-Six

The Procurator Fiscal leaned back in his chair, set his finger-tips together, gazed from under his thick bushy eyebrows at Charles and Ann, and said,

"Imphm—"

This is a very ancient Scottish word. It means exactly what you want it to mean. It may express doubt, dissimulation, dubiety. It can agree, or disagree. It can convey any shade of surprise, pleasure, or annoyance. It can interrogate, deprecate, or assent. It is strange that other nations manage to get along without it.

Charles, not being a Scot, was not quite certain of his ground. The sound was strange to him. It did not encourage him to make any further remarks.

"Imphm—" said the Procurator Fiscal again.

Then, still leaning back, he inquired, "May I ask if you are a writer, Mr. Anstruther?"

Charles coloured under the scrutiny of a pair of very shrewd eyes, was furious with himself for colouring, and said,

"No."

"Imphm—" said the Procurator Fiscal. There was a further pause before he resumed ordinary speech, which he did as if there had been no pause at all. "Because what you've been telling me would make a grand tale, I've no doubt."

Ann put her chin in the air and looked at him indignantly.

"Imphm—" said the Procurator Fiscal. He sustained a flashing glance with calm. "Now, Mr. Anstruther—as I've been saying, that's a very interesting tale you've just been telling me, and you told it very well. Now mind you, I'm not saying I don't believe you, so there's no need for you to get angry. In my private capacity I can believe as much as any man and perhaps a bit more, for I've Highland blood in me. But as Procurator Fiscal "—he paused and waved a hand—"let me tell you this. If it is your purpose to engage in writing one of those works of fiction commonly known as thrillers, you may put into it as many warlocks, bogles and sea-serpents as you will, but I must freely tell you that I do not propose to extend the hospitality of my office files to any such creatures."

Charles had got over his annoyance. The shrewd eyes had a twinkle in them.

"All right, sir," he said. "But those two men are dead, you know."

"Imphm," said the Procurator Fiscal in full agreement. "And by all accounts they'll be no great loss. There's no difficulty about that that I can see. You have deponed that they were drowned. Let us leave out your sea-serpent, Mr. Anstruther, and we have a plain tale. They'll not be the first, nor the last, to be drowned in Loch Dhu. The place has an ill name—imphm. As to the man Halliday, he'll be gone before the police can get there. You'll be right about the drug-running, I've no doubt, and it's a pity he'll have had time to get away. I doubt there'd be no evidence. Now you'll just leave me your address and Miss Vernon's—"

Half an hour later Charles came into the lounge of the King's Arms hotel and sat down by Ann. She looked up at him dreamily. Sitting here by herself, she had come very near going to sleep. She had not really slept the night before. They had stayed at a little country inn where a kind landlady had fussed over her, and brought her hot milk to drink in bed, and told her that if she wanted anything in the night she had only to knock on the wall and she would be with her. She had been coward enough to keep her light burning, but the early dawn had found her still awake. It was easier somehow to go to sleep in clear, safe daylight.

Charles sat down on the couch beside her and patted her on the shoulder.

"Wake up and listen—I've got things to tell you."

"Charles—what?"

"Well, to begin with, Elias Paulett died yesterday. I got on the telephone to his house, and they told me."

Ann said, "Oh!" She looked at him with startled eyes. Presently an expression of distress came into them. She fingered his sleeve and said, "It's horrid not to be sorry when someone's dead—but I didn't ever see him."

"No," said Charles. What he had heard of Elias Paulett convinced him that she had not missed much, but it didn't seem quite the moment to say so. He put her hand against his cheek and said, "I wouldn't worry, darling."

"I hope someone is sorry about him.... Perhaps Hilda is—"

Charles felt profoundly sceptical. He said nothing however.

Ann sighed.

"You didn't speak to Hilda?"

"No. I'll have to write to her. I suppose she was fond of that fellow Anderson, but she seemed awfully afraid of him. I expect she'll get over it."

"Charles, we shall have to do something for her."

Charles made a face.

"I suppose so. But for heaven's sake don't ask me to have her to stay—I draw the line at that."

"Charles—be good!"

"I am being good. You do realize you're an heiress then? If I was all stuck up with pride like you were, it would be my turn to say I couldn't possibly marry you."

Ann snuggled up to him.

"But you're not proud—you told me you weren't. Charles, you *will* be able to keep Bewley?"

"I expect so. Now listen! We're going to catch the next train south, because Scotch marriage law is too complicated for me, and I know we can get married in three days in London."

Ann wasn't dreamy any more. She was pale, and her eyes were bright. She sat back in her corner.

"Charles, we can't!"

"Oh yes, we can. It's all in train. I've sent my solicitor a wire and told him to get busy. And I got on to my sister—the one that's married to the bishop—and she's meeting us, so Mrs. Grundy can't so much as lift an eyebrow."

Ann gazed at Charles. Had he told his sister that she was Elias Paulett's heiress? Would she be meeting them if he hadn't? She opened her lips and closed them again. Some questions are better not asked.

"Well?" said Charles.

They were side by side on a big couch at the far end of the lounge. The lounge was empty. A stag at bay gazed at them from the left-hand wall. Another stag in the act of challenging a foe to mortal combat looked over their heads from the right-hand wall. Heads of other stags partially obscured the wall-paper, which was also of the Landseer period. The couch was covered with horse-hair and had three neat antimacassars laid along its back. Charles slid along the horse-hair, deranged the middle antimacassar, and put both arms round Ann.

"We'll be married in three days," he said.

Ann's cheeks were as bright as her eyes.

"I didn't say I would."

"But you will," said Charles.

"Perhaps," said Ann.

THE END

Postscript

I DO NOT APOLOGIZE for my sea-serpent; I justify him—taking evidence on the one side from folk-lore, and on the other from fact.

In Mr. J. J. Bell's delightful book *The Glory of Scotland* he refers to the monster of Loch Morar, whose appearance is believed to presage disaster. So much for folk-lore.

In Lieut.-Commander R. T. Gould's enthralling work *The Case for the Sea-serpent*, to which I herewith make grateful acknowledgment, he prints as frontispiece a map upon which round black spots mark the various appearances of some unusual sea-monster. Three of these spots lie touching one another upon the west coast of Scotland, and a fourth sits on the top of John o' Groats like a cap. These appearances are well authenticated, and occurred in the years 1808, 1872, 1893, and 1920 respectively. So much for fact.

I am informed—most passionately and even threateningly informed—that it is impossible that a sea-serpent should have luminous eyes. To this I reply that Charles Anstruther *says* he saw luminous eyes staring up at him out of the dark.

PATRICIA WENTWORTH

P.P.S.—This book was written in the autumn of 1932, before I had heard so much as a whisper about the Loch Ness Monster.

Lightning Source UK Ltd.
Milton Keynes UK
UKHW022153301019
352617UK00009B/1762/P

9 781911 413257